HUNTED
RESURRECTION

BOOK TWO

ABOUT THE AUTHOR

Donna Collins was born at home in Romford, Essex, England. Five minutes later, she was one-hundred-per cent a bookworm. Her favourite novel, Enid Blyton's *The Children of Cherry Tree Farm*, was a gift from her parents and now the most worn book on her bookshelf.

It was this book, and her love for 70's and 80's TV shows such as *Hart to Hart*, *Charlie's Angels*, *Hunter*, and *Dempsey and Makepeace*, that lured Donna to the dark side of mystery and thriller writing. Since then, Donna has racked up many favourite authors, including Paula Gosling (*A Running Duck* is the second most worn book on her bookshelf), Jonathan Kellerman, Patricia Cornwell, and A.J. Quinnell.

Although Donna loves to write, she also loves crime - and her career proves it. Having founded her school magazine, her professional career includes not only working at OK! Magazine but also for Essex Police, Ormiston Prison Services, and Essex Offender Services. With publishing credits for freelance and commissioned magazine articles under her belt, Donna has now turned her attention and imagination to what she is best at – storytelling.

In her spare time (what spare time?), Donna loves anything scary that will get her adrenaline pumping, including storm chasing, fright nights, zombie-infested shopping malls, and séance panic rooms - with her all-time goal involving the open sea, a cage, and a whole heap of great white sharks. Donna also proudly boasts finishing the 2010 London Marathon, but you'll have to ask nicely if you want her to tell you where she was placed and who overtook her.

The HUNTED series is Donna's first trilogy.

Visit her website at www.donnacollins.co.uk
Twitter @donnacollinsUK
Facebook.com/donnacollinsUK
Instagram @donnacollinsUK

Also by Donna Collins

HUNTED: RESURRECTION

Donna Collins

Willow Books

AUTHOR'S NOTE

One thing I love about storytelling is the ability to research things I would never normally think about. Things like the devices I use in this novel's torture room. So, I feel compelled to share with you a little place nestled close to London's Borough Market called *The Clink Prison*. I'd never been before and took some writer friends who were visiting from the States (I know, of all the tourist places in London, I find the goriest to showcase). Luckily, they are as mad as I, and loved it.

Definitely check this place out. I also recommend a lovely fish and chip restaurant aptly named Fish!, which is a short walk away and just around the corner to Bridget Jones' flat.

For Megan and Jamie

aka *Meg The Peg* and *Ab Boy*
You are both my whole world

CHAPTER ONE

SATURDAY
The Chamber, Purgatory

Not even the lad's screams could cover the sound of his arms being dislocated from his shoulders.

The Sheriff cranked the handle again. The already-taut rope pulled further, and the gurgled cries the Sheriff loved to hear spat from the young lad's throat.

Shame. The boy passed out before his pelvis had a chance to splinter apart.

The Sheriff slapped him across the face. The lad's head just whipped from left to right, then lulled against his dislodged shoulder. He wasn't going to give anything more tonight – and that infuriated the Sheriff. He hadn't frequented this chamber in little over six months. His involvement with the rack had been even longer than that. And now the eagerly anticipated build-up of brutalising this peasant for the best part of the night left him feeling deflated and unfulfilled. He'd have to choose his next victim more carefully, and make him pay in spades.

Behind him, he heard one of his aids approach.

The Sheriff glanced once more at the lad lying stretched on the rack, his head of orange hair hardly discernible beneath the clotted blood, his skin lacerated and shredded from the whipping the Sheriff had administered earlier that afternoon. It would be an age before the Sheriff's main duties of overseeing these torture chambers would allow him the time to come down and indulge again.

Damn it. Humans just weren't as strong as they used to be.

The aid nervously cleared his throat.

The Sheriff sighed. "You'd better have something worthy to report."

"Sir, we've located prisoner 4429."

The Sheriff lost interest in the red-haired lad. He spun towards the aid, unconcerned if his sudden elation and sadistic delight were obvious. "It's about time. Where is he?"

"England. South"

"Be more specific."

"Somewhere around the Cornwall area."

Disappointment momentarily quenched the Sheriff's joy. He inhaled. Held it. Drummed his long fingernails against his leg. Exhaled. "I can't fetch him from *somewhere*. I need an exact location."

"I'll get one for you straight away."

"I don't want you to get it – I want to you to already have it before you come here and disturb me." The

Sheriff's fingers paused drumming. He glanced at the pathetic red-haired boy and thought back to better times, when his prisoners could handle hours of torture before they finally died. He grabbed the rack handle and twisted. He didn't stop until the young lad's body completely severed apart. The bloody sight failed to calm the building rage he felt. He noticed the aid. "You're still standing there, which would suggest to me that you now have the location."

The aid's eyes widened with fear. He cleared his throat. "No."

"Then why are you standing there?"

"I have the men ready to move upon your command."

"Without a location?"

"I'll get it now, Sir." He bowed. Turned. Scampered to the doorway.

"And tell the men to stand down. I will do this capture myself."

"But, Sir, the support of your men is a requirement."

The Sheriff reached the aid in two long strides. He slapped him across the face. Watched the disfigured skin redden almost immediately. "Your job is not to preach the law. Your job is to get me the exact location before I slaughter you."

The aid bowed again. He backed away as quickly as he could, and made haste. The Sheriff waited until his scampering footsteps disappeared down the passageway. Then he sighed. He was surrounded by nothing but incompetent fools.

He turned his thoughts to prisoner 4429. The same sadistic delight returned. It would do him good returning the escapee back to Purgatory. He had, after all, been one of the Sheriff's unapologetic pleasures back in the day. Not his most favourite victim, mind you, but the man could suck up pain like nobody else. It would be a pleasure to hunt him down and bring him back to the fold.

It would be just like the good old days.

CHAPTER TWO

St. Catherine's Castle, Fowey, Cornwall

Eliza drew her knees to her chest and rocked like a small child.

Coldness had battled its way through the velvet robe that wrapped her semi-nakedness, and her body shook under the attack. A tear rolled down her cheek, but instead of giving in to the many more that wanted to follow, she wiped it away.

Her father had vanished.

Her brother had died.

Her neighbour had been murdered.

And herself? Well, she'd been strung up on a crucifix and sacrificed like the Messiah himself.

It was a colossal, disturbing mess, and she understood none of it.

Well, apart from the fact that she now watched the one man irrefutably stuck in the center of it all limp away from her.

Not that Roman – the man she watched walk away now – had been the one to sacrifice her. No. That small feat belonged to her own dear, psychotic father. Roman had in fact saved her from that outcome. But, he was the one man alive who knew how to help her now.

Eliza shook her head. Had it really only been two days since Roman first walked into her life? Two days ago that he'd first stopped the Shadow from choking her to death. A Shadow that, according to Roman, had been sent by God himself, because her blood happened to be the key into Heaven.

She wanted to laugh.

How absurd did all that sound? Even just thinking it?

In fact, just believing what she'd lived through in the last forty-eight hours was enough to convince her that a nut home was where she really needed to be.

She continued to watch Roman. The man had saved her, kidnapped her, drugged her... Jesus, he was more screwed up than her. And yet, deep down inside, she felt sorrow at the prospect of never seeing him again. Maybe she did need that nut hospital.

She pulled the robe tighter around herself. She had a choice to make, and very little time to make it. First choice – the better choice – was to remain crumpled on the dirt and allow Roman to disappear from her life forever. After all, danger followed the man around like a virus. To even consider her second choice, and follow him, would be rubber stamping her own death warrant for sure.

Besides, she hated Roman... Didn't she?

She'd spent the best part of two days trying to flee him. Now she was finally rid of him, was she actually considering following him again? What in the hell was wrong with her?

She slowly got to her feet. Around her, the inside of the tower looked ransacked. The Cross her father had assembled no longer dominated the centre of the area. Just like her brother and father, it had vanished into thin air. Her neighbour, Mr. McKenzie, on the other hand, lay flat out on his back. His eyes were open, and fear seemed to distort the whole of his face. Eliza turned away. She desperately wanted to believe he deserved whatever Roman had done to him, but wouldn't that make her just as bad as he?

She glanced towards the tower exit. Roman continued to limp away, but he moved slowly, and hadn't made much progress.

The earlier rain had ceased, and the wind had died to little more than a light breeze. Still, the previous weather had left its mark. Water trickled over rocks and raced towards the cliff steps, leaving a muddy and slippery bog in its wake that looked to test Roman's balance to the limit. He certainly hadn't walked away from this mess unscathed.

She wished him gone – she truly did. But the truth was, she owed it to her brother, Billy, to call Roman back… Roman was the only person alive who knew what had happened here tonight; he was the only one who could find Billy. The only one who could save him. And Roman owed her.

Eliza's first step towards him was unsteady. Stones and storm-shredded foliage tore at her bare feet. When she reached the exit archway, she leaned against it for support and took a deep breath. She thought about calling out after him, but somehow she sensed he already knew she was there.

She pushed herself away from the stone wall and continued on. Strength slowly found her, and her steps grew into strides. She expected him to stop and wait, but he didn't even look back. Anger bubbled to the surface. When she finally reached him, she grabbed his arm. It wasn't hard to spin him to face her.

"Eliza, I don't have time to deal with shit from you."

For a brief second, Roman's gaze met hers. Was that sympathy she saw there? Bizarre really; Roman didn't do sympathy. He tried to pull from her grip, but he was weak. Weaker than she'd ever seen him before.

She tightened her hold. "What in hell's wrong with you? Why didn't you wait for me back there?"

"Let go of my arm."

"Not until you tell me what went on here tonight. Where's my brother?"

"Dead. But I told you that already."

She resisted the pain the words struck in her heart, clinging instead to a knowledge she still couldn't define. Didn't understand. "You're wrong," she said.

"See, now that right there's your problem." Roman shrugged free. "You always think you're right."

"But you saved me?"

"Yeah. So?"

"So, you're the only one who can help me find my brother."

"You're delusional."

"You owe me."

Roman chuckled. "Owe you? For what? Ruining my life?"

"Your life? I died. My brother is gone."

Roman turned from her and limped to the edge of the cliff, where stone steps led down to the beach.

"You kidnapped me," she continued, undeterred. "You tied me up. You drugged me. You bloody stuffed me in the smallest car boot in the world—"

"And, boy oh boy, do I wish I had it here again now." He reached for the rusty handrail.

"You'll never make it down those steps alone." Roman's irritated sigh didn't stop her. "If you help me, I'll help you."

His jaw tensed. "I don't need your help."

"That's one hell of a drop to the beach."

Roman paused. He glanced up, and Eliza expected to see his blue eyes twinkle the way they had when he'd arrived at her door the day before. Instead, they remained dull and grey. In fact, she saw nothing but hatred inside them.

"And just how are you going to help me? What, you going to sling me over your shoulder and carry me down?"

Eliza stared at him. "What the hell's gotten into you?

"I don't like being blackmailed."

"I'm not blackmailing you. Just proposing a business arrangement."

Roman scoffed. "That's the sort of crap your father would say."

Eliza slapped him across the face. His legs seemed to buckle and, for the briefest moment, she thought he was going to fall. She went to reach for him, but his hand tightened around the handrail and he steadied himself. The hatred in his eyes deepened. His lips pursed tight and, although she was sure he had a barrage full of obscenities to throw at her, he remained quiet.

"What is wrong with you? Why are you so weak?" she asked.

"You're why I'm so weak."

"Me?"

"What? You think dragging a soul back from the dead is easy?"

Eliza took a deep breath. Where had the man who'd begged her father to spare her life vanished to? "What have I done to suddenly make you hate me so much?"

Roman's face softened slightly. Again, he looked as if to speak, but chose to remain quiet.

Eliza placed her hand on his shoulder – a show that she didn't judge him. And she certainly didn't want to argue. "What happened here after I died?"

"You lived again."

"That tells me nothing."

"Well, that's all you're getting."

"I just want my brother back."

"And I want to get the hell out of here…without you." He turned from her and hopped down onto the step.

"Please. I'm begging you. Help me find him."

"No." He hopped another step. His shoulders tensed, and he stopped for a second.

Eliza stepped down behind him. Her robe tangled around her ankles and she scooped it up. She manoeuvred herself beside him and propped his arm around her shoulder. To her surprise, he didn't fight her intervention.

"You helping me changes nothing."

Eliza chose not to answer.

The previous rainfall still gathered in pools on the uneven steps, and Eliza wasn't entirely convinced they were the easiest choice to go with. If she was being totally honest with herself, she expected the pair of them to have slipped and fallen way before reaching the fourth step. She was pleasantly surprised when they both still held strong by the sixth.

She glanced at Roman. Pain creased his face with every step he hobbled down. He paused for a moment and drew a deep breath.

"Are you okay?"

"Just get me the hell down." He lowered another step.

It took a good ten minutes to finally reach the bottom, and regardless of the obvious excruciating pain that consumed him, Roman looked exhilarated when his feet hit the surf and sunk into the sand.

Eliza mirrored his relief with a short intake of breath. But, the comfort of the tide quickly turned cold, soaking her bare feet and freezing her body to the core. The cold had the same effect on Roman. Within seconds, his teeth chattered together, and shivers rocked his whole body. Hell, her medical training as a nurse told her he'd probably pass out before he made it back to her father's house, and there was no way in hell she could drag him up to her father's house. She released her grip on the robe, watched its hem fan across the surface of the water, and repositioned herself under his arm. He didn't give one of his bad-tempered rejections as she'd expected. Instead, like before, he swallowed what was probably his pride and allowed her to take as much of his weight as she could handle.

They made it to the cave, the ocean air pushing and urging them through the tunnels, and it wasn't long before the dull flicker of torches lit the main corridor that led to the library. The bookcase remained ajar, and Eliza pushed it open.

She spotted Davis's highly polished shoes first, and then the butler himself. He lay on his back, his eyes wide open, his face twisted in pain. "What did you do to Davis?"

For a brief moment, Roman's gaze froze on her. A flicker of disbelief betrayed his eyes, and then anger reignited them. He removed his arm from around her shoulders. "Why is it you see a dead body and immediately ask what *I* did?"

Eliza stared at him. "You seem to kill a lot of people."

"Yeah, well, this one was on your brother."

"Billy did this?"

"He hit him."

Eliza knelt beside the old man and checked for a pulse. "And that killed him?"

Roman shot her a look. "The heart attack afterwards killed him." He hobbled towards the library door.

"And what about my father? He couldn't have just vanished into thin air."

"Wanna bet?"

"Did you kill him?"

Roman looked at her. "Contrary to what you clearly believe, I haven't killed everybody I've ever met."

"Then where'd he go?"

"Heaven."

"Really?"

Roman rolled his eyes.

Eliza's patience hit the boiling point. "Where the hell are they?"

Roman sighed. He looked fed up to his back teeth with this conversation. "I altered the pathway to Heaven."

"Altered it? To where?"

"Purgatory."

"Purgatory?"

"Yes."

"What's Purgatory?"

"You really don't know much of your history, do you?" Roman rolled his eyes again, a mannerism that was beginning to aggravate Eliza. "Every soul has to be processed and go through a kind of inventory stock-take."

"So you can get Billy back? Like you did me?"

"It's not that simple."

"But you got me back—"

"There are only five routes for a soul to take. First and foremost, you have to die. Then, your soul is registered. After that, it remains in a sort of waiting room until its number comes up. That's when you find out if you're heading to Heaven, Hell, being Reincarnated, or just getting a second chance with your own life with the good old Resurrection card. I just pulled you back out before the powers that be had time to place you."

"I don't understand."

"You were destined for Heaven. I sensed that much. By bringing you back, your soul had to be replaced... Keep the waiting room's stock-take balanced."

"With Mr. McKenzie?"

"With Mr. McKenzie."

"So, he went to Heaven?"

"It is a slight drawback, I admit."

"But he did so much wrong."

"Would you have preferred it to be you?"

Eliza stared at him. "How could evil like Mr. McKenzie even be allowed in Heaven?"

"Does it really matter?"

No. In the big scheme of things, it didn't matter one bit. "What about Billy? We can still save him, right?"

Roman shook his head again. "Your father and Billy didn't die in the conventional sense. They physically entered Purgatory. They completely bypassed the whole waiting room process. Their presence will do more than unbalance things. Purgatory will be in chaos, and they'll be hunted down."

Eliza paused. She wanted to know exactly what Roman meant by that, but was too afraid to ask. "You said there were five choices."

Roman swallowed. He shifted position. "Nobody speaks of the fifth path – and for good reason."

Eliza didn't say anything, dread building in her chest as she waited for his next words.

Finally, he continued. "When a soul doesn't fit any of the first four choices, it's thrown into the depths of Purgatory itself, and tortured for all eternity."

"And this is where Billy will be sent?"

"No. This is where Billy is. I told you, I altered the path."

Eliza stared at him through glazed eyes. "He's being tortured?"

Roman looked away.

"But he has to be caught first, right?"

"Your father and Billy will stick out like two sore thumbs. Trust me. They've been caught."

"Then they can escape? I mean, we know where he is. We can get him out."

Roman turned back to her. "Your optimism is misplaced and stupid. This place is reserved for the worst of the worst. Once you're sent there, you never get out."

Eliza digested his words, her tears ready to overflow. Instead, she blinked them back. "If nobody speaks about this place, how do you know it really exists? How did you know to send them there?"

"Have you forgotten I'm a Reaper? And I wasn't sending *them* there. I sent your father there. Billy should not have been in that light."

"But how can you be so sure? Maybe you made a mistake. Maybe Billy can escape."

Roman looked her in the eyes. For a moment he seemed to contemplate whether to actually answer. Finally, he said, "I know, because I've been there."

He turned from her and walked into the corridor.

"Where are you going?" she demanded.

"Away."

"Away where?"

"Away anywhere."

Within seconds, Eliza was behind him, the damn robe wrapping her legs and nearly tripping her. "You need a hospital."

"I'll be fine."

"What about Billy?"

Roman paused. "Are you deaf?"

He turned to face her, his broken arm cradled against his chest. "What part of 'your brother's dead' do you not understand? How many times do I have to say it before it registers inside that head of yours?"

"I was dead."

"And, if you carry on, you're gonna be again – very soon."

Eliza ignored his idle threat. "You're a reaper. That means you have the ability to bring people back. To bring *him* back."

Roman clasped her by the shoulders. His hands trembled. He stared at her, just as he had in the cabin after he'd taken her from the hospital. But even then, when she'd thought him a psychopathic killer, there had been warmth in his eyes. Right now, there was only desperation. "You're stupid and deluded."

Fury at his lack of remorse flooded Eliza's veins. "And you're an arsehole." She pushed his hands from her shoulders, unbothered if he collapsed, and glared at him.

He turned to leave, but Eliza blocked his path. "I'm not done with you yet."

"But I'm done with you, and this fucking place."

The movie reel inside her head began to play. Unwelcomed, this time. She desperately tried to shut it off. She didn't want to hurt anyone else. Nevertheless, the table lamp behind Roman – and the table it sat on – started to rattle violently.

Roman steadied himself against the wall. He shifted his weight from his injured leg. "Is your telekinetic party trick supposed to scare me?"

"Why not? It scares the hell out of me." A picture left the wall and flew across the hallway.

Eliza's heart raced. Now her irritation matched his. "You're going to get Billy back, you hear?"

"Or what, Eliza? It's death by oil painting?" Roman side stepped her and hobbled along the corridor.

An ornament catapulted towards him. He ducked and watched it smash into the wall.

He straightened, his face doing its best to hide the pain that obviously crippled him. "You think you're the only one who's lost someone? We all lose people,

Eliza. We all make sacrifices. You need to grow up and live with yours."

"And what sacrifices are you living with? Who, other than yourself, have you ever put first?"

Roman stared at her. When he spoke, his voice didn't convey the anger that remained in his eyes. "You."

She hadn't expected that answer. In fact, she hadn't expected any answer. The furniture stilled, and the movie reel faded.

"I sacrificed being with my son and his mother because I chose to save you instead."

Eliza remained silent. She didn't know what to say. Thank you? Somehow it sounded more patronizing than sincere.

"And now I wish I hadn't."

"You bastard." The words left her lips before she had a chance to stop them.

"Probably, but I'm a bastard who's now outta here."

"No." Eliza pulled him back. "You need to help me get my brother back first."

Roman stumbled. His knees shook under the pressure to remain standing, and he leaned against the wall again for support. "I'm getting fucked off with this demanding shit of yours."

But he didn't straighten. He bent over and just stared at his boots like they were a safe haven to hide. When he finally glanced up, the colour had drained from his face.

"Roman, you are not well. You need to rest."

"I don't have time to rest."

"Then tell me how I can get my brother back."

"I told you, Billy is dead." His hands slipped down the wall, no longer able to hold his pathetic body up. He fell to the floor and sprawled across the marble tiles. When he tried to get back up, his body shook, his arms unable to hold his own weight.

Sweat and blood soaked his jumper, and when his eyes met hers, fear was the only thing she saw.

His last words were little more than a whisper. "Don't let them take me back."

CHAPTER THREE

Billy opened his eyes.

For a moment, he thought it was the stone walls of the Cornish tower that still surrounded him. He lifted his face off the gritty floor and spat the dirt from his mouth. His head throbbed worse than any hangover he'd ever suffered.

A flick-book of images pushed forward, but they were unclear and blurred, and he struggled to make out what they meant. He glanced again at the walls. Definitely not the tower.

Where the hell am I?

The flick-book continued to race through the images. The ache around his skull intensified, and the pressure inside his head built until he thought his eyes would pop. He squeezed them shut and let the darkness block out his otherwise unsettling surroundings. It didn't offer much security, but at this moment he'd take whatever he could get.

Unfortunately, it didn't last long.

A small glow of light formed in the vast blackness of his mind. As it neared, it grew in size. Closer and closer it came until, at last, he saw what it was: Eliza, hanging on the Cross, all signs of life snuffed from her blood-covered body. Tears sprang to his eyes. Anger surged his veins. He'd failed to save his sister.

In a flash, other events flooded back – way too fast, and the hammering behind his eyes intensified. He remembered his father trying to kill Eliza, and he remembered Roman trying to save her. He remembered battling with Mr. McKenzie, and he remembered jumping into the white light in pursuit of his father just before the darkness came and took them both. *Shit*. He remembered the whole goddamn nightmare.

So, what did that mean?

Had he died?

Was he now in heaven?

Had his father died? God, he bloody well hoped so.

He opened his eyes, and again stared at the stone walls.

This place wasn't Heaven. This place felt more like Hell.

He clambered to his feet and reached for his taser. The leather clasp on his police belt was empty. *Shit*. He'd thrown it at a dead guy who'd tried to eat him outside the police station earlier that afternoon. *Shit*. *Shit*. Where in the hell was he?

He got to his feet, a little unsteady, but he had to find a way out of here. Corridors extended to his left and right, each side stretching on for what seemed miles. Stalactites hung from the ceilings. In places, the icicle-shaped formations almost blocked the passageway from view.

It occurred to him that Eliza could also be here, wherever the hell *here* was. Maybe he could find her. Maybe he could still save her.

No. Eliza hadn't been anywhere near the light, and this location certainly didn't strike him as the kind of place good-hearted people like his sister were sent to by choice.

On the other hand, his father more than likely *was* here. Somewhere.

Billy glanced to his right. The passageway stretched so far its end eluded him. To his left, it was no different.

Which way to go?

He remembered a trick his mother had taught him as a child to find his way out of a maze. It had never let him down, so he turned to his right, placed the back of his hand against the wall, and walked.

He walked, and walked, and walked, and began to wonder if he'd chosen his path wisely. His surroundings never changed, regardless of the distance he thought he covered. Stalactites routinely blocked his way, and when they didn't, he had to squeeze past stalagmites, their bases spreading the floor and almost touching the tunnel walls.

He wiped his brow and aimlessly checked his watch. It showed five to ten. It seemed much later. He stopped walking and leaned against a stalagmite.

Where in the hell was this place?

Images of Eliza tried to force their way to the forefront of his mind, but he pushed them away. He needed to focus. He needed to find a way out of here.

Water dripped from the ceiling and soaked his bare skin. A few hours ago – before the walking dead and the sacrifices, when all he'd had to worry about was school fetes and noise complaints – the dripping water would have irritated him. He held out his hand, palm up. His dry mouth itched at the anticipation of tasting the water.

When a small pool had formed, he eagerly sucked it up. Not even enough for a mouthful, but he was still grateful for this small mercy. And he kept being grateful with the second slurp, then the third.

Gruff voices filled the passageway some way behind him. Billy spun on his heel, but saw no one. More voices, this time to his right. Or was it to his left? He couldn't tell anymore. He turned again, using the stalagmite for cover. Still no sign of anybody, and Billy wondered if the stress of being stuck wherever the hell this was had started to play tricks on his mind.

The voices faded. Billy stood and peered over the top of the stalagmite. Apart from himself, the passage looked to be void of anyone...or anything. He continued onwards. Again, voices emerged behind him. Words were yelled, but Billy couldn't decipher what they were.

He hurried on, and didn't look back. His only goal was to find the exit.

A deafening scream filled the air.

Billy halted. His boots skidded through the gritty floor. His body tightened. The hairs on the back of his neck raised.

He heard a whip crack against flesh, and a second, terrifying scream burst through the passageway.

Frantic, Billy searched the corridors. Nothing behind him. Nothing in front.

Another scream cried out.

Where in the hell was it coming from? Billy glanced at his hands. They shook uncontrollably. He rubbed them. Held them tight against his chest. Another crack of the whip. Another scream. His knees weakened. Fear immobilised him. He didn't care where the sounds came from, and he didn't want to find out.

Billy ran.

Still, the tortured screams followed him through the tunnel, bouncing off the walls and echoing around him. Another shriek – deeper than the first – yelled for mercy. Then back to the whip cracking, and the first scream was with him again.

Cries of pain surrounded him and, for all he knew, he was running straight towards the source of them.

The earlier mob of voices he thought he'd imagined still chased some way behind him. Were these the people inflicting the pain? Did they know about him? Were they chasing him?

Another stalagmite slowed Billy's sprint. He crawled around it and quickly regained his pace.

The first opening he stumbled across, he bolted through. Warning bells shouted inside his head. He should stop and look first. Check it out. He may be rushing straight into the lion's den. But he ignored them all. Escape was the only thing on his mind.

He kept on running.

And he didn't stop, ducking through every opening and charging down every passageway he passed. Any additional distance he put between himself and the hoard of voices – that may or may not be chasing him – could only be a good thing.

The corridor gradually fell silent. The screams and voices faded, and all Billy heard was his own boots hitting grit. He slowed enough to see he stood in a corridor almost identical to the one he had woken in. He wanted to hide. To curl into a ball, but he knew then he'd never find an outcome to the situation he was in.

Rapid breaths dried his mouth. He wanted to cry. He wanted to scream. If he had a gun, he actually believed he would shoot himself dead to escape this hell he found himself trapped in.

He waited. His heartbeat sustained its rapid pace. Hasty breaths continued to draw in air. He had to get a grip. He had to stay focused and regain some control. He glanced around once more – properly this time. Another corridor. More icicle formations. Only, something was different. Up ahead, he saw a darkened shape lying on the floor.

The tightness returned to his shoulders. Warnings bellowed at him not to go closer. But Billy had to check. After all, what if it was Eliza?

Slowly, he approached the shape. It didn't move.

Billy stepped nearer. It looked to be that of a man. His father? Billy paused and checked the corridor.

Once certain there was no immediate threat, he edged closer.

James lay on his back. His eyes were closed and, for a moment, Billy thought he was dead. He certainly looked dead. Blood stained his shirt, but when Billy investigated, he found no injury. He knelt beside his father, and checked for a pulse. When he found one, the immediate relief and joy most children would feel at finding a parent alive eluded him. Instead, anger returned. Billy wanted to destroy the man.

He stood and glanced down at the despicable person he used to call Dad. He should kill him right now. Give both his mother and Eliza some retribution. But Billy was no killer. And he sure as hell was a better man than his father.

But, could he leave him here? Easy game for when the mob of voices caught up? It would certainly buy Billy some time while he found a way out on his own.

He checked his watch again. Still five to ten. Damn thing must've stopped when that white light hit. He stepped over his father's body. A despicable man who deserved to rot down here for all eternity. Let him fight his own battle with the voices.

However...

Billy paused. He had no idea what danger lay in wait in these tunnels. Did he really want to face those threats alone?

Alone had to be better that trusting his father.

Or was it better to fight alongside the devil you already knew?

Shit.

Billy turned. He kicked his father's foot. When James didn't move, Billy kicked it again. Harder.

His dad stirred.

Aware that at any moment somebody could come along and find them, Billy knelt beside him. He grabbed James by the shoulders, and shook him awake.

James's eyes fluttered open. He didn't look around. Instead, he stared directly at his son. "What happened?"

Billy's anger grew. He wanted to punch the shit out of that face. "We need to get the hell out of here."

"Out of where? Where are we?"

"I have no idea, but it isn't anywhere good." Billy encouraged him up off the floor. However, it quickly dawned on him that his father didn't appreciate the severity of the situation they were in.

James swept his hair back, and patted down his trousers. "Son, I am exactly where I want to be."

"Really? Look around, Dad. Do you honestly think you're in Heaven right now?"

James glanced around. The confident look remained, but Billy knew a poker face when he saw one.

He grabbed his father's arm "We need to find a way back home."

"Are you insane?" James shrugged free. "I sacrificed my entire existence to find a way out of that place."

"We cannot stay here."

"I am not going back."

Billy looked at his dad. "Then I'll leave you here."

James said nothing, and Billy realised every moment he wasted trying to get his father to see sense was a moment closer to the voices finding him. He turned away.

Several voices echoed through from the adjoining passageway. One voice, a male, ordered others to search the levels above and below.

"Last chance, Dad."

James smiled.

Billy didn't look back at his father. Instead, he just ran.

CHAPTER FOUR

Tiny pockets of air bubbled the water.

Eliza turned off the kitchen tap, and knocked back the two aspirin she held.

Outside, the dark night hid the garden from view. She glanced at her reflection in the window. Although not all that clear, she could still see her cheeks flushed soft pink. She continued to drink. Her throat felt drier than the Sahara Desert, and her ability to focus trailed two seconds behind her eye movement.

She thought of Roman. Did she honestly believe the cock-and-bull story about his son?

She poked out her tongue. It looked a normal colour.

Felt her head. A little warm, but nothing to be alarmed about.

She couldn't believe Roman. Hell, if she did, that would make her just damn too stupid for her own good. She held her wrist and counted the tiny pulsations. All normal.

Stress. That was what was wrong with her.

She stared at her reflection. No shit she felt stressed.

Nausea hit, and a green tint coloured her usually brown eyes, giving her a brief oriental appearance.

The girl's green eyes darkened to brown.

He retched over the sink and spat the remaining vile from his mouth. When he straightened, he immediately panicked. Roman was nearby. He spun from the window. The strange room he stood in was empty. Where was he? He'd been outside. Roman had been there. Where was Roman?

In the corner of the room, a door offered a way outside. Clammy hands – a girl's hands – reached for its handle. He paused. What was out there? Maybe Roman was out there. He turned back to the room. Spotting the large knife in a wooden block, he slid it free – just in case Roman appeared.

Maybe Roman hadn't seen him earlier. No, Roman had looked straight at him. So why hadn't Roman reacted when they saw each other. Why had he not shown the slightest glimmer of shock, surprise, anger, or the need to kill?

One thing was for sure, this room didn't seem to hold any of the answers. However, that see-through box in the corner of the room, stocked to the brim with liquor, sure as hell did. Yes. If in doubt, drink, and lots of it.

The glass door swung open, and a frosty white cloud floated out.

So many bottles of wine to select from, and the winner was…a red one.

He put the knife down. Thought better to keep it close, and slipped it inside the robe's pockets. The blade was too long to be completely concealed, and the handle stuck out like a sore thumb. Nevertheless, that is where he left it.

Small fleuron etchings engraved glass tumblers – important-looking and only for the rich and noble. He poured the wine, quickly filling one to the brim. The first gulp hit the back of his throat. My God, it was good. Better than anything he'd ever tasted in his life. The second and third gulps tasted just as good, if not better. The fourth guzzle drained the glass dry. He started to fill it again. Hell, forget the glass. More productive to just swig straight from the bottle.

He glanced back at the reflection in the window. The beautiful woman that stared back at him wiped the back of that soft hand across those luscious lips, and formed a small smile. Of course, it was obvious. Roman hadn't reacted because Roman hadn't seen him. And if Roman couldn't see him, it would make a long-awaited revenge so much sweeter… and easier.

So, where in the hell was Roman now?

Another gulp of wine, followed by a sensual lick of the girl's lips and a caressing wipe to dry them. He liked the way this girl felt. He glanced down at the form he took. Let his gaze linger on her perfectly formed body. If there were more time, he'd give her body a more thorough examination. Instead, he headed outside to the long hallway for a quick check to see if the coast was clear. There was no sign of Roman, or anyone for that matter. But Roman couldn't be far away. Maybe in another room…wherever that was?

He took another swig of wine. Although feeling confident, he took each step with caution. Another swig of booze – a second one just to be on the safe side – and the exploration of the rooms began. The house seemed massive; far bigger than anything he'd ever been in before. Trust Roman to land on his feet, and end up here. He downed another mouthful of wine and – what was this room? A study of some sort? Lots of books, and a large mahogany desk, the likes of which were not entirely unfamiliar to him – albeit this study was on a much bigger scale.

He walked back into the corridor. Another room, this one home to a funny-looking green table covered with some coloured balls and two sticks. Another swig of wine, this gulp an extra-large one, and his stride emanated much more confidence. Another drink, and he grinned.

Roman didn't know what was about to hit him.

CHAPTER FIVE

Roman felt extremely comfortable.

An oddity, considering the last thing he remembered was collapsing on the hard, marble floor in the hallway. He opened his eyes, expecting to find himself lying in a king-size bed, given that his head was buried deep in the most luxurious pillow he'd ever had the pleasure to encounter. But he wasn't in a bedroom, and there was no bed. He lifted his head, disturbing the soft blanket that covered his body, and glanced around. He wasn't even on a sofa. He lay on the shag pile rug in the library.

He fully sat, and the security of the blanket sagged around his waist. Light-headedness seized hold, and it took several seconds before he could focus again. He was still in James Hamilton's library, but this was not how he'd left it. The secret passageway had been concealed behind the closed bookcase, and Davis' body no longer lay anywhere that he could see. Fire roared in the fireplace, and everything looked, well, normal.

Damn it. Normal made Roman nervous.

He prepared himself for the onslaught of anxiety to kick in, but the warm glow of the flickering flames produced a surprising calmness. He had no idea what had happened, he had no idea how he came to be snuggled under the blanket, and he had no idea how long he'd been out. And for that split second, he didn't care.

Roman rubbed his head. An eruption of pain exploded down his arm, supporting the fear that his earlier break still hadn't fully healed. *Shit.* He should have recovered by now. What the hell fucked-up shit had that butler done to him when he broke it?

A bottle of water stood beside him, the lid already loosened. He took it, flicked the cap free, and gulped back the contents until only half remained. He had to leave this house – and Eliza – behind for good.

Eliza?

He should find her.

No, he shouldn't. She'd just start on about saving Billy again.

Now was Roman's time to slip out unnoticed. He'd already wasted too much time here. There were people on their way to get him, and they could be here at any moment to take him back.

He stood. On the sofa lay a clean shirt. He glanced down at the blood-soaked jumper he already wore, and quickly removed it. The softness of the shirt's fabric felt good on his skin and, for a moment he wondered if leaving was the right thing to do. Yes. It was the right thing to do.

He grabbed the water again. If his watch was anything to go by, he'd dozed for no more than forty minutes. The strength in his legs had returned and, still holding the bottle of water, he shuffled towards the door. Dizziness no longer stalled him, but it was still there, lingering somewhere at the back of his head, just waiting to pounce. He gulped back what was left of the water, and glanced into the corridor.

Empty. No sign of Eliza. That was good.

He stepped out, and slowly made his way along the hall. He saw the front door. Placed the empty water bottle on the table as he passed.

It was a grand house, there was no disputing that. The majority of people would probably offer their right eye to live in such a place. But, it was cold and un-homey. Thinking of Eliza as a child growing up here bore a huge sadness. Like Eliza, Roman himself had grown up in a relatively prosperous household.

His clergy father had held good standing within the local community, and his childhood residence had been one of the more enviable in the area. Although at a time before the invention of electricity and many other luxuries that today's youth took for granted, Roman and his younger brother had always been well provided for. But Roman had learned at an early age that money didn't make happiness. Eliza had undoubtedly learned that, too. Money, and every other good thing received in life, also brought with it a sacrifice. Unfortunately, in Roman's case, the sacrifice was an absent, workaholic father who lived to serve God more than his own family. Because of this,

Roman's mother had suffered, too. Duty-bound, she had stood by her husband's side, and whether through fear or respect, she failed to ever raise an objection about just how much harm his obsession with religion did to the rest of the family.

Instead, she'd accepted it and made the best of a bad situation. Roman's brother had done the same and followed in his father's footsteps to carve out a living for himself within the Church. Not Roman, though. Religion was a farce and the root of all evil. Liquor, sex, and carefree living suited Roman much more. For eight years, he'd travelled the land testing that theory, whoring and drinking, and pissing up the wall what little money he earned working in the fields.

Then, one day, he returned home... and set eyes upon his brother's new wife, Jane.

God was no saviour, and Roman fucking hated him for it.

He passed the library, James's office, and even the billiards room. Eliza wasn't in any of them. Just as well. It meant he could make a break for the main entrance and leave before she tried to stop him again.

He quickened his pace, ignoring the dull ache that still dominated his leg, and headed for the front door. Billy's police hybrid would still be outside and, as much as Roman hated its little electric arse, it would have to suffice as his getaway vehicle.

The bottom of the stairs came into view, and he stopped in his tracks. Eliza stood on the third step, her back to him, leaning over the bannister and staring up as if trying to see the first-floor balcony. When she finally straightened, he saw she held a knife in her left hand and a bottle of wine in her right. Then, she drank.

And she didn't stop.

Roman watched air bubble after air bubble replace every guzzle she swallowed. "What the hell are you doing?" he finally said.

Eliza jumped. Red wine dribbled down her chin, and she glared at him. Her eyes widened like a child who'd just been caught with their hand in the cookie jar.

Roman limped towards her. "Are you okay?"

Eliza raised the knife at arm's length. The frightened expression in her eyes grew the nearer he got. A green tint brightened her pupils for a second or two, then faded away. She glanced at the bottle in her hand. A frown creased her brow, and she looked to him for an answer. Before she had time to ask, she leaned forward and vomited.

Her legs buckled, and Roman caught her. The tip of the knife slashed his shoulder, and a newfound pain surged through his arm. He couldn't stop the wince of discomfort from morphing into an infuriated cry. Even so, he held her steady until her light-headedness passed. It took less than thirty seconds.

"I didn't know wine was your tipple." Roman took the knife from her hand, and stepped back. His blood already reddened the fabric of his shirt, but when he stretched back the collar he saw the slashed skin had already healed. At least his normal injuries mended like they should. It was just the earlier break Davis inflicted on his leg that caused him grief now.

Eliza wiped her mouth and stared at the bottle through glazed eyes. Her cheeks flushed pink, and she swayed slightly until the banister behind re-balanced her. "I was getting some water."

"Uh-huh." Roman slid the knife into his back pocket.

"I need some air."

"You need more than that." He took the bottle from her and sniffed its contents. Swigged back a mouthful to be sure the poison he'd consumed the day before didn't mar this drink as well. "Trust me when I say you really don't want to drink any alcohol in this place. It could literally kill you."

"I hate wine."

Roman eyed her. She genuinely seemed confused.

"Is it hot in here?" Eliza wafted the neck of the robe.

"No."

"I don't feel too good."

"Because you're pissed."

"But I haven't drunk anything."

Roman glanced at the bottle and decided to hold back on the mounting sarcasm. Something didn't sit right with him. Not the drinking. She'd been through so much in the last thirty-six hours. If getting pissed was how she needed to deal with the shit she'd been dealt, then hey, who was he to stop her? But trying to deny it? Eliza didn't care for his opinion, so why lie? And what the hell was the knife all about?

Shit. The nagging voice in the back of his mind pounded away. He took a deep breath, and rubbed his shoulder. A knot had formed right between his blades, and bugger him if he couldn't reach it. He closed his eyes and inhaled a deeper breath. Calmness still eluded him. Something wasn't right with Eliza. He knew it – could see it as clear as the nose on her face. But, at the moment, he could only deal with one problem at a time. And she wasn't his problem. He opened his eyes and looked at her. She couldn't be his problem. He'd saved her from her father. He'd earned the right to walk away with a clear conscience. He deserved to be able to have a go at sorting out his own shit now. He turned from her and started towards the door.

"Where are you going?"

"Somewhere that ain't here."

"But you owe me."

"I don't owe you shit."

"What about my brother?"

"For the love of God. He's dead." Roman turned to face her, those big brown eyes drawing him in so he'd agree to anything she wanted.

"Then what about me?" Eliza pointed towards the library. "I have my father's dead butler lying on the other side of a bookcase in that room. I know this because after you collapsed I bloody well dragged him in there. How the hell am I supposed to explain that to the police?"

"Shit. A grouchy drunk. That's just what I need."

"And what happens when, in a day or two, people start asking where the hell my father is, huh? What am I supposed to tell them? He just fucking disappeared?"

Her sudden use of the F-word surprised Roman.

Eliza walked down the couple of stairs and marched towards him, her steps short but rapid. "You goddamn owe me."

"I don't owe you anything. I fucked up, yeah, but I've put that right. Now I need to get the hell away from here." Standing on his leg had become more painful than he cared to admit. He turned and opened the front door. Moonlight brightened an otherwise dark sky, which suited him. It would be easier to run while the nearby towns slept. The hybrid was still parked at the bottom of the steps, the doors open. He had no idea what Billy had done with the keys, but Roman had yet to find a car he couldn't hotwire.

He stepped outside, the autumn air not as cool as he'd expected it to be.

Eliza was in front of him before he'd even reached the bottom of the steps. "You walk like John Wayne."

"So would you if I broke your leg." Even though he towered her by a good five inches, she still managed to stare him down. "I'm losing my temper with you, Eliza."

He tried to sidestep her, but she blocked his path. Again, she lost her balance and he steadied her. "For fuck's sake. I don't have time to play this fucking game. People are coming for me."

"You keep saying that, but I'm not seeing anyone."

Roman lowered his head. The ache in his shoulder crawled across his spine and pulsated up into his brain. He took a deep breath and looked at the bottle in his hand. It would be so easy to say fuck it and get drunk too.

"So, the way I see it, getting Billy back is our first and only concern."

Roman gave up. He closed his eyes, and stretched his head back as far as it would go. Immediately, he felt a little of tonight's tension loosen. He needed rest. He needed sleep. And most of all, he needed to get away from this house. When he opened his eyes, Eliza remained in front of him. Still staring through alcohol-glazed eyes. Still waiting. And, still ready to give him another belly full about saving the cop.

Roman glanced back at the bottle of wine, and sighed. *Fuck it.* First, he was going to drain the remainder of the bottle. Then, he was going to stick Eliza, and her constant nagging, in the boot of the car...again.

An owl hooted, and a sudden rush of birds flew from the woods that bordered the property. Roman glanced up. Beyond the first few trees there beckoned nothing but darkness. Probably just his imagination in overdrive, but the hairs on the back of his neck pricked to life. He sensed something, he just didn't know what. Eliza continued to talk, but he pushed her voice to the back of his mind. For maybe half a minute more he continued to watch the trees...just to be sure.

Again, his senses pricked to life. Something was seriously off. Eliza continued to rattle off what he assumed were her plans to save Billy, but Roman hushed her. He glanced across the grounds. Small lights illuminated the length of the winding driveway. Several Victorian lamps circled the fountain and brightened the area where the hybrid was parked. He glanced towards the forest. Did he just see something move? A light wind blew through the trees and everything seemed to shift. Shit. He was allowing it to play tricks with his mind.

No. His senses never let him down. Somebody was there, hiding in the woods, and an uneasy feeling weighed down on his shoulders.

"Are you even listening to me?" Eliza pulled on his arm.

Instead of answering, Roman kept his attention on the woods. Seconds passed, and still he saw nothing but the trees. Then something stepped out into the open. A dark-suited figure, hunched over but still well over seven feet tall, with arms hanging longer than any human limbs Roman had ever seen on this earth. It stopped, and seemed to take a moment to evaluate the area. Then, as Roman had witnessed many times in the past, it slowly twisted its bony neck until the whiteness of its face – partially hidden beneath coarse black hair and a top hat, which was pulled so far down it covered the tips of its ears – pointed towards the front of the house.

Grey eyes illuminated yellow and glared in Roman's direction.

The wine bottle fell from Roman's hand and smashed on the floor. He edged back from the top of the steps, the glass crushing beneath his shoes. He wasn't a man easily scared, but the sight of this thing frightened him to the core. Images resurfaced from his past: the endless torture he'd endured, the agonising screams of the other prisoner's he'd been forced to listen to. The monster that eyed him now had inflicted every ounce of it, and now Roman's worst nightmare – Purgatory's own Sheriff – had hunted him down to repeat it all over again.

CHAPTER SIX

Eliza ran.

From what, she had no idea.

She certainly hadn't seen whatever it was that had spooked Roman.

Her first instinct when he'd screamed at her to get inside the house was to argue with him, but when she saw how ghostly white his skin had turned, and the fear that dominated his eyes, she did as she was told.

The kitchen at the end of the hall was where she headed.

Roman grabbed her arm and pulled her back.

"We can get out through the back door."

"He'll have people there."

"He who?"

"The Sheriff."

"The police?"

"Not the police." Roman pushed her towards the stairs. "Up there."

"And go where?"

"Just get up there."

He clambered up the stairs behind her, his hand clasping tight onto hers until she felt as if it was she who were dragging him up. She glanced over her shoulder. Every step he climbed, his face creased in pain, and a short intake of breath escaped his lips. He paused at the top, presumably to catch his breath and wait for the pain in his leg to subside. Roman's current lack of fitness was going to get them both caught.

"What the hell is going on? Who are we running from?"

"I told you." Worry lines crumpled Roman's face, and anxiety darkened his eyes.

"You're not making sense."

"That thing down there is Purgatory's Sheriff."

"What does he want?"

"That thing ain't no *he*."

"Then what does *it* want?"

"Me."

Roman hobbled towards the room on their left – her father's bedroom. Far too large for just a place to sleep, and way too extravagant: Four-poster bed, silk sheets, mirrored ceiling - the dirty bastard – and a multitude of sophisticated art hanging on the walls. It had everything except what they needed: a panic room.

"There's nowhere to hide in there." Eliza pulled Roman back.

From below, heavy footsteps entered the house. Thud after thud, Eliza listened. They crossed the foyer and reached the stairs.

She froze.

Roman, however, didn't. He grabbed her hand and dragged her along the corridor, far away from her father's bedroom, and far away from the stairs. Eliza ran with him, passing room after room until they reached the end wall. It left them with nowhere else to go. She looked to Roman for an answer; for him to put some plan into action and get them both out of this mess like he had done numerous times already, but he seemed lost and unprepared.

Suddenly, reality slapped her in the face and she was petrified. The strong, arrogant control freak who had forced his zombie-killing self into her life and turned it upside down now looked scared and incapable of saving either of them.

"Why does it want you?"

"It wants to take me back."

"Back? Back where?"

"Purgatory."

The apprehension Eliza had seen on Roman's face moments earlier intensified. For the first time since she'd met him, she longed to see his cocky brashness return.

The first of the Sheriff's footsteps stomped onto the stairs.

"I can hold him off using my telekinesis."

"It won't be enough." He held her stare for a second, then spun her towards what had been her old bedroom. "Get inside that room and hide."

"Hide? Hide where? Under the bed?"

"Just do it."

"And what about you?"

Over Roman's shoulder, a man reached the top of the stairs. He stared blankly at the wall for a second or two, then turned towards Eliza. The familiar police uniform, dirty and dishevelled; his hair, chaotic and messy – just how he'd looked when Eliza last saw him. *Billy.* She fought free from Roman's grip and tried to run towards him, but Roman bundled her into the bedroom. He shut the door and locked it, immediately wedging a chair under the door handle.

"That's Billy out there," Eliza said, fighting to get back outside. She reached for the door handle, but didn't stand a chance against Roman. His strength far outweighed hers, even though he still struggled with the recovery of a broken leg.

"That is not Billy." He removed her hand from the door and restrained her from going for it again.

"But I saw him. You saw him. He's found a way back."

"I'm telling you, that is not Billy."

Eliza went for the handle again, and again Roman stopped her. "You are not going out there."

"I am."

Various items on her dresser started to rumble and shake. On her bedside table, the drawer flew out and smashed against the opposite wall.

Roman saw and loosened his grip on her. He drew in a controlled breath, as though to calm a tense situation. "If you go out there, that thing will kill you."

"But it was Billy. I saw him. You saw him."

Roman slowly shook his head. It spoke volumes.

The random items around the bedroom stilled. Fear replaced the fire in Roman's eyes, and now all Eliza wanted to do was get out of this bedroom and as far away from her father's house as possible. "Who is it?"

"The Sheriff."

"How can he—"

"Eliza, hush. Let me think."

"How are we going to get out of here?"

Something whacked the other side of the door, and Eliza jumped.

Roman was already at the window. "This way," he said, lifting the sash as high as it would go.

"You can't be serious."

Another thump, harder and more violent, walloped the door.

"I am serious."

"You said there may be more of these things out there."

"There aren't."

"How do you know?"

"Just get out the window."

"But we're a floor up."

"There's a drainpipe. Climb down it."

Eliza hurried to the window. It was a long drop to the garden below. She hated heights. Always had, ever since childhood, and by the time she'd reached her teens, it had gotten so bad she hadn't even been able to stomach the altitude of her tree house. She wiped her forehead. Her hands trembled. In fact, her whole body shook. She climbed on to the windowsill. To her left, the drainpipe descended the house a metre to her left. Again, she looked down. The autumn grass swirled below her. "I can't do this."

"Yes, you can."

She turned back to Roman, but he'd returned to the bedroom door. "What if I fall?"

"Make sure you don't."

A third blow bashed the door.

A fourth blow.

A fifth.

On the sixth, a hand punched clean through the wood. It wrapped Roman's neck, yanked him backwards, and pinned him against the door. Roman gripped the wrist. Twirling like a dancer, he spun free from its hold and twisted the Sheriff's arm into a lock.

Eliza stretched for the drainpipe, body overextending, her fingertips brushing the plastic cylinder until they found their grip. She inhaled deeply, and tried her best to ignore the distance separating her and the ground. She swung her legs over the ledge and lowered herself down a little further. The tips of her toes scraped the brickwork for extra grip until her foot found the pipe bracket. Terror paralysed her, and her panicked brain begged her not to let go of the sill. So, she hung there. Straddled between window and drainpipe. One foot struggled to stay on the bracket while the other foot dangled mid-air. The ends of her fingers whitened under the strain of carrying her weight, and gradually she started to slip.

From the bedroom, she heard the door cave in.

Roman.

But she was powerless to help. Her hand slipped from the ledge, and she swung from the window like a pendulum, slamming against the drainpipe some fifteen feet above the garden. Adrenalin failed to overpower her inner fear, and her hand trembled and weakened, unable to hold on to the pipe. Her foot slipped from the narrow bracket. She fell to the ground, the rain-soaked garden cushioning her fall, and the wet grass saturating her velvet robe.

She rolled on to her back and stared up at the window in time to see Roman leap out feet first. He landed beside her, his boots sinking a good inch or two into the muddy ground. His face contorted with pain under the impact.

He stood, but the look of discomfort remained in his eyes. "We need to get out of here."

Eliza already knew this. Whatever had smashed its way into her bedroom could at any moment jump through the window after them.

"Hurry." Roman gripped her arm and pulled her up off the floor. "Get to the front of the house."

Eliza didn't question him and instead ran with him, aiding him to the spot where the police hybrid sat in front of her father's house, doors still open, back window smashed in.

"Get in," Roman said.

Eliza did as she was told. She climbed in the passenger side and pulled the door shut. Roman was quickly beside her and reaching beneath the steering wheel. He broke a section of the dash away. Within seconds, he held a mass of wires in his hand.

"What are you doing?" But even as the words left Eliza's lips, she knew. Roman would get them away from this situation, and out of harm's way. After all, wasn't evading danger what he did best?

He singled out two specific wires and tapped them together.

Nothing.

No roar of an engine. No spark of life in the motor.

Roman slammed back against the seat, his head hitting the head rest. He tried again. Each tap became more agitated than the last. Finally, he dropped the wires and punched the steering wheel.

Any other time, Eliza would have seen his anger as the arrogant manner she'd come to expect: rapid breath, clenched fists, perspiration covering a face so taut it was as if he were made of stone. But anger wasn't what consumed him now. It was fear. Roman Holbrook was terrified.

"Can you hotwire a Roller?" she asked.

"What?"

"My father's Rolls Royce. Can you hotwire it?"

Slowly, the tightness in his jaw relaxed a little, and a faint smile turned the corners of his mouth. "I can hotwire anything."

Ignoring the fact that he'd just failed to do such a thing with the hybrid, Eliza chose to believe him. Why wouldn't she? He was Roman, after all.

Together they fled the tiny police car and raced to her father's garage. Eliza pulled open the newly painted door, and a laser of moonlight bounced off the Flying Lady of a 1921 Silver Ghost. It certainly was a magnificent-looking car – that unfortunately held nothing but bad memories for her.

"What the hell am I supposed to do with that?" Roman said, gawping at the aged vehicle.

"The other door," Eliza gestured.

Roman swung back the second door, and a look of satisfaction replaced his disappointment. A brand-new Drophead Coupe. It cost a fortune, made more than a statement around the town of Fowey, and had been her father's pride and joy.

"Now this I can work with."

He opened the car door, surprising Eliza that her father hadn't locked them, and ducked for the dash. Eliza checked the grounds behind her. Still no sign of this thing Roman said had come for him. A slither of doubt that perhaps Roman had been wrong started to nag at her. Maybe it *had* been Billy at the top of her father's staircase after all, escaping the hell he'd supposedly been trapped in and proving Roman wrong.

The Drophead roared to life, and Roman revved the engine until Eliza turned to face him. "Hurry up," he yelled out the window.

Eliza gave the scenery behind her one final, if not hurried, glance. Many times in her life she'd dreamed of fleeing this house, and now, like a wish gone bad, she was doing just that. The engine revved again and, as if on cue, she dashed to the car. She hadn't even closed the door when Roman punched the gear into drive. Tyres momentarily squealed on the highly polished garage floor, and the car shot forward.

Roman handled the accelerating vehicle with a welcomed skill. A different experience from Eliza's previous car journey with him, which she'd suffered from inside the boot of his Aston. That trip made her doubt Roman could in fact drive at all. However, she'd been very wrong. The Drophead glided around the curves of the driveway like a professional skater and, instead of grabbing for the seatbelt, a newfound confidence washed over her. They were going to get out of this. Roman was going to get them out of this.

Ahead, the secured gates blocked their path, but the car continued to speed towards them with no sign of slowing. Eliza reached for the dash and, as much as she wanted to scream for Roman to stop, she readied for the vehicle to smash through. Closer and closer. She shut her eyes. Held her breath.

Tyres screeched to a halt, and the driver's door opened. When Eliza looked up, Roman had already pushed the exit button, and the gates had begun to swing open. That was it. They'd escaped. They were free.

Roman turned from the gate, took a step towards the car, and froze.

Eliza froze, too.

Her breathing quickened. She sensed the person approach the car and, from the corner of her eye, watched it bend down and peer in at her through the passenger window. She turned her head, and there he was. Billy.

She wanted to smile, to open the door and wrap her arms around him. She knew she hadn't imagined him back at the house. But Roman had been right; she could see it now. This wasn't Billy. Darkness clouded his eyes, and the usual warmth in his smile was nowhere to be seen. This was pure evil sent from Purgatory to get Roman, just as he'd said.

A crease crinkled the tip of Billy's nose, and his nostrils lifted to sniff the night air. Without warning, Billy's face whipped towards Roman. "You?"

Confusion seemed to sweep over Roman and, for moment, neither man moved.

"Well, well, well. I'd just about given up looking for you, Holbrook."

"Well, now you've found me." Roman's cocky demeanour failed to hide his fear.

"Yes, I have, haven't I?" High-pitched amusement cackled from the Sheriff's throat. "You know, I saw you standing at the door, but it just didn't register. My eyesight must finally be failing me, eh?"

"Old age'll do that to you."

The Sheriff straightened. The smile fell from his lips. With fists clenched, he pounced at Roman with a speed Eliza had never before witnessed. One moment he was beside her window, and the next he was hammering Billy's police boots into Roman's stomach. Neither a show of retaliation or resistance surfaced and, to Eliza's dismay, Roman curled into a ball and took the beating.

Anger suddenly consumed her. Maybe Roman had given up, but she sure as hell hadn't.

The gates rattled open to their full extent. In less than ninety seconds, if the sensors picked up no movement, they would begin to close again. Freedom was only metres away. Once the car was moving again, nothing – not even the speed of the Sheriff – would ever be able to keep up.

Eliza shifted over to the driver's side and whacked the horn. The Sheriff stopped kicking Roman, and straightened. The Drophead's engine purred like a kitten, and Eliza could see only one option open to her. She moved the gear out of neutral and into drive. Her heartbeat pounded so hard she could hear it.

Roman stared at her, eyes wide, a sure sign he was dead against what she was about to do. But she had no choice. She revved the engine, and slid her hand to the brake. The Sheriff saw and smiled, revealing blackened teeth and a grey tongue – definitely not Billy.

He raised his hand and waved his finger at her like a parent scolding a child. Then his smile widened. Before Eliza's eyes, his physique transformed. The fullness that had been Billy's face thinned and shrivelled away. Coarse, straw-like black hair lengthened past his ears to frame a pointed nose; dry, reedy lips; and eyes so yellow they were almost illuminate. Gone went the blue of the police uniform, and spindle-like fingers – pale and thin, with nails resembling daggers – jutted out from beneath the sleeves of a long dark overcoat.

His height increased at least an extra two feet and, although hunched, Eliza still had to lean forward just so she could see the top of him through the windscreen. He whipped his fingers across the brim of his tall and newly appointed hat, and flicked back the tails of his coat – just how a cowboy would – to reveal the shiny badge pinned to the waistband of his trousers. A Sheriff's badge not too dissimilar to Billy's.

What in God's name had Roman done to have this thing come for him?

The Sheriff moved towards the car, his fingernails scratching paint from the bonnet as he closed in. Roman remained on the ground, coughing blood and struggling to breathe, but at least no longer a priority. Now the Sheriff had his sights set on her. He raised his nose towards the sky, closed his eyes, and sniffed in the night air until his inflated chest looked as though it would burst. Eliza's grip tightened around the hand brake. Her father's car could squash this Purgatory monster like a fly. The Sheriff whipped his head towards her, and in the blink of an eye he materialised beside the open driver's door. Eliza reached for the armrest to haul it shut, but the Sheriff's inch-long nails curled the frame and stopped it. He ducked his head until he looked her in the eyes. Hairs sprung from his chin, and tiny potholes cratered his blemished skin.

When he spoke, a stench warmed the air. "Just how many souls do we have hiding in here?"

Eliza pulled on the door again, but the Sheriff's grip didn't give an ounce. He reached out for her face, the tips of his talons touching her cheeks. Eliza hit his hand away, and scurried back across to the passenger seat. The Sheriff smiled again, but his eyes revealed he wasn't amused at having to chase her. He leaned in further, and grabbed her around the neck. Eliza screamed, but his cold fingers tightened their grip and yanked her towards him.

The dash, the steering wheel, the handbrake, everything she grabbed slipped from her grasp. The movie reel inside her head started to play, and the driver's door slammed hard against the Sheriff's legs, just as she willed it to do.

He didn't yell out in pain, and his hold around her throat tightened further. "I see Roman finally found his witch."

The car door opened and closed again, only this time without Eliza wishing it. Again, it opened. And again, Roman smashed it shut against the Sheriff's legs. The grip around Eliza's neck released, and she scampered back to the safety of the passenger seat. The Sheriff turned and his fingers coiled the frame to prevent Roman hitting him again.

The iron gates began to swing shut across the driveway, and Eliza knew the window to get the hell away was closing. Roman must have known it too, because he swung a clenched fist towards the Sheriff — a lucky punch considering his weakened state. It connected against the bony white of the predator's chin, and knocked him clear from the open door. The Sheriff straightened, and Roman pounced again. The Sheriff's longer reach found Roman first. His talons clawed into Roman's chest, ripping apart his shirt and slicing through his skin. Roman's face creased in pain, and he fell back against the car. He wasn't up to fighting this monster. The Sheriff would kill him for sure.

The Sheriff lifted Roman off the ground by his throat. Roman kicked at the air, his feet struggling to find the ground.

The Sheriff smiled, unbothered by the Reaper's weight. "I can't wait to get you back." He cast Roman away as if he were nothing more than a crumpled ball of paper.

Roman hurtled through the air and landed on the road just outside the house gates. Eliza clambered back into the driver's seat and released the handbrake. The gates had half closed, and she was unsure if the width of the car would get through unscathed. She punched down the accelerator and sped forward. Both wing mirrors clipped iron, and the edge of the gates ripped them clean from the bodywork.

Roman was in the road, already on his knees. Disorientated, he didn't notice the car alongside him until Eliza screamed at him to get in. He got to his feet and staggered towards her.

Before he'd even had time to close the door, Eliza accelerated away.

CHAPTER SEVEN

The Sheriff moved quickly.

He darted through the iron gates. The car swerved across the road, the wheels struggling to stick to the tarmac. A cloud of smoke wafted from the exhaust, and the Sheriff heard the gearbox groan for the next gear.

The Sheriff gave chase. Roman turned in the passenger seat. He glared with the same pretence of strength he'd shown endless times during his torturous ordeals back in Purgatory. Roman's defiance had angered the Sheriff back then, and it angered him now. One thing for sure, when he caught Roman this time, he'd break him once and for all.

Brake lights illuminated the dark lane. The Drophead rounded the bend, tyres screaming to hold on to the tarmac. The Sheriff reached for the car. His fingers brushed the car boot, and his talons punctured the metal bodywork. The country lane straightened, and he heard Roman scream for the girl to hit the accelerator. She did, but the Sheriff dug deeper. The car pulled away, dragging the Sheriff with it. He quickened his sprint, trying to regain control. He was proud to boast he could move like the wind, but this car was too fast even for him. The Sheriff started to lag. His claws tore through the metal until there was no boot left to hold onto.

But, he continued to chase. The gap between both him and the car increased, until he could no longer make out the number plate. And after two miles, even the glow of brake lights was no longer visible.

The Sheriff could run forever. He never tired. However, his speed was never going to match that of the car. He slowed to walking pace. Then, finally, admitted defeat and stopped altogether. He glanced at his hands, the illumination from the moon enhancing their skeletal appearance. One of his talons had been ripped clean off his finger.

And he was angry at that.

He was also angry that he had lost inmate 4429. The very person he'd been sent to retrieve.

He wanted to console himself with the knowledge that he had located another inmate. 2322. Roman Holbrook. Someone who had eluded him for many, many years. But, he couldn't. Because the Sheriff had lost him, too.

He sniffed the air. All he picked up now was the smell of damp grass and waning exhaust fumes. That's not to say he had forgotten Roman's scent. In fact, he remembered it now as well as the day they'd first met way back during the Salem witch trials. Roman's cocky facade and refusal to show any fear had outshone the other prisoners. That defiance was the basis of their entire relationship. A relationship where the Sheriff tortured Roman, and Roman pretended to not be affected by it. However, breaking Roman Holbrook's spirit had been a challenge. A challenge the Sheriff had eventually lost.

Hundreds of years passed, and that loss followed the Sheriff around like an STD. For the first hundred and fifty years, it had tormented him. After that, it just plain angered him. And the Sheriff did not like to lose. Swore he never would again. Especially not against Roman Holbrook.

Damn it. The Sheriff *had* just lost. For the second time. He'd be damned if he would lose a third.

Anger simmered beneath his skin. Now, though, after seeing Roman again, he couldn't help but feel a little excited.

Because now, finally, the Sheriff had a chance to redeem himself.

He sniffed the air again. Caught the faint whiff of cow dung. He may not be able to locate Roman's scent straight away, but patience was a virtue. The odour would present itself again. And the Sheriff would be waiting.

He heard the hum of a vehicle approach from behind. Before the headlights found him, he cracked his bony knuckles, stretched his long neck, and closed his eyes. He felt his body compact. His hair lifted from around his shoulders. His talons shortened. When he opened his eyes, his dark coat had been replaced once again by the police uniform.

Lights behind brightened the lane in front of him. The Sheriff held out his hand, and the car stopped beside him. Use of a car would be good right about now.

The window lowered, and a young girl peered up at him. Before she spoke, the Sheriff grabbed her hair. The girl screamed, but the Sheriff yanked her from the car. He threw her to the ground and could have left it there. He had the car after all. But he needed to ease his feeling of failure with a kill. The girl scrambled to her knees, but he stamped down between her shoulder blades. He heard her spine crack, and she collapsed. He flipped her over. Fear stared up at him, and contentment found him.

"Please, don't kill me." Tears streamed her face, but she did not move. Could not move.

He turned to the sky. Reckoned he had ten minutes spare to fulfil his need. He closed his eyes, and it was only seconds before he was once again his old self. The girl's eyes widened. She screamed. Her head whipped from side to side, but her body still didn't attempt to move.

The Sheriff flapped open his coat. Pulled a saw from an inside pocket. Old blood and rust dirtied the blunt blade. He knelt beside the girl. Spread her legs. Placed the blade at the juncture. He didn't have time to string her upside down between two trees — much to his dismay. This spur-of-the-moment method would have to suffice.

Death by saw had always been one of his top-five torture methods.

The girl screamed. Cried out for help. Begged God for her life.

The Sheriff began to saw. Up past her navel. Through her ribcage. Her throat was very accommodating. Her skull – not so much. The saw finally cracked free and the girl divided into two.

The Sheriff slid the saw back into his coat – uncleaned – and stepped over the body. He opened the car door and stole into the driver's seat. He glanced at the girl, wished he could take her with him, and closed the door.

Give or take a year or two, it had been thirty years since he'd last visited this area. No doubt, after sunrise, he'd see the place would've changed, just like every other place he had visited over the years while trying to locate Roman.

But now he had found him.

Now, the Sheriff's perseverance was finally going to pay off.

CHAPTER EIGHT

Different shades of green whizzed past Eliza in a blur.

The countryside, as dark as it was, couldn't slow the Drophead down. Instead, the car powered on through the narrow lanes, clipping dirt banks and flicking mud from its back wheels.

"Is it following us?"

Roman turned in his seat. "No." He settled back, a faint groan of discomfort leaving his lips.

"Are you sure?"

"No. It's pitch black. I can't see a damn thing."

She threw a glance his way. He was doing nothing to calm her nerves. His arm wrapped his stomach, and although he looked better than he had five minutes earlier, it was clear he'd suffered another injury back at her father's house. She turned away and, having learned well enough by now that he'd never voluntarily admit to weakness, peered up at the sky. It was hard to believe this glorious starry night had borne so much horror.

"What are you looking at?"

"I'm checking."

"Checking what? Whether we're being followed? It's a Purgatory Sheriff, not Superman."

"For all I know, he can teleport."

"Eliza, relax. He's not following us."

Eliza eased her foot from the accelerator. The needle fell to forty, and she held it there. "Is that the thing you said was coming for you?"

"No. That back there was much worse."

"So, there's still something else coming for you?"

"No."

"Are you sure? How'd you know?"

"Because he's the Boss Man."

"What does he want?"

He glanced at her. "Me."

"Why?"

Roman shrugged. He lifted his jumper to check his stomach. He saw Eliza staring. "Just a couple of broken ribs. They're already healing."

Roman's ability to change subject and avoid her questions grated on Eliza. "Does he want me as well?"

"You? No. That's a different department altogether. Besides, I replaced your soul. You won't even be on their radar."

"How did he become Billy? Has he seen my brother?"

"He can take different forms."

"But it was so real."

"That's the whole point."

Eliza slowed further, until the needle hit thirty. Roman didn't look too good. They needed to find somewhere to hole up, and she had more questions she wanted answered. Lots more, in fact. "How did he *know* to be Billy?"

"He just does. Hones in on someone's weak spot – in your case, you and Billy – then manipulates the hell out of it."

"Why does he want you?"

Roman answered with a sigh.

"Tell me."

"I already did. I spent some time in Purgatory. Then I left. He wants me back there."

"About that… You said you were imprisoned in this inescapable place that's Purgatory, yet here you are. How?"

Roman shifted position. Wrinkles of discomfort creased his eyes.

"Did you escape? Can Billy escape?"

Roman glanced out the window.

Eliza stared at the back of his head for what seemed an age. "Answer me!"

Roman's fists clenched. "It's impossible to escape Purgatory."

"But you did?"

Roman nodded.

"So, it is possible to escape. Billy does have a chance to escape."

"No."

"But you just said—"

"You have to forget about Billy. Billy is dead."

"He is my brother. I will never stop looking for him."

"Then you're in for a lot of disappointment." Roman turned away from her again. "Where exactly are you driving to?"

Another change of subject. As much as she didn't want to, Eliza decided to let the conversation drop. First they'd get to a safe place, then she'd make Roman go and get Billy. "My house. You need to rest."

"I told you I'm fine."

"Well, I'm not." Eliza paused. She took a deep breath. When she spoke again, she purposely kept her voice calm and even. "We need time to catch our breath, regroup, come up with a plan, grab supplies,—"

"The zombie apocalypse is over, remember?"

"Yeah. Now we have some freak from Purgatory after us. After you."

Up ahead, three army trucks dominated the right-hand side of the road. Spotlights lit two soldiers clambering across the upturned field. They reached the tarmac, a decaying corpse swinging between them like a neglected rope bridge. They threw it up into the back of the nearest truck. The body landed on a heap of carcasses and descended into a roll before finding its place nearer the bottom. Then, the soldiers dropped the khaki canopy and climbed into the truck's cab. The vehicle pulled out in front of Eliza with no indication, and she slowed until the Drophead's speedometer hardly moved. The truck pulled away, but Eliza was apprehensive to follow.

"What's wrong?" Roman said.

Seriously? He actually expected a civil answer to that question? Tens upon tens of zombie bodies stuffed the back of a truck just metres in front of her. Possibly the same zombies who'd killed her colleagues and patients at the hospital. Possibly the same zombies who'd also tried to kill her. And Roman had the gall to ask what was wrong? What the hell was right about this situation?

Across the landscape, it became evident the government's clean-up (cover-up) operation was in full swing. Soldiers scattered floodlit fields in pairs, looking alert and anxious, with guns ready to shoot anything that moved. A soldier stepped from between the remaining parked trucks and hurriedly waved Eliza past. Reluctantly, she sped up, catching up with the truck again in next to no time.

She needed a distraction. "I won't stop asking why this Sheriff wants you, you know."

"Please, just drop it."

"And you know why? Because if he finds you, he will also find me."

"Trust me, he has no interest in you. I pulled a Houdini." He looked at Eliza. Probably noticed her confusion. "I swapped your soul with McKenzie's. The waiting room wouldn't have had time to log you. Purgatory has nothing to do with the waiting room, other than to take anyone sent to them. It's impossible that he is here for you."

"That does little to reassure me." The army truck turned off to the right, and some of the unease that gnawed at Eliza's nerves lifted. "Look, suppose you're right–"

"I am."

"– and the Sheriff hasn't come for me. How did it find you at my father's house?"

Roman shrugged. "Probably when I brought you back from the dead."

"But it looked surprised to see you – at the car, I mean."

"I don't know what else to tell you."

"Then why didn't it take you? Why did it come after me?"

Roman sighed. His body tightened, and irritation marred his voice. "You did honk your horn like a mad woman."

"He was going to kill you. I had to do something."

"Killing me was not on his mind."

"Then what was?"

"I told you, he wants to take me back."

"To Purgatory?"

"Yes."

"Why?"

"Why not?"

"Really? After everything we've been through. Why won't you just tell me?"

"Because I don't want to relive it!" Roman pulled on the steering, and the Drophead swerved to the side of the road. Eliza braked, but before she could say anything, Roman got out of the car and slammed the door shut behind him.

Eliza remained seated and watched him. He walked to the edge of the field, arms crossed, and stared into the darkness.

She opened the door and got out of the car. Should she console him? Would he appreciate it? Would he turn on her again?

He glanced over his shoulder as she approached, but didn't say anything.

It was down to Eliza to make the peace. She placed her hand on his arm. "We'll sort this out."

"No, we won't."

"So why the hell are we running? Why the hell didn't you just let him take you back at the house?"

"You don't understand."

"That's right, I don't. Because you refuse to explain it to me."

Roman turned to her. "I fucked up."

"Does it matter?"

"Of course it matters."

"Why? Because you never fuck up?" She smiled, trying to diffuse the tension between them. "We can fight this thing. I'll help you."

Roman frowned, clearly not sharing her buoyant approach. "If you interfere and try to stop him, he will either kill you or take you, too."

"I don't care."

"Then you're a fool. Because of something I've done, we're both in danger. Why can't you get that in your head?"

"Oh, for Christ's sake, man up."

Roman stepped closer to her, teeth clenched, pulse throbbing in his jaw. "There are only three outcomes to this mess. The first: He takes me back to Purgatory and tortures me for the rest of eternity. The second: He takes you back to Purgatory and tortures you for the rest of eternity. Or third: He takes us both back and, well, you know the drill. I'm not comfortable with any of those endings."

"Have you even considered that maybe there's a fourth option?"

"Oh?"

"We find a way out of this mess and nobody gets tortured in Purgatory?"

Roman snorted, but his jaw softened. "There goes that misplaced optimism again."

"I don't think it's misplaced." Eliza checked the road. Still no sign of the Sheriff, but she really didn't want to stand out here any longer than necessary. She needed a different tactic. "Let me ask you a question. Why did you bring me back from the dead?"

"What do you mean?"

"It's a simple enough question. You said yourself, you could be with your son and his mother now. Instead, you saved me. Why?"

Roman's lips tightened. "Because you didn't deserve to die."

"And now I do?"

"What are you talkin—"

"I think you saved me because you couldn't live with the guilt if I'd died."

"You're wrong. I have no conscience. I thought you'd have learned that by now."

Eliza stared at him. "My mistake, then." She walked back to the car.

"Where're you going?"

Eliza opened the door. "Back to my father's. If the Sheriff is going to take me, it may as well be now." She got in the car and shut the door.

Roman turned back to the darkness. Had her instinct about him caring for her been misread? She hoped not, because she very much wanted him to stop her right now.

At the very least, she expected him to talk her into going somewhere safer. She pulled the seatbelt across her and buckled it. Still, Roman made no attempt to intervene. She turned the key, and the engine roared to life. Obviously, she'd misjudged everything about him. He clearly didn't have a conscience, just as he said. She waited for the reaction of anger and betrayal to overpower her emotions, but instead a twinge of sadness trounced her. For the first time since she had met Roman, it dawned on her that she didn't want to be apart from him. Realisation was a harsh thing when at last it happened.

Her throat tightened, and tears filled her eyes. She put the car into gear and reached for the handbrake.

The passenger door opened. "I should drive."

"I'm fine."

"You've been drinking."

"I've also been driving."

"Still, best not to tempt fate."

Eliza didn't look at him. "Jumping out my bedroom window and fighting monsters from Purgatory has surprisingly sobered me up." Relief that she'd not been wrong about Roman overwhelmed her, and further tears, these of joy, threatened to spill.

He climbed back into the car – the passenger side. As much as she wanted to turn to him and seek comfort, exposing her confused affection for a man she'd convinced herself she hated was not something she was willing to share – at least, not until she understood it herself first.

She started the car and pulled away from the verge. An annoying beep warned that something had gone amiss, and a red light illuminated the dash.

"Are you still planning on going home to Polperro?" Roman plugged in his seatbelt and the beeping stopped.

"Yes."

"You should go somewhere else."

The Drophead was a much bigger car than she was used to, and navigating the corners took immense concentration and skill. She threw Roman a quick glance. "Why?"

"Your neighbour. She's lying dead on your kitchen floor."

This news should have shocked Eliza. It certainly would have shocked her on any other day. Today, however? Today, it seemed acceptable. "You killed Mrs. McKenzie?"

"In self-defense. The woman was a psychotic nut-job."

"So, tell me somewhere you haven't killed anyone, and we'll go there." Eliza's vision blurred. Dizziness swooned inside her head, and her eyes closed.

When they opened, a dark road lay ahead. Then, Roman came into view.

Nausea set in. Then panic. Thunderous palpitations made it hard to breathe. Dainty hands gripped the steering wheel, and fear of the unknown would not allow him to release it. Outside, trees and darkness sped past in the opposite direction. His skin dampened with perspiration. Where was he? Where was the house he'd been in last time? The vehicle veered towards the edge of the path.

Roman grabbed the wheel. "What're you doing?"

Frightened, he forced the dainty hands to release the steering wheel. Trepidation seized his spine. In a split second, dread turned into immense terror. The girl's hands clenched into fists and started to bang against the driver's window, desperate to smash the glass and escape before Roman killed him. Darkness was everywhere. The car accelerated. Swerved. Shot forward across the road.

"Brake! Brake!"

The car gathered speed.

Roman screamed for the car to stop. He pulled on the steering wheel, and yanked up the handbrake. The car spun, and the Drophead skidded across the road. It crashed side-on into a tree.

"Eliza. Eliza."

Eliza opened her eyes.

A cool breeze swept across her skin. Glass littered her lap, and when she turned to look at Roman, giddiness consumed her again. "What happened?"

"You crashed the fucking car." He reached for her hand.

Eliza didn't remember any of it. She moved her hand away from him. Threw up in his lap. "I'm sorry," she mumbled, and tried to open the door. The tree wedged it shut. She tried again. Claustrophobia consumed her. She pushed at the door again. "I have to get out of here."

"Hey, just calm down." Roman unclipped his seatbelt. He reached across, his hands quickly finding her shoulders. He forced her to face him. "You're okay, you hear me?"

She flinched away, but he held her still. She tried again, but her whole body felt heavy and tired. She stopped struggling.

"Okay, now are you hurt?"

Eliza shook her head. At least, she didn't think she was hurt.

"Good, because I'm going to fucking kill you." He released her shoulders and unlocked her seatbelt. He glanced down at his lap. Cursed. Looked back at her. "What the hell were you thinking?"

"I don't remember crashing."

"How can you not remember?"

"I don't know." She tried to open the driver's door again, and this time Roman didn't try to stop her. Finally, after it was clear it wouldn't budge, she sat back in her seat. "I couldn't have done this."

He pulled a tissue from the silver dispenser on the dash and wiped his trousers. "Well, you did."

"Why can't I remember?"

Roman leaned away from her. "Your head's just frazzled." He flicked on the interior light.

Several cracks fractured the windscreen. Beyond that, she saw nothing. "There's something wrong with me, isn't there? I can't remember drinking. I keep being sick. And now this."

"You're being sick *because* you keep drinking. And you're drinking because you're in shock over what happened last night. That's all." He stared at her for what seemed minutes. Finally, he sighed. He kicked open the passenger door. "We need to get out of here."

"And go where?

Again, Roman sighed. "Where does Billy live?"

"Millendreath."

"Then that's where we're going."

"But it's miles away. We can't walk that kind of distance."

Roman climbed out of the car. "That's why we're gonna get another car."

"What car? We have no money."

"I wasn't planning on paying for one."

Eliza climbed over the passenger seat. Murder, kidnapping, and now thieving. "There really is no end to your talents, is there?"

"Hey, you wanna walk, be my guest." He offered his hand to help her from the car, but she declined it.

Sickness swirled in the pit of her stomach. She felt like crap. "This is all your fault."

Roman gave a disbelieving snort. "How the fuck is you crashing the car my fault?"

"It just is." Of course, it wasn't his fault. If he hadn't bulldozed his way into her life, she'd be dead right now.

Roman sighed. He walked to the back of the car and forced open the mangled boot.

Eliza didn't follow. Instead, she leant against the bonnet, and waited. The coarse tarmac hurt her feet, but to complain seemed futile. Ironically, the cold air soothed her aching soles. However, within seconds her toes numbed and a new ache began.

The boot closed, and Roman swaggered back to the front of the car. "Come on, let's get out of here." He wrapped a blanket around her shoulders.

"And how far do you think we'll get?"

"We won't know if we don't start walking."

The blanket warmed her slightly and, although pleased, she'd have given it up in an instant for a pair of shoes – or even socks.

Roman didn't wait for her. By the time she began to walk, he'd already put several strides between them. She turned her head and stared behind her. Darkness swallowed the lane. Maybe it also concealed the Sheriff. Eliza broke into a run. She quickly caught up with Roman, but her apprehension that at any given moment the Sheriff could jump from the darkness didn't diminish. The blanket slipped from her shoulders. She caught it before it hit the floor and re-wrapped it – tighter this time. "We're sitting ducks out here."

"That's why we need a car."

"You're delusional. We're in the middle of nowhere, and it is stupid-o'clock. We're not going to find one."

Roman didn't answer.

"So, let's just say that – by some miracle – we find a car. We make it to Billy's…and then what? How long before that monster finds us again?"

"Can you just shut up for five minutes while I think?"

"I'm just saying. If we get a car, why not drive further? Like Scotland? Daddy has…" She paused. *Daddy.* How could she ever call him by that name again? "There's a place in Scotland. Inverness to be exact."

Roman smiled. Supercilious. "Do you think you'd be safer there?"

"Fine. Don't stay at the house. We can get a flight instead. Go to Europe or something."

Roman took a deep breath, and Eliza could hear that his patience wore thin.

"At least I am trying to think of a way out of this mess."

Roman's smile widened. Again, he was being a dick and patronizing her. For the briefest moment, a sliver of moonlight filtered past the treetops. It shimmered against the side of his face, drawing attention to the scar that curved his lips. Suddenly, Eliza felt a calm sweep over her.

"We need to head to the river, see if we can get across it," Roman said.

"Have a boat in your back pocket, do you?" She felt Roman's glare bore into her.

"We're not far from Milltown."

"So?"

"So, Fowey River becomes a stream from there on in. We can cross it and get to your brother's place a hell of a lot quicker than sticking to the roads." He seemed to give her a second to digest what he said. "Unless you want to take the long way round? All twenty miles of it?"

Oh, hell. She hated it when he was right.

He took off for the trees, and again she had to quicken to a jog to catch up. "You do know how we can kill this Sheriff thing, don't you?"

Roman paused, and the rustle of branches ceased. "There is no way to kill the Sheriff."

CHAPTER NINE

Boconnoc was as good a place as any to steal a car.

Although finding one along the deserted path was proving more than just a challenge, even to a more experienced thief like Roman.

He stopped for breath. Walking ten miles used to be easy – heck, a week ago he could have run it backwards faster than he moved now. But, even he was smart enough to realise he'd never reach Milendreath on foot. He rubbed his ribs, and stretched. No soreness there. They'd completely healed. His leg? Not so much. That ached like hell. Best he tried to ignore that altogether.

Across the landscape, the morning sun stirred. Roman wore no watch and had little idea of how early it was, but golden rays warmed the countryside and reawakened memories from a life he'd long since left behind. It also reminded him of how much time had passed since he and his brother had spent time here. God, he'd loved this area. The views, the quietness, the time spent away from his father. Good times, good drinking, and even better, good women.

He arched his back and tried to stretch the ache from his spine. Across the way, a clump of trees, much more matured than when he'd last been here, formed the perfect circle in the middle of the field. Guilt stabbed his heart. He'd brought Jane here the day she'd told him he was to be a father. The day he told her she'd be better off staying with his brother. The day he told her he was leaving. He glanced at the trees again and thought of his own child, and what could have been. He heard Eliza approach, and his thoughts turned to her and what could still be.

Roman shook his head. Goddamn Eliza messing with his head again. "You need to keep up or you're going to get us both killed."

"I'm trying." Eliza pushed past him. Now, she led them.

But Roman didn't follow.

She walked on, probably aware that he wasn't behind her – maybe even aware that he watched her. He'd been stupid not leaving the house before the Sheriff found him. And now Eliza was involved. Maybe he'd been stupid saving Eliza in the first place. No. he'd been right to resurrect her, of that he was certain. When his dear Jane had died, it was two years before word of her death reached him. He hadn't possessed the power back then to save her or his child. But now? Now he could save a life, and what better life to save than Eliza's? *Shit.* He knew using his powers to save her would alert Purgatory, but he hadn't expected the Sheriff to come for him.

He shook Eliza from his thoughts and continued onwards across the field after her, annoyed that once again his feelings for her had taken him somewhere he didn't want to go. It didn't take long before he'd overtaken her and resumed the lead.

Ahead, in the midst of overgrown grass, the tip of a church spire reached towards the clouds. Although unfamiliar to Roman and probably built many years after his time on this earth had ended, he headed towards it. Going by the direction of the sunrise, the church looked to be somewhere over by the coast. That's where they needed to head.

Rough weather and years of neglect had brought the church to its knees. Outside, crumbled stone had fallen away from its walls, and windswept tiles left holes in the roof. Inside, the sea air had eaten away most of its history, only to have late night revellers replace it with a more modern, twenty-first-century look. Church candles filled every nook and cranny – some melted into nothing, others hardly used. Empty beer cans and used condoms scattered the dirt around old sleeping bags, and in the far corner, a used syringe. Someone had enjoyed one hell of a time.

Roman left, and walked around to the back of the building. The long grass tangled around his ankles, slowing his pace further, and he wished that, just for once in this whole godforsaken mess, some luck would come his way.

An old Ford Escort was not the kind of luck he had been hoping for. It was parked alongside the wall. Rust ate away most of the faded red paintwork, one rear light was smashed, and polythene covered the missing back window.

"You're not thinking of taking that thing?" Eliza said.

Roman ignored her and peered inside. Two teenagers snuggled together on the back seat, fast asleep. In the front, empty beer cans and the remains of a spent joint. Roman turned and gave the surrounding area a quick once-over. No other vehicles and, over by the trees, no sign that there could be any other remaining partygoers taking a piss. Roman smiled. Not his usual choice of transport, and clearly not Eliza's, but it had wheels. If the engine worked, he wanted it.

Roman banged on the roof, but neither occupant moved. *Jesus.* They were more stoned than he'd first thought. Roman banged harder. "Wakey, wakey. Time to rise and shine, lovebirds."

The young girl stirred. Her eyelashes pulled free from the smudged mascara, and her eyes flickered open. She stretched, yawned, and crooked her neck at the young man lying beside her. "What time is it?"

"Time for you and your boyfriend here to get on home."

The girl turned to Roman. Her eyes widened. "What do you want?"

"This car." Roman opened the door. He reached for her hand and encouraged her out of the vehicle. "Now, apart from lover boy here, is there anyone else with you?"

The girl shook her head.

"Good. Let's get Sleeping Beauty up, and I'll be on my way." Roman slapped the guy around the feet.

The man groaned, and turned over.

Roman looked at the girl. "Just how many drugs did he take last night?"

"None. Honest."

"Uh-huh." Roman grabbed for the boy's ankles and pulled him out of the car.

The boy landed on the grass. Disorientated, he spotted Roman and froze. "Who the hell are you, man?"

"As I've just explained to your girlfriend here, I'm in need of a vehicle." Roman reached into the back of the car. Over his shoulder flew a pair of sandals, a denim shirt, and an old blanket.

The boy caught the shirt. "You're going to steal my ride?"

Roman straightened. "I prefer to call it borrowing, but if stealing works for you then I'm good with that."

"But that's my ride."

Roman slammed the door shut. "Does it work?"

"Of course it works. How the hell'd you think I got here?"

"Good." Roman opened the driver's door. It creaked and grated, and he expected it to fall free. The keys hung from the ignition, and he turned them. Surprisingly, the engine fired up the first time, sounding like a drag car. Roman fought the urge to take a gander beneath the bonnet.

He glanced at Eliza. "You coming?"

Eliza stared at the two teens. "I am so sorry for this." She ran around to the passenger side and got in the car.

"Hey, man." The boy jumped up from the grass, still struggling to pull his shirt on. "I can't let you take my ride, man."

Roman settled in the seat and reached for the door handle. "What's your name, son?"

The boy stopped, now unsure what to do. "Josh."

"Well, Josh, I'd worry more about what would happen if you tried to stop me." Roman let the words sink in, then pulled the door shut.

Neither Josh nor his girlfriend gave chase.

CHAPTER TEN

Billy heard them looking for him.

By *them*, he meant people.

At least, it sounded like people – a bloody lot of people.

He crouched deeper into the crevice. The rock face dug into his back, and he prayed to whatever God was listening that a way out would hurry up and come his way.

Voices echoed around him. One, louder than the rest, shouted orders for the two unauthorised souls to be found, and Billy knew that referred to him and his father. It also meant that his father had so far also eluded capture or maybe even escaped altogether. Footsteps hammered up and down the adjoining passages, and shadows washed across the dimly lit walls. Billy closed his eyes. This place was different from anything he'd ever known. Never-ending tunnels with nowhere to hide. Even the largest of gaps, like the one he now squeezed into, didn't hide him completely.

His knees stuck out. His head couldn't quite get under the ridge. He was a sitting duck.

He opened his eyes again. The voices had drifted off in another direction and, by the sound of it, the army of followers had gone with them. Billy turned his head. First left. Then right. To his relief, he saw no sign of anyone, or anything. But he knew that, sooner or later, those footsteps would charge down this passageway and, if Billy remained where he was, he'd be found.

He crawled away from the wall and took refuge behind a stalagmite. Still, he could hear voices somewhere at the end of the long corridor. He turned from them and headed in the opposite direction. Never had he wanted to get out of a place so badly. His hesitant footsteps gradually quickened, and soon desperation outweighed his cautiousness. He sprinted along the passage, squeezing and ducking past obstructing stalagmites and stalactites.

The tunnel continued on and on. Identical rocks and stones passed by, and Billy wondered if he was stuck in some kind of *Groundhog Day* scenario – only without Bill Murray annoying the shit out of him.

Behind, echoing voices seemed to keep up with him. *Shit.* The search party was hot on his trail, even if they themselves didn't know it. Billy moved faster. A stitch pierced his side, but as much as he wanted to stop for breath, he carried on running.

Ahead, he saw a shadow darken the already dim tunnel. He slowed, crouched behind a stalagmite, and watched.

Definitely a shadow. Somebody was coming. *Shit.*

Behind, the hoard of voices gained on him. In front, only one shadow blocked him. Could it belong to only one person? Could he be that lucky? His heart hammered against his chest. He had no choice but to push on, and pray that the lone person between him and the end of the passage was weak, short, and bloody stupid.

He stuck close to the tunnel edge. Every step he took moved at a creeping pace until he reached the next stalagmite. The person in front of him was close – like Billy, not moving too fast, and being almost as quiet.

Billy crouched, and waited. His heart pounded harder than he'd ever thought possible. Droplets of sweat trickled down his forehead. He wanted to wipe them away, but fear of being heard paralysed him. The person approached the other side of the stalagmite. Billy's body stiffened, and he readied himself for attack. He listened. To his right, the person began to squeeze past the rock formation. Billy rounded the formation to his left. The crowd of voices echoed through the air. The person hesitated. Billy pounced from behind.

The person, a man, yelled. Billy wrapped his neck, and covered his mouth. The yell quietened into a muffle. Now the man fought back. Billy tightened his hold, but when the man's struggle failed to weaken, Billy punched him in the side of the head. The man continued to scuffle, albeit weaker and less aggressive. Billy punched him again, and kicked him to the floor. He raised his foot, ready to stamp the man's throat out.

Billy halted his assault. "What the fuck…Dad?"

James glanced up at him. Pure hatred filled the old man's eyes. Billy held his father's stare for a second, then forced the anger away. James went to speak, but Billy lowered to his side and hushed him.

The voices were louder. Closer. Hunting them.

"We have to get out of here."

Being given an order ignited another hateful glare in James' eyes.

Billy had witnessed that look more times than he could count. "I don't have time for your shit." He stood.

James struggled to get to his feet. Billy didn't offer to help him. Instead, he peered over the stalagmite and watched for the pursuing troops.

"Can you see them?" James hovered close beside him.

"No." But Billy could hear them. Moving closer and closer.

"Who are they?"

"I have no idea, and I have no desire to find out." Billy faced his dad. "What's down that way?"

"The same as this."

The voices grew louder.

"Any way out?" Billy pressed.

"If there was, I can assure you I'd have taken it."

Billy swallowed back the urge to argue. "Well, that's the way we need to go."

"I told you, there's no exit that way."

"Then you carry on going your way." Billy didn't wait for an answer. He pushed past his father. And he ran.

James' footsteps soon ran close behind him. Billy didn't turn back. He didn't care for his father. In fact, he wished the dear old bastard dead. The man was a monster – possibly even worse than the evil that chased them down here. Again, Billy pushed back the rising anger. Anger that he may actually need his father's help to escape.

Together they ran along identical-looking passageways, with identical-looking rock formations.

The voices followed. Shouted. "Here. I see one of them. Go around. Cut them off."

Billy quickened his pace. His father kept up with him.

More yelling. "Get to the corner. Release the Hellhounds."

What the hell was a Hellhound? What the hell was Billy running towards?

Dread gnawed his insides, but Billy continued to sprint along the corridor.

Ahead, ear-splitting barking drowned out all sounds of their footsteps. Billy slowed, as did his father. Billy covered his ears. These were no dogs he'd ever heard before. He stopped, smart enough to know he'd die if he went any further. He needed options. Maybe climb a stalactite? *Stupid*. Outrun the dogs or whatever the hell they were? *Even more stupid.*

"Shit." Billy was out of options before he'd even thought of any.

He stopped.

"What's wrong?"

The sound of his father's voice was proving hard to listen to. He wanted to kill his father for all the evil he'd done, not strike up an alliance. "We're stuck with no way out."

"There's always a way, son. You just have to look for it."

Billy snapped. "You're bloody delusional."

"I'm a survivor."

Billy punched his father. His dad's knees buckled, and he collapsed to the floor. Maybe he should kill his father. Go out on a high? He tilted his head back and glanced into the darkness above him. There seemed no end in sight. He trailed the blackness back down until the rock walls came into view.

The rock walls.

Large rocks, jutting out at all angles. What did he have to lose?

His father got back to his feet. Saw what Billy was thinking. "You're not serious, are you?"

"Do you have a better idea?"

James remained silent.

"Good. Get climbing." Billy felt for the first rock.

Gripping hold, he hauled himself off the ground. His boot found a small jut. He jammed the toe cap in and pushed himself up another couple of feet. His father also climbed. Not as fast, but enough to be hidden from sight before the pack of dogs and hunters reached them.

Billy touched the darkness first. He glanced down, losing sight of his own shoes as he climbed higher. Six feet below, he watched his father climb into the black veil, and hoped it was enough to throw the predators below off their trail.

Billy paused. He didn't want to climb any higher than he needed to. As it was, he reckoned he was about thirty feet up. If he slipped? Well, a fall from this height and it wouldn't matter who was waiting for him below.

He saw the dogs arrive. At least, they resembled something from the canine family. Five in total. Bigger than any mutt he'd ever seen before. In fact, bigger than any bear he'd seen before. They growled and snarled. Shuffled around the area erratically, sniffing the floor, the air, the walls. Three seconds, then, in unison, they leapt to their hind legs and barked up into the darkness.

A group of hooded men joined them. They also stared up into the darkness. One of them ordered several of the others to climb the walls. Billy held tight, and prayed. His father moved and brushed against his calf, and Billy knew they had to keep climbing. He clambered for a higher rock and scaled another foot, hoping his father would follow.

A hand grabbed his ankle. Billy looked down. Was his father in trouble? Had the hooded men reached them already? The hand tugged down. Billy tried to shake it free, but the clasp tightened.

"They're only after you." James yanked Billy's ankle harder. "And like I said, son. I'm a survivor."

Billy scrambled to regain his footing. Fingertips slipped from the tiny ledge, and he tumbled away from the wall.

He plummeted towards the ground.

But he didn't hit the floor.

The goddamn stalagmite skewered him first.

CHAPTER ELEVEN

Millendreath seemed normal.

And by that, Roman meant it seemed unaffected by the horror of the last few days. No dead bodies littered the street. No smashed windows decorated chocolate-box cottages. It was as if Millendreath had dodged the whole zombie nightmare.

Roman cut the engine and glanced at the apartment building. "Which one's your brother's?"

"Top left."

"Right. Let's get up there before someone sees us."

"And then what?"

"What do you mean?"

"I mean, and then what? You're gonna leave, aren't you?"

Roman opened the driver's door. He really didn't need this crap. Not right now. "Let's just get up there."

He crossed the car park and headed inside the apartment building, Eliza sticking by his side the whole time. Only one flight of stairs, and he took it to the first floor. The pain in his leg had lessened to no more than an annoyance and displayed much more strength than he could have hoped for. In a couple of hours he'd be fighting fit again. And God knows, he was going to need it. At the end of the short corridor was a window. Outside, he saw the beat-up car he'd nicked. It would have to go before the kids reported it stolen. He turned to his right – Billy's door. "You have a key?"

Eliza glanced down at her robe. "You want a civilised answer?"

Roman held up a hand. No arguments. "So how are we supposed to get in?"

"The way you do everything. Illegally."

Roman ran his hand along the top of the door frame. "Doesn't he have a key under a mat or something?"

"Tell me, honestly, how many people have you met in your lifetime who were stupid enough to actually hide a key under their doormat?"

Roman bit his tongue. He glanced at the lock. Yale. Pushed on the door – just on the off chance. "If I kick this door in, I'm gonna wake the neighbours."

"Can't you pick it?"

He glared at her. "Wait here."

"Where're you going?" Eliza started after him.

"To do illegal shit." He reached the top of the stairs and, against his better judgment, turned to look at her. Worry lines creased her forehead, and her eyes pleaded for him not to leave her. "Stay right there. Do not move an inch, you hear me?"

Eliza nodded. A lot of good that meant.

Outside, he felt like he could breathe again. Roman didn't like being crowded. Never had. Not since being locked up in Purgatory. He walked around the side of the property and stared up at Billy's apartment. Unfortunately, there appeared to be only one option. To climb. And Roman hated climbing. He dragged next door's garden table, which clearly hadn't been used all summer, across the concrete patio, and hopped up onto it. Hauled himself over the balcony rail and landed firmly on his feet.

For a cop, Billy didn't seem too security conscious. The patio door was locked, but the cliché key beneath the plant pot opened it easily. He filed that one away to use on Eliza the next time she thought she knew it all. With one foot through the door, Roman glanced back and checked out the scenery behind him. Just the car park, trees and fields, and far off in the distant, the faint hum of a lorry as it travelled along a road Roman was unfamiliar with. But it was what he couldn't see that pleased him. The lack of people. And that was good. Because hopefully, nobody had seen him break in.

He opened the front door expecting to see an impatient Eliza standing there. She wasn't. Instant panic swept over him. The Sheriff couldn't have found them this quickly. Roman rushed into the hallway. At the top of the stairs stood Eliza. She glanced up and smiled with relief – a gorgeous smile that only she could do.

She ran towards him and, without thinking, he opened his arms ready to embrace her. A stupid move. She darted straight past him and into Billy's apartment.

Roman lowered his arms and followed her in. What in the hell was he thinking? He wasn't thinking, and that was the problem. He never thought clearly while around her. He closed the door. He had to get away from here...from her.

He flopped onto the sofa. Twenty minutes to rest, then back on the road.

"When can we talk about getting Billy back?"

"Jesus fucking Christ." Roman got up. "You never fucking stop."

He walked towards a room. A bedroom. Left it, and peered into the room opposite. Another bedroom. "Where the fuck is the bathroom?" Didn't wait for an answer. Found it at the end of the corridor.

He slammed the door behind him. Hard. Enough for Eliza to know that he was pissed with her. Goddamn it. She was like a dog with a goddamn bone. Didn't she understand that Billy was never coming back? He stood at the sink – a bloody clean sink. In fact, this whole goddamn bathroom was spotless. Billy had to be gay.

Roman sighed, and turned back to the mirror. He looked like utter shit. Dark shadows circled his eyes, something he hadn't seen since the drug-fueled sixties. Of course, he blamed Eliza for it. He ran the tap. Let the sink fill with water, and splashed his face. When he glanced back into the mirror, he was none the wiser as to what he was going to do. He wanted to leave –

put as much distance between himself and the Sheriff as possible. But he wasn't blind. He could see there was something wrong with Eliza. He himself had been in extreme pain at the time of resurrecting her. Maybe he'd made an error somewhere along the way? Or, maybe Eliza's erratic and confusing behaviour – the drinking binge and the amnesic episodes – were in fact nothing more than grief rearing its ugly head.

No.

There was something else. Something not so easy to explain. Maybe he imagined it. No. He hadn't imagined it. Her eye colour changed a split second before her personality switches. It happened on the stairs back at her father's. And it happened in the car just before she crashed. In fact, it happened every time before she vomited.

Shit. If there was even an ounce of a chance that he'd somehow brought her back wrong, how could he abandon her?

He reached for the hand towel – fluffy with a scent of magnolia – and dried his face.

Shit.

He glanced at his shirt, now covered in blood and torn to shreds. His trousers, now stained and smelly from her puke. Roman opened the door and crossed the corridor, ripping the shirt off as he went. He entered the bedroom opposite. Threw the shirt on the floor, and stepped out of his trousers. He opened the door to the wardrobe. Good call. Billy was about his build. Roman reached for a black pair of denims and a jumper – a khaki V-neck – and headed back into the living room.

Eliza sat on the sofa. The TV was on, tuned to some shopping channel about toning your abs in three days flat.

"I'm gonna ditch the car."

Eliza stood. She waited until he'd pulled the jumper over his head, then said, "I'll come with you."

"No. I'll be gone ten minutes. Fifteen max."

"You won't come back."

"I am coming back. Take a shower. Grab a change of clothes."

"I can do that now, then we can go together."

"You're safer here."

She reached for his hand. "But we're stronger together."

Her skin felt soft and warm. *Don't let her get to you.* "You shower. Let me ditch the car. I'll be ten minutes."

"What if the Sheriff arrives?"

"He's not after you. He's after me. Remember?"

He withdrew his hand from hers and reached for the door latch. "Be ready for me. We're leaving as soon as I get back."

CHAPTER TWELVE

Eliza's shower lasted exactly six and a half minutes.

That included a hair wash.

Not a hair-dry, though. Billy didn't seem to possess a dryer.

She found some jogger bottoms, and pulled the drawstring as tight as it allowed. Still too big, but at least they didn't fall down. The jumper was just plain baggy, but she liked it that way. She paused for a minute. Never could she remember seeing Billy wearing this tracksuit. The realisation made her feel stupid. Stupid because she'd believed her father over her brother. Stupid because she'd ignored Billy when he labelled their father a murderer. And stupid because she'd allowed that belief to come between them.

A knock on the front door snapped her from her thoughts. She walked through to the living room, glad that Roman had returned as quickly as he'd promised, and opened the door.

Eddie, the young cop who worked with Billy, stood on the step with his hand poised, ready to knock again.

He looked tired. His clothes hung, dishevelled, and the cast that wrapped his right leg caused him to stand in a way that appeared awkward and uncomfortable. He stared at her, looking surprised that it was she who'd opened the door.

"Eddie. What are you doing here? I thought you were on sick leave."

"Station was attacked last night. I've been called in to help deal with the calls." He winced and tried to rub his leg, but the cast prevented him. "Is Billy here? He's not answering his phone."

Panic set in. "Er, no."

"Oh." Eddie shifted position. "Do you know where he is?"

"No. No idea."

He looked past Eliza. Seemed to search the room behind her. "I'm worried. It's not like him to just disappear."

He knows. He knows. "He's probably just caught up dealing with stuff. Maybe his phone is switched off, or out of battery?" She needed to stop rambling.

Eddie didn't look convinced. "When was the last time you saw him?"

"Yesterday. At the station, actually."

"Time?"

"Afternoon."

"Was he okay?"

Eliza shrugged. "Yeah, he was fine. George was with us. He may know where Billy is."

Eddie's eyes clouded with sadness. "You haven't heard."

"Heard what?"

"George died last night."

Mixed emotions flooded Eliza. "What? How?"

"I'm not completely sure. Nobody is. Main division headed over last night after several CB calls about a crowd attacking…" Eddie pause. "Hell, I don't know what the hell was supposed to be attacking the station. Anyway, the boys from main found him."

Eddie swallowed. "He'd been ripped apart."

Eliza said nothing. That was no way for anybody to go. Not even an arsehole like George.

"Seems like you're now the last person to have seen your brother. I'm worried."

"Billy will be fine."

"Bet George thought the same thing when he got up for work yesterday morning." Eddie winced again. He was clearly in pain.

Roman would kill her, but Eliza said, "Do you want to come in for a minute?"

"I can't. Girlfriend's waiting in the car. She's driving me in."

An awkward silence followed. Eddie showed no sign of leaving. Instead, he just stared as if waiting for her to confess everything. Eliza felt her face flush and prayed it hadn't turned a bright shade of pink.

"Maybe I will come in. Just get a quick glass of water."

Oh God, he knows. "Sure." Eliza stepped back from the door.

Eddie entered, but instead of heading towards the kitchen, he turned and said, "I'm a little confused as to why you're not freaking out?"

"What do you mean?" Eliza closed the door.

"George has been mutilated and Billy, your own brother, is missing. I know you guys had a few issues, but you don't seem the least bit worried."

"I am worried."

"No. You look spooked."

Eliza felt her skin go clammy. This was it. He was going to arrest her and drag her down to the station. Maybe she could tell him what happened to Billy. Maybe he'd believe her. Then again, he probably wouldn't. She wouldn't believe her if she was standing there in his shoes...or cast.

"Eliza, if you know something, you have to tell me."

Her heart rate accelerated. Palpitations pained her chest. Then her vision dulled, and the room darkened from sight.

When it brightened, the first thing he saw was the young man standing in the middle of the room. Beyond that, the unfamiliar area gave little clue as to what was happening.

Roman? No sign of him.

"Eliza, are you okay?"

Sickness threatened to spew over. "Who are you?"

"Eliza, it's Eddie." Eddie frowned. "Hey, you don't look so hot. Let's get you to the sofa."

"Where the hell is Roman?"

"I'll get you some water?" Without waiting for an answer, Eddie turned and limped awkwardly towards the kitchenette.

The path to the front door was clear. The urge to get out of here beckoned.

Eddie returned. Glass in hand. He held it out. "Drink this. You'll feel better."

In one swift motion, Eliza's slender leg extended out and kicked Eddie back.

He crashed against the armchair. Surprise distorted his face. He felt his head. "Eliza, what the hell..."

Another room adjoined this one, and with that came the sudden threat that Roman was nearby, and had heard. After a moment listening, it seemed clear that either Roman wasn't here, or he hadn't heard.

Eddie started to get up. He was quickly kicked back down. "Where is Roman?"

Eddie looked confused.

Eliza's dainty hand grabbed him by the balls.

"I don't know any Roman."

"Don't lie to me, son."

"I have no idea who you're talking about. Please, Eliza..."

A quick nod towards the adjoining room. "What is out there?"

"What?"

The dainty hand tightened its grip. "Answer me."

"You know what's out there," Eddie cried out.

"Remind me."

"Bedrooms and a bathroom."

"Is there anyone else here?"

"I don't know. I don't think so."

"If I discover you are lying..." The dainty hand twisted its grip.

Tears sprang from Eddie eyes. "I'm not. Oh God, I'm not. I promise. I think it's just us."

Eliza's hand released its hold. "Remain here, and do not move."

Eddie slid off the chair. He curled into the fetal position – one leg remaining outstretched – and cradled his bollocks. He wasn't going anywhere.

A quick check of the hallway. Just as Eddie reported, unoccupied. Next to the kitchen counter, an array of knives sat in a knife block. So many to choose from. Ah, the big one. It felt good to hold a carving knife again.

Eddie was on his feet again, but didn't look to be a threat. He could hardly stand with that white thing around his leg. "What is that?"

Eddie glanced at his cast, but declined to answer. He wiped the tears from his eyes. "Eliza, I don't know what the hell is up with you, but you just assaulted a police officer."

"Assault?"

Eddie looked more confused than ever. "Eliza, what on earth's gotten into you?"

"Where am I currently?"

"What?"

The tip of the blade pressed against Eddie's balls.

A whimper left Eddie's lips. When he spoke, the words couldn't get out quick enough. "Billy's house. You're at your brother's house."

"And where is that, exactly?"

"Sheila Road."

"Sheila what?"

"Road. Road. In Millendreath... Cornwall for crying out loud."

The knife lowered. "Cornwall, England?"

"Yes, yes, oh God, please tell me what's happening here."

"What year is this?"

Eddie frowned, and the blade rose again. "Twenty Eighteen."

"Two thousand and eighteen? That is impossible."

"Eliza, do you know what happened to Billy? Did you do something to him?" Eddie reached for his belt. He held out an object that looked remarkably like a pistol. "Eliza, tell me or I'll have no choice but to take you in for questioning."

Watching this young man was amusing. But it was clear he had no more information to give. The girl's hand jabbed the knife towards him. Suddenly, agony pierced just left of the girl's navel. It halted the knife from jabbing into Eddie any further. At first the pain felt like a ball bearing. Then, the female body he occupied started to convulse. Her fingers curled together, and the knife fell from her dainty grasp. Her arms tensed, and finally those slender legs gave way. Spasms rocked every bone, and he felt every inch of it. Regaining control seemed impossible. But, no blood meant no gunshot. What in the hell was happening?

"Oh my God, Eliza, I'm so sorry." Eddie kicked the knife away. "I don't know what the hell's gotten into you, but you need help."

Teeth gritted back the scream that wanted to escape. The pain was unbearable. "What did you do to me? What is that thing?"

Eddie released the charge. Two wires dropped free, and he reloaded it. Still clutching the pistol, he leaned over – awkwardly, with his plastered leg. "Just breathe, Eliza. Just breathe."

The seizures lessened slightly. "Who are you? Why would you attack the girl?"

"Oh shit, Eliza. What in the hell is wrong with you?"

Eliza's hand wrapped the small dart, and pulled it from the slender stomach it embedded. It was more discomforting than expected.

"Eliza, just take it easy." Eddie straightened.

It was enough of a lull in concentration to raise the girl's legs and kick out. Eddie stumbled back, his broken leg stopping him from keeping balance. He smashed against the far wall, and dropped onto his arse.

The girl's body movement was great. He got to his feet, and strolled over to where the young cop lay.

Eddie fumbled for his belt.

Without reaching for it, the carving knife flew up from the floor and into the girl's delicate palm.

Eddie's eyes widened – first with fear. "How did you do that?"

"I have no idea." A laugh left Eliza's lips. "But I like it."

And, then Eddie's eyes filled with horror.

The blade plunged downwards and penetrated Eddie stomach. God, it felt good to kill like that again.

Eddie's eyes bulged. A groan warbled past his lips. He wrapped his hands around the blade, but couldn't stop the blood from spreading across his shirt.

A smile twitched Eliza's lips. Her dainty hand twisted the handle and, in one sweep, sliced across the cop's abdomen. Spasms consumed the young man, but they were brief. Adrenaline surged forth. Blood sprayed the door, the floor, the furniture. It felt good to be alive again. Over and over, the blade sank into Eddie's chest, neck, arms. The last gasp of life left Eddie's lips, but the knife didn't stop. It penetrated the skull, the abdomen, the ribcage. Blood splatters morphed into red pools.

Then nothing.

Energy buzzed through every vein, more than it had in decades. He could not have found a better person to hide inside. He started to whistle "Greensleeves" past dry lips, the girl's female tones making it sound almost magical.

Casual as you like, the delicate hand wiped the blood from the knife. In the near-clean steel, Eliza's reflection stared back.

And another smile twitched her lips.

CHAPTER THIRTEEN

The stench was everywhere.

The Sheriff could smell it: the lingering sweat, the reek of body odour, the pain, the panic. So many smells. And they all disappeared off in the direction of the trees — somewhere he could not take the car.

He turned from the crashed Drophead, and began to run. The scent overwhelmed him. It assaulted his nostrils. His target had to be less than twenty-five miles away. It was a distance he could make up in next to no time, but he had to act quickly. The stench wouldn't last forever, and he was damned if he would let the opportunity to throw Roman back in Purgatory slip through his fingers.

The Sheriff raced into the trees, the morning sun at first lighting his way. Fallen leaves crushed under foot. Trees whipped by until they were no more than a line of emerald green. The lure to see his old adversary was one he could not pass up. Roman's capture was personal, an old score to settle, and one that would reclaim the Sheriff's prominent standing within the realm of the Underworld.

Two birds for the price of one.

Roman Holbrook. The reaper thrown into Purgatory by his own brother. Ordered to endure an eternity of torture that stretched even the Sheriff's vivid imagination. Even the mere thought of that brash and irritating man elicited an anger the Sheriff found hard to control.

Further in, the trees started to house bushes. He pushed his way through. His black coat caught on twigs and brambles. It was not enough to stop him – or even slow him down. He wanted to catch Roman so badly, he was willing to sacrifice his own prominent standing in Purgatory to achieve it.

Then, as he feared, the scent dissipated.

He slowed. Now the brambles annoyed him. He hadn't moved quick enough, and now he had lost the scent. A bramble caught his coat, and he pulled it free. He needed to stop for a second and think. Protocol ordered that he return to Purgatory until the scent resurfaced, but that just meant he would waste more time. No. He would continue on with this path. Be well-placed for his next encounter. He started to walk again, not stopping until the sun began to filter through the trees again, and slowly daylight could be seen. Then it hit him.

The scent.

He closed his eyes and opened his mind, welcoming the flicker of images that came to him: the room, the chairs, the knife. He sensed the kill. Felt the warm blood on the girl's hands. Tasted the urgency to slaughter again.

He hastened his pace into an abnormally fast sprint. The new scent now led the way.

He knew where he had to be.

CHAPTER FOURTEEN

Each parking space outside Billy's apartment block was numbered.

Roman parked the little Volkswagen Beetle in the one marked 12. Not the car he went out for.

He patted his trouser pockets for a cigarette, annoyed when he realised he didn't have any, and glanced at the windows. Along the bottom, drawn blinds obscured three of the six windows. The ones he could see into were in darkness and showed no sign of occupancy. The row above – the top row – was more accommodating. No blinds, and in most cases, no nets either. Just balconies and glass doors.

Not Billy's window, though. The blinds were open. The balcony door was ajar. And there was Eliza, bobbing and rotating around the room, and looking as though she didn't have a care in the world. Was she bloody dancing?

Roman couldn't deny his admiration for the way her body moved with such technique. It could have held his attention all day. But, his confusion at her carefree attitude – and the obvious anger he felt towards her for leaving the balcony door open – tore through. Eliza just didn't seem to be Eliza anymore.

He stopped.

Eliza didn't seem to be Eliza anymore.

Possession? No. He shook the thought from his head, and opened the car door to the pounding bass of Roxy Music blasting through the air. Yes, under the current circumstances, her behaviour was strange to say the least. Something wasn't right with her, but possession? It was impossible. A one-in-a-trillion chance – and he'd already filled those odds.

He entered the building and took the stairs to the first floor. Music pounded from Billy's flat. Roman slipped Billy's spare key into the lock. The door opened less than an inch. He tried again. Something seemed to be obstructing it. He tried again. Banged his fist against it when the door still didn't open.

"A policeman should know better," a female voice yelled behind him.

Roman pulled the door shut, and turned. An older woman, short, plump, and well into her eighties, stood tapping her hands against her hips, her silver hair scooped back into a bun. "I'm sorry?"

The woman stepped out into the hall. "It's been like this for over twenty minutes. I called the police...the other police that aren't him... But nobody's available—"

"I'm sorry. I'll sort it out."

"Best see you do. I expected better behaviour from a police officer."

Roman whacked the door. The old woman still watched, and he flashed her an uncomfortable smile when Eliza still didn't answer. Having this old biddy eyeing his every move made him feel like a suspect in a Miss Marple mystery. He pounded his fist against the door one last time, smiled at the old dear. "I'll go around back."

The garden table was where he'd left it, and the climb over the balcony was easier than the first time. Deafening music pounded out through the open door.

Inside Billy's apartment, Roman watched Eliza, her back turned on him, bopping to the music while she made herself a sandwich. The kitchen knife went down on the counter, and she reached for an open bottle of wine. Gulp after gulp, she drank until a good quarter of the bottle emptied. Then, the music tempo fastened, up raised her arms, and she began jumping on the spot while her head swayed from side to side. She turned, eyes closed, head still banging to the beat. Blood drenched the front of her clothes, and splatter marks painted her face – clearly not hers going by the energetic way her body still moved.

Roman reached out. He held her by the shoulders. "Eliza?"

She opened her eyes. He waited for her to focus on him, and then her eyes widened. She swiped his hands away from her, and stumbled back against the counter. It was brief and rapid, but Roman saw the flash of green discolour her pupils. A trick of the light it definitely wasn't, he was certain of that now.

Eliza stared back at him for what seemed a good minute before she noticed the wine bottle she held in one hand, and the half-eaten sandwich in the other. She swayed, unable to keep her balance steady, and dropped the sandwich to the floor. "I think I'm going to be sick."

Roman grabbed the bottle before that too slipped free from her grasp. "You're covered in blood. What the hell happened? Who did this?" he shouted over the music.

Eliza glanced down at her bloody clothes. "I don't know. Is it mine?" The words slurred past her lips.

"I doubt it, considering you're still alive."

Eliza slid down the cupboard door until her arse hit the floor. Drawing her knees to her chest, she wrapped them in her arms. Tears filled her eyes, and she buried her face. When she spoke, it was muffled and incoherent. Roman couldn't hear a word of it over the music, let alone understand it. So he let her cry, hoping she'd sob the alcohol right out of her system.

The next record hit the playlist, louder than its predecessor. Roman swiftly killed it.

A deafening silence followed.

He turned back to Eliza, who remained crumpled on the floor. Could she be possessed? Was it possible that the trillion-to-one shot he'd accomplished could actually happen twice? She certainly didn't seem possessed at the moment. So, what did that mean? And, what the hell did he do with her now?

He sighed, bent down, and offered out his hand. When she declined to take it, he took the initiative and pulled her up from the floor. "Tell me what happened."

"I don't..."

"You're covered in blood. So, let's start with who it belongs to?"

"I..." Eliza's attention wandered from him.

Clearly this line of questioning wasn't getting him anywhere. He clicked his fingers until her focus found him again. "Tell me what you did after I left you."

Eliza wiped her eyes. "I had a shower and changed, like you said."

She wobbled, and Roman steadied her again. "And?"

She glanced towards the living room. "There was a knock at the door. It was Eddie."

"Who the hell is Eddie?"

"He works with my brother."

"He's also Police? Why was he here?"

Eliza bowed her head. Her shoulders started to tremble, and she swayed against Roman's chest for support. Having her body this close to him felt good. Too good. Roman wrapped his arm around her and lightly pressed his face into her hair. Still that strawberry scent lingered, and he closed his eyes. For a couple of seconds, he allowed himself to believe life was normal. That Eliza pressed against him was normal. However, it was anything but. Her behaviour was off the scale, and she was covered in blood. Until he had some answers as to why, he couldn't let it rest.

Now was definitely not the time to let these damn emotions of his get the better of him.

"Let's get you sat down." He walked her around the kitchen unit and into the living room.

It was the blood-splattered walls that first caught his eye. He heard Eliza gasp. She pulled from his grip, and fled back into the kitchen. He checked over his shoulder. Watched her hurl over the few items of washing-up sitting in the sink. He glanced just to her left – out through the open curtains, thankful that the car park was empty and the fields were not a housing estate. Nobody could have witnessed this.

He turned back to the massacre in the living room. It was an impossible long shot if the amount of blood soaked into Eliza's clothes was any indication, but maybe he was wrong. Maybe Eliza hadn't actually killed this Eddie character, or anybody else for that matter. He tiptoed forward. Listened for the slightest noise that would suggest someone else was alive in the house: the murmur of the television, the toilet system refilling, footsteps in the hallway. But the place was quiet. Dead quiet.

Bloody handprints smeared the front door and, from the corner of his eye, he noticed the one thing he'd hoped not to find. The cop, Eddie, slumped against the back of the door, his blue police shirt soaked in blood. At least Roman knew now why the door wouldn't open. Eddie's neck had been sliced to within an inch of being severed completely. Multiple stab wounds pierced open every part of his body. Intestines sprawled across his abdomen. Blood puddled the floor. Roman had a strong stomach, but this sight tested even him. He also didn't need a medical degree to determine many of the wounds had happened long after the man's death. This frenzied attack was more than just an act of self-defence or revenge; it was satisfying a lust to kill, a hunger to inflict pain and torture. No restraint had taken place, no self-control or discipline. This was the aftermath of a psychopath, and whoever had done this sure as hell didn't care about being found out.

Bloody footprints scattered the whole of the carpet, some even marking their way to the hallway. Roman stood. Eliza remained in the kitchen. He couldn't – wouldn't – believe she had done this, no matter how strange her behaviour had been of late.

Nevertheless, he followed the footprints into the first bedroom. Pretty much the same sight as the living room. A young girl sprawled across the bed. Her blood saturated the walls, the sheets, the floor. Roman walked around the body, careful not to add his boot prints into the mix, and checked for a pulse. Stupid really. Even if he couldn't sense, she looked as dead as a person could look.

"What's in there?" Eliza called out.

Roman walked back to the door. A bad feeling festered in his stomach. Could Eliza really have it in her to commit such horror? Was this her telekinetic power acting out? Had Roman brought her back from the dead somehow broken or wrong? He closed the door behind him.

He refused to believe either option. Someone had hitched a ride back with her. All the evidence before him supported that: Eliza's drinking, her personality changes, her blacking out. Jesus Christ, two bloody murders. Somebody else had to have a hand in this.

Roman headed back into the kitchen, his main focus being the cupboard under the sink. He grabbed a rag and a bottle of bleach, and went back to the hallway. Eliza hadn't done this. He started to bleach down the front door. But, as he tried to wipe the blood clean, he couldn't help but wonder...

Who the fuck *had?*

"What was in the bedroom?" Eliza slurred as she spoke.

Roman looked up at her. Was it still her who looked back at him, or was it now someone else?

"We need to leave here as soon as possible." Roman stopped scrubbing. Who was he kidding that he would be able to clean this mess up? "At some point, the police are going to wonder where in the hell your brother's at and, when they come looking, they're gonna find this massacre waiting for them. You can't be here for that."

"Maybe I should be here. Maybe I deserve what's coming to me."

"I don't believe that. Now go wash. Grab another change of clothes."

"I'm a monster." Her voice was desperate.

"I don't think you are. I don't think you did this."

"But I was the only one here."

Roman twisted to face her. Her brown eyes pleaded for answers, and it pained him that all he had to offer was an assumption. He walked her back into the kitchen and sat her on a breakfast stool. "Wait here."

Roman rushed into the back bedroom. The wardrobe was full of clothes, all of which would be useless for Eliza. He pulled a navy shirt from a hanger. Grabbed some shorts and socks from a drawer. A pair of oversized biker boots would be better than no shoes at all.

He rushed back into the kitchen. Eliza hadn't moved. "What's the last thing you remember before I turned up?" He pulled the bloodied jumper over her head and quickly replaced it with the clean shirt.

"Eddie wanted to know why I wasn't concerned about Billy."

"That's it? There's nothing else?" He motioned for her to stand.

Eliza shook her head.

Roman whipped the tracksuit bottoms down. Threw them into the corner of the kitchen and held out the shorts. "Step in."

Eliza did. "I'm a murderer, aren't I?"

Roman paused. He cupped her face, her skin soft against the roughness of his fingertips. "Your father was a murderer, and you are nothing like him."

Eliza nodded, but it was unconvincing at best. "If I didn't do this, then who did?"

He slipped her feet into the socks. "I think I know what's happening." Followed by the boots. He looked for some buckles. Found none, so stood. Took a deep breath. "Don't freak out, but I think someone may have hitched a ride out of Purgatory with you."

Anger ignited her eyes. "What do you mean?"

"I mean, somebody used you to escape." Roman paused, giving Eliza a minute to let the information sink in. He spotted a baseball cap beside the stereo.

"You mean I'm possessed?" Eliza's cheeks reddened, and her breathing quickened. The wine bottle rattled on the counter, as did the ashtray beside it. "I'm possessed?"

Roman pulled the hat onto her head, and prepared to block the objects should they fly his way. "Now calm down."

But Eliza didn't hear. Her eyes hardened, and her nostrils flared. "Who the hell by? You said I was okay. You said what you did had no consequences."

She stood, and Roman didn't attempt to seat her again. Sleep wanted to take him so badly, but he couldn't rest. Instead, he sat back and let her vent the shock and frustration of the situation. All in all, he'd expected her to take the information much, much worse. "You are okay. And there shouldn't be any consequences."

"So who the hell's possessing me?"

"Going by the state of Eddie, and the girl in the bedroom—"

"There's a dead girl in the bedroom?"

"—I'd say someone very unstable."

"Unstable? You think?" She paused, remembering. "Eddie's girlfriend was waiting for him outside in the car."

"So now we know who's occupying your brother's bed."

Eliza's face reddened. "Stop being to blasé about all of this. People have died."

"People I don't know, nor do I care about."

"Stop talking like that."

"Like what?"

"Like an uncaring arsehole. A freaking psychopath may be controlling me, but those people died by *my* hand. Don't tell me you don't bloody care." The ashtray flew from the counter and smashed into the wall.

"Look, Eliza—"

"And what now? I'm supposed to spend the rest of my days killing people?" Eliza paced the kitchen, the biker boots slopping up and down on her feet until finally her strides shortened, and she calmed a little. The anger in her eyes died ever so slightly, and she turned to Roman. "How could this happen? How could you let this happen?"

"The odds are a zillion to one."

Eliza snorted at his response. "And you'd know that how?"

"Because I stand for the *one* in that equation."

The anger in her eyes reignited. She glared at Roman, hatred oozing through every pore in her body. "That's how you escaped Purgatory? You possessed someone?"

Roman said nothing. He didn't need to. Eliza had answered her own question.

"You did to someone else what this psycho inside me is doing now?"

"No." Roman stood. "I used the soul for transport only. As soon as I was free of Purgatory, I was gone."

"So why hasn't this bastard inside me gone, too?"

"I don't know. There's no reason I can think of for this person to stay."

"And yet he is," she screamed. "And what about Billy? This whole time you knew there was a way out of Purgatory."

"It's not a way out."

"Clearly it is. You used it. This person inside me used it. Why can't Billy use it?"

"Because you never know when or what soul is destined to be returned. I got lucky. This person inside you got lucky."

"Billy could get lucky, too."

"No, he can't. Face it, Eliza. Billy is gone."

Eliza banged her fist on the counter. Put her head in her hands. Her shoulders shook, and the tears flowed. "I want this person out of me."

Roman wanted to reach out to her, to comfort her. Instead, he remained where he was. "I do too."

"Then how do we do it? How did you get out?"

"I waited for my vessel to fall asleep. Then I just stepped out. There are no boundaries, no obstacles when the host is asleep."

"So then I need to sleep?"

Roman shook his head. "The person inside you has to leave of their own free will. I have no idea how to make them."

She lowered her head again. "Are you even you, or did you steal the body you're now wearing?"

"This is my real body."

"But a soul is like…air."

"You watch way too many movies."

"I mean, how could you even fit inside another person?"

Roman sighed. "Eliza, I did not die. My body is not buried in a grave six foot under. I was sent to Purgatory. Imprisoned there. My whole body was sent to Purgatory, and my whole body escaped."

"Like Billy?"

"Shit. Back to that."

"Damn right, back to that."

A flicker of green flashed across Eliza's brown eyes. Roman saw it clear as day. No trick of the light. Not a figment of his imagination. Who the hell was he looking at now? Eliza? No. He now stared at the entity inside her. It stared back at him through Eliza's eyes, the initial look of shock quickly fading to mild panic. The two watched each other, each waiting for the other to make a move.

Finally, everything made sense. The Sheriff hadn't initially returned for Roman or Eliza. It had returned for the soul hiding inside her. And until Roman figured out how to extract him – or her – Eliza was like a beacon for the Sheriff to follow. Every time the entity inside her showed itself, the Sheriff would hone in and he'd know exactly where they were.

Shit. That meant the Sheriff was already on his way here now. That put both of them in the firing line.

Roman needed to get the hell out of there. They both needed to get the hell out of there. Any thoughts of dumping Eliza somewhere safe while he went on the run evaporated. The Sheriff would rip her apart to get the soul inside her.

Roman ran his fingers through his hair, and grabbed Billy's jacket from the chair. Just play it cool. Don't want to spook the little shit possessing her. Make him or her believe they remained undetected until he knew what the hell to do about them. "We need to hit the road before the police show up."

Eliza licked her lips and wiped her mouth dry with the back of her hand. Roman stiffened. He'd seen her do it before, but hadn't registered the familiarity of it.

Eliza turned from him, and glanced towards the kitchen worktop.

Roman knew she searched the knife block. Fortunately for him, the largest of the group embedded the head of the girl in the bedroom. The next largest was lying on the work top. He just hoped Eliza's uninvited guest realised they'd never have time to reach it, or one of the others, before Roman intervened.

Eliza turned back, and smiled. It was a nervous smile, like she wanted to get the hell out of there and run as fast as she could. "Where are we going?"

"We'll decide once we're on the road."

She grabbed the open bottle of wine from the counter and strolled past him, whistling "Greensleeves" as she went.

Roman froze. His whole body tightened until his jaw locked and his arms ached. It had been decades, no, centuries, since he'd heard that tune whistled in that way. It couldn't be who he thought it was.

Please, God, don't let it be who he thought it was. Not Jacob Witenie.

CHAPTER FIFTEEN

The Volkswagen's windscreen misted over.

Roman had panicked.

Goddamn it, he could kick his own arse right about now.

He pulled the cuff of his jumper down over his palm and wiped the glass clear until he could see the car park again. He'd fled Billy's apartment so quickly after realising it was Jacob he spoke to that he hadn't thought twice when Eliza failed to follow him. And now she was alone inside her brother's apartment with just Jacob's warped, sick mind for company.

Roman clenched the steering wheel, his eyes flitting between Billy's apartment window and the building entrance. Jacob would look for any opportunity to kill Roman or to make his life a living hell. That could be the only reason he still possessed Eliza. Good old-fashioned revenge. Roman needed to think. But first, he needed to panic at the situation he'd put Eliza in without Jacob seeing. Because if Jacob sensed even the slightest hint that Roman knew...

Roman turned the key. The engine clattered to life, and he glanced at the dash clock. Seven minutes had passed. He was sure Jacob wouldn't run for the hills, but stick close by until such time that he saw fit to exact a suitable vengeance. And God knew what that would entail. Jacob had spent hundreds of years in Purgatory, and had it not been for Roman double-crossing him, he'd have escaped centuries ago. Hundreds of years spent plotting his retaliation. What could be the worst he could come up with?

Brutalization? Roman had handled worse in Purgatory.

Torture? Jacob didn't have the imagination.

Hurting a loved one?

Roman looked at the clock again. Eight minutes gone.

Dread darkened his thoughts. Images sped through his mind like a flick-book and, hard as he tried, he couldn't turn them off. Instead, he watched helpless as, slice after slice, Jacob reigned the knife down into Eliza's body: her face, her neck, her back, all mutilated until she had no fight left to give, and her life drained away.

Roman reached for the door handle. He couldn't breathe. He needed air. He needed to go back for Eliza. This was the worst kind of retribution Jacob could bestow. This was how Jacob would find his justice. It was the ultimate payback. By hurting Eliza, Jacob would destroy Roman.

The passenger door opened, and Eliza peered in. Her hand clenched around the neck of the wine bottle, and her face hardened with distrust. "Where are you going?" It was Eliza's voice, but Jacob's words.

Roman turned to her. The morning sun emphasised the subtle golden lights in her hair. She was alive. Jacob hadn't hurt her. Yet. But how long before he did? He lacked creativity on the best of days, but even he had enough brain capacity to eventually work out that Eliza was Roman's only weak spot. Every emotion possible raced through Roman's mind. He wanted to destroy Jacob, to rip him in two.

Roman shrugged. Alcohol glazed her eyes, and Jacob's words slurred from her lips when she spoke. "Where are you going?"

"Dartmoor."

"Dartmoor?" Jacob slouched in the passenger seat, and slammed the door shut. "To do what? That place is barren."

It became clear that Jacob had no idea the Sheriff had come for him. And Roman wanted to keep it that way. He didn't want Jacob bolting – not while he had control of Eliza. "You killed someone. A cop. We can't stay here."

"On whose say-so?" Jacob swigged another drink, unbothered by the notion he could be in trouble. He wiped his lips dry, glanced at the bottle, and took another drink.

Roman answered with little empathy. He didn't fully understand his feelings towards Eliza, other than he liked her. A lot. Something he'd never let Jacob see. "You can stay here if you want. But you'll be on your own. Your choice."

Jacob took another drink, pouring that poison down Eliza's throat. Right there and then, Roman wanted to reach deep down inside her and yank Jacob's worthless soul out. But that would kill Eliza.

"How long we going for?" Another succession of gulps, nearly draining the bottle dry, finished with a belch.

Roman spun to face Eliza, slightly more aggressive than he'd planned. "Until I say so. D'you have a problem with that?"

Defence mechanism kicked in, and Jacob leaned away from him. A flicker of green highlighted Eliza's eyes. Jacob disappeared, and Eliza spluttered out a mouthful of wine.

"God, I feel sick." She wiped her lips – her way, not Jacob's – and searched the car. "It was here again, wasn't it?"

"Yes."

"Oh God, please tell me I didn't hurt someone." She felt her head, and Roman could see she struggled to focus.

It was good having her back. "You didn't hurt anyone."

Eliza's eyes narrowed. "You saying that cause it's what I wanna hear, or cause it's the truth?"

"Because it's the truth. Now buckle up."

Eliza handed Roman the bottle, and wiped her hands down her top. "What did it want?"

"Revenge."

"Against who?" She twisted for the seatbelt, her top pulling tight across her body.

Roman forced himself to look away from her, and opened the driver's door. Confusion over the way he felt for this girl muddied every decision he made. When exactly had he started to like her? He stood the bottle on the car park tarmac, and stared at it until he heard her belt click into the clip. "Against me."

"You know who this person is?" Still the words slurred from her lips.

Roman closed the door. Yet another can of worms about to open. He took a deep breath, and put the car into gear. "His name is Jacob Witenie."

"And you're the reason I still have him stuck inside me?"

Her question hadn't been harsh or malicious, but the words still managed to sting like hell. He felt the need to apologise for that fact, but before he could say anything further, Eliza quickly opened the passenger door. She leaned out, the seatbelt restricting her somewhat, and vomited. Roman patted his jumper for a tissue. Opened the glove box. A packet of handy wipes – perfect for the job in hand. He pulled one free, flapped it open, and passed it to her.

Eliza took it. "What did you do to make him hate you so much?"

"I befriended him, double-crossed him, and stole his ride out of Purgatory." Roman was too ashamed to look at her. He waited for her to comment, but she remained quiet and continued to wipe her face. He hated the silence, the not knowing and having to surmise what she thought of him. He tried to think of something to add that didn't make him sound like such an arsehole, but the truth was simple. He was what he was, and no amount of words could change that. "What are you thinking?"

"I'm thinking, what are we going to do about him?" Not an ounce of resentment or anger distorted her delicate, if not inebriated, voice.

To say her calmness unnerved Roman was an understatement. "Is that it?"

"What'd you expect?"

Roman shrugged. "Shouting, screaming, a string of obscenities as long as my arm. Even a couple of punches thrown my way wouldn't be out of place."

"The day's still young." She plucked a clean hanky from the pack, and pulled down the visor. "Do I look or act different when he's here?"

Roman shook his head. He wanted to tell her that she looked beautiful no matter what. He coughed, worried for a moment he'd spoken his thoughts aloud. "You're still a pain in the backside."

"And apparently a drunk psychopath as well, it would seem." She flicked the visor shut and adjusted her seatbelt. "How are we gonna get out of this mess?"

"I'm trying to think of a solution, trust me."

"Can't you just kill him?"

"Of course I can."

"Then why don't you?"

Again, he wanted to look at her, but images of her mutilated body resurfaced. "Well, for one, I risk killing you."

Eliza quietened for a second. "What's the other reason?"

"If I kill Jacob – bearing in mind I won't because I'd also be killing you – he'll go to the waiting room as a newly deceased soul. Purgatory will not be notified until he's processed, which means the Sheriff will still be hunting him – us. He knows I'm here now. He'll come for me."

"So, what do you suggest?"

"The Sheriff has to physically take Jacob back to Purgatory first before he can come for us."

"How can you know that?"

"Because even he has to follow orders. Jacob is who he's been sent here for."

"So, how's he gonna get this Jacob character while he's inside me?"

"He'll rip him out." Finally, Roman glanced at her.

Eliza pulled the door shut and wound down the window a little, tilting her head and allowing the breeze to find her. "Can't we just kill the Sheriff, or send it back to Purgatory or wherever?"

"I told you. He can't be killed."

"I can help."

"No. I don't want you involved in this."

Eliza laughed half-heartedly. "I am involved. I'm the problem."

"Even the two of us together won't beat him. We could have an army, but he cannot be killed." Roman watched her. This was his fight, not hers. How the hell had he gotten her involved in all this? "There is something else."

Eliza didn't ask him to elaborate. Instead, she closed her eyes, and lulled her head against the window. Whether she wanted Roman to continue or not, he said, "The Sheriff is tracking Jacob. Every time he shows himself, it's like a Disneyland firework going off."

"So he's on his way here now?"

"Yes."

"How long do we have?"

"I don't know. Ten minutes. An hour. Maybe even two."

"I'm guessing that suppressing Jacob until the day I die isn't something that would work?"

"From what I can tell, he's able to overpower you when your emotions are heightened."

"So as long as I stay calm and refrain from getting pissed with you, we should be okay?"

"In theory." Roman looked at her. The breeze still filtered through her long, auburn hair.

"Best keep on our toes then."

Her nose crinkled. She turned and smiled, and in that second Roman knew he would happily die just to keep her alive.

"And," Eliza wound the window back up, "if this Jacob shows himself again, please stop him from drinking. I feel like utter crap."

CHAPTER SIXTEEN

Adrenaline rushed the Sheriff's veins.

So much so that he nearly called out and gave his position away.

He smiled, taking a quick moment to enjoy the calm before the storm. Roman and Eliza had no idea he was here. They had no idea he'd spotted them. They seemed too busy talking to even notice he was right there – watching. This was going to be fun.

He gave a quick glance around the car park. It was devoid of anyone else, which meant little interference. Shame. He liked a good, bloody massacre. The little Volkswagen's engine turned over, and the Sheriff quickened his pace across the car park. He reached Roman before the car's first gear had been found.

And that's where he stood, and waited.

Roman spoke to the girl, unaware of the fate that awaited him. It was the girl who first looked up and saw the Sheriff watching them. Her face froze. In fact, her whole body tensed. Maybe because it was the mirror image of her brother staring back at her, or maybe because she knew she was about to die. Roman also stopped talking. He slowly turned forward and faced the Sheriff. His face hardened, but the Sheriff saw the defeat that clouded his eyes. The cat had cornered the mice, and the chase had come to an abrupt end.

"A little discourteous of you running out on me earlier, Roman."

Roman's hand slipped from the steering wheel.

The Sheriff tutted. "Now, even you're smart enough to know you will never outrun me in this thing."

The gearbox groaned for first gear.

"Clearly you think otherwise." The Sheriff raised his arms. With one swoop, he hammered his hands down against the car bonnet. Fingernails, yellow and dirt-stained, tore through Billy's fingertips. They punctured the hood, severing the metal apart.

Gears grated and groaned as Roman frantically tried to find first gear. Above the noise, the girl begged for him to hurry. Their distress was music to the Sheriff's ears. His claws hooked hold of the metal and he ripped the bonnet from the car.

First gear found, but it was too late. The Sheriff extended his index finger, and smiled. Roman pumped the accelerator, and the engine growled. The Sheriff readied for the car to shoot forward, but Roman seemed reluctant to release the clutch. His hesitation was all the Sheriff needed. He reached down into the engine and swiped his claws across the fuel line. The pipe severed apart, and fuel spilled over the hot exhaust manifold.

The driver's door opened before the engine had time to die. Roman jumped out, pulling Eliza along with him.

He turned towards the Sheriff, his body clearly positioned to protect her. "I know you're here for Jacob."

"Aye, that I am."

"But if you drag him out, you will kill her."

"Aye, that I will."

"She is an innocent in all this."

"That is of no concern to me."

"If you take Jacob without hurting her..." Roman glanced towards Eliza. His rigid posture couldn't hide the war going on inside the man – do I run, or do I fight? "I will let you take me back without a brawl."

The Sheriff tapped his chin. "It's tempting, but I plan on taking you back anyway."

"But my way will be quicker. You can only transport one of us at a time. If you kill her, I will be long gone by the time you return."

"Maybe I will just take you back first. Jacob will not be so difficult to find."

Sweat beaded Roman's forehead. When he spoke, his words were rushed. "You were sent here for Jacob. You will be crucified if you ignore orders and return with me first."

Irritation itched the Sheriff's skin. "I follow nobody's orders, Holbrook."

"No?" Roman stepped forward. "Then take me."

Eliza grabbed Roman's arm. "What are you doing?"

Roman stared at the Sheriff. He held his arms out, wrists together. "I can't make it any easier for you."

The Sheriff dropped his arms to his side. He tapped the side of his leg, the irritable feeling becoming almost unbearable. He'd searched for Holbrook for so long, and now to have him so close – the temptation to break the rules was too much. "You underestimate me, Holbrook."

"Oh? And why's that?"

The Sheriff grabbed Roman's jumper and dragged him closer. "Because taking you back first will be worth every severe penalty I receive."

"Then stop wasting everybody's time, and just do it."

Flames burst across the Volkswagen's manifold and engulfed the engine. Roman and thc Sheriff spun towards the car. The heat quickly reached them. Roman used the distraction to twist free of the Sheriff's grip. The Sheriff stretched to re-grab him, but Roman easily dodged his grasp. Fumes choked the air, and the Sheriff almost lost sight of Roman behind the fog of black smoke. When the Sheriff lunged for him again, Roman had already pushed the girl towards the back of the car.

"Get to Billy's bike," Eliza shouted out. She turned back to the Sheriff and positioned herself as if to do battle.

Roman yanked her away. "Are you insane?"

"Just get to the bike." She pointed. "By the entrance."

"Sod the bike. Get up to the road."

The Sheriff knocked Eliza out of the way with a flick of his hand. She hit the side of the Volkswagen and dropped to her knees. Roman's fist retaliated. It connected with the Sheriff's jaw quicker than he was prepared for.

"I see you've found some of that strength you lacked during our last encounter." The Sheriff spat out one of Billy's teeth. "But it's not enough to beat me."

Anger filled Roman's eyes. He swung his fist again. The Sheriff caught it in the palm of his hand. He wrapped Billy's fingers tight, and squeezed. Roman's bones crushed together, and he could only hold back his cry of agony for a few seconds.

"Just a little taste of what's to come." The Sheriff tilted Roman's hand back, forcing him down to his knees. He glanced down at Roman, and smiled. "Remember our torturous days together? The devices I used on you? The bones I broke. The castration."

The Sheriff leant closer. "Remember when I scalped you?"

"Go fuck yourself."

The Sheriff released Roman. He glanced at Eliza. Pulled her up, and wrapped his arm around her neck. "You know what? I'm feeling in a generous mood. I think I will extract Jacob without killing you."

Roman got to his feet. "Let her go."

"I think I may take her back instead." The Sheriff laughed. "Tell me, Roman. How long would it take before her pain stopped dominating your nightmares?"

A rock hurtled through the air. It whacked the Sheriff in the face. He laughed harder. "Witch, your powers are weak."

Another rock headed towards him. Like the first, it hit him. The Sheriff bellowed with laughter. The fence post came as a surprise. It whipped from the ground and hurtled through the air like a javelin. It speared through the right-hand side of his face and landed on the ground behind him. The Sheriff shoved Eliza down to the ground. Felt the fleshy hole.

Roman's attack came from the left.

The Sheriff stumbled and dropped to his knees. Took two more punches to his face. Wrapped his arm around Roman's leg when the kick hurtled in towards him, and hammered his elbow down into Roman's knee cap.

Roman cried out and collapsed to the ground.

The Sheriff got back onto his feet. Staggered. Only having one eye obscured his vision. He turned from Roman to Eliza.

She was gone.

The Sheriff glanced back up. Searched to his left. Then his right. A sickened feeling that he may have lost Jacob rose in his throat.

"Distraction's a bitch when it works." Now it was Roman who laughed.

"You think your silly games will save her?"

"I do."

"Then you are a bigger fool than I gave you credit for."

The fence post smashed through the Sheriff's chest, and held position. He shook his head, but the acute pain held strong. He looked down for Roman, but Roman was no longer on the ground; now, the Reaper stood before him.

"I'll see you in Hell." Roman grabbed the pole and swung the Sheriff towards the car. He gritted his teeth and pushed the Sheriff against the burning car.

The Sheriff didn't have time to react. Flames caught hold of Billy's uniform. Within seconds, the fabric melted into the Sheriff's skin. He cried out – more from the frustration at being caught off guard than the pain the fire caused. He reached again for Roman, but Roman had set off limping towards the bike. The blaze quickly took his face, his vision, his hair.

"Roman!"

Roman leapt onto the bike. The girl jumped on behind him.

The Sheriff's sight darkened. He heard the motorcycle engine rev. The screeching of tyre. And then, gradually, nothing. The engine quietened as, the Sheriff assumed, the bike hightailed it out of there.

The Sheriff cursed. He pulled the post out from his stomach and dropped it to his knees. Stopped moving. Inhaled long and slow. And allowed the warmth of the embers to lull him back to the memories he cherished from his days spent in Hell. Darkness blacker than anything he'd ever known, even though fires raged beneath, above, and all around him. He should have remembered it as nothing other than torment and excruciating pain. He'd endured horrors. His skin had continuously been melted from his body.

But he held no malice towards those days. He only remembered the security of it all. God, he missed them. Hell had gifted him with inner peace, and liberated him from the murderous thoughts that had once crammed his human head. Hell had shown him the light; that he needn't lock his demons away like some freak – especially from a weakened society that ultimately condemned him to the life he now loved so very much.

He turned his hands palms up and admired the black-tainted scars that scratched so deep they touched his bones. On the left, the figure of infinity etched into his wrist, a sign that he would go on forever; and on his right, a reverse pentagram – the sign of evil. Neither of them had faded with age, and he smiled at the irony of it all. Yes, Hell had become his saviour. And the Devil had become his friend.

Just under thirty seconds passed before he calmed enough to think clearly again. Then he straightened. The fire that consumed him died, and the cop's body stretched back into his own. The Sheriff looked down at the smouldering fabric and watched it morph into his own attire. He flexed his hands, bones reshaping, nails lengthening to their usual claws.

The Sheriff repositioned his hat and glanced towards the road. As he thought, Roman and the girl were long gone. He kicked the wooden post from his path, and walked towards the apartment. The girl had escaped him twice, and in doing so, saved Roman's good-for-nothing soul. Now, for the second time that day, the Sheriff was left empty handed and filled with rage.

Jacob's odour lingered in the air like a black cloud. However, it did not lead him in the direction Roman had travelled. Instead, it directed him into the apartment building. Not that Jacob was in there now, but it may house a clue as to where Roman and the girl had fled.

Sirens began to fill the air. The Sheriff cursed again, and although he didn't want to, he morphed back into the cop – brand-new uniform intact once again.

A fire engine came hurtling down the road. It pulled into the parking area, and four firemen jumped out and headed straight for the burning Volkswagen. Spectators gathered, and suddenly the car park was overcrowded.

The Sheriff clenched his fists. He wanted to follow Roman and the girl. He wanted to hunt them down and drag their sorry souls back to Purgatory. But if firemen had turned up, chances were the police wouldn't be far behind. The Sheriff entered Billy's building, and followed the scent up the stairs to the blue door at the end of the corridor. No handle. Just a lock and doorbell.

Behind him, a door opened.

"There you are, Billy. I have to complain about those friends of yours."

The Sheriff clenched his fists and turned. An elderly woman stood behind him, arms crossed, looking ready to give him a severe dressing down. "Ma'am?"

"I have been trying to telephone the station, but nobody is answering. I don't know what is happening to this town. It's all going to hell."

"I'll be sure to pass your comments on to my superiors." The Sheriff turned back to the blue front door. The small hallway reeked. Jacob's odour lingered here, but other smells also enveloped him. There was no mistaking the stench of death. It welled up from under the door like overgrown weeds.

"Is everything all right in there?" The old woman was beside him. "Your sister has had an awful lot of people coming and going over the last hour or so…"

The Sheriff's curiosity stopped him from killing her where she stood. He hid his murderous intentions with a smile. She was old – like, really old. He couldn't remember ever killing a living human this old before.

"…And the last young man, oh there was something very odd about him."

"Young man?"

"He just looked suspicious, you know?"

"No. I don't. What did he look like?" But the Sheriff already knew her description would fit Roman. His scent also hung in the air.

"Well, let's see. He had brown hair, and was very tall. Not like a giant, but taller than the average man. Oh, and his dress. My, my. Very untidy."

"He wore a dress?"

The woman cackled. "No. I mean the clothes he wore – looked like he'd slept in them, if you know what I mean?"

The Sheriff lost interest. "I think it best if you go back inside now."

"Don't you need me to make a statement?"

"No crime has been committed, ma'am." The Sheriff examined the door. He could easily kick it in. He glanced at the eagle-eyed pensioner who watched him.

"Forgotten your key, dear? The other man got in around the back."

The Sheriff planted his foot against the door, and kicked it open. Wood splintered from the lock, and he entered. He pushed the door shut behind him. It didn't close. The catch had ripped away with the wooden frame. So he pushed it, too, enough to stop the old woman from looking in.

He breathed in a lungful of air, unconcerned whether others inhabited the house or not. Yes, both Roman and Jacob's scents were all around him – Jacob's stronger here, Roman's towards the kitchen. He fought back the urge to stay focused on Roman, and looked at the blood-splattered walls. He glanced down at the mush of human remains lying behind the door. Definitely Jacob's work.

But this wasn't the only death he smelled.

He walked to the bedroom. Saw the mutilated girl drenched in her own blood and sprawled across the bed. Oh, Jacob had enjoyed himself.

Damn it. Tracking Jacob Witenie had become somewhat of a pain. And the longer it took to reign him in, the more incapable the Sheriff appeared to his peers – with or without Roman Holbrook in tow.

There was nothing in this apartment that held a clue as to where Roman had gone. The Sheriff walked to the apartment door, and opened it. Two police officers, one male, one female, stood before him. Both seemed nervous.

The female officer more so. "Billy, where have you been?"

The Sheriff glanced down at the officer's form he still used, then across to the dismembered officer lying behind the door. He closed the door a little to hide the blood-soaked carpet, smiled, and said, "What can I do for you?"

The female officer threw a quizzical look at her partner.

The male officer scratched his head. "Billy? Are you okay?"

"I'm fine. Why?"

"We need you to come to the station."

"I cannot do that at this present time."

Now the male officer gave a quizzical look. "Sergeant Collins has been murdered."

"That is of little concern to me." The Sheriff pushed past the two officers and stepped out into the hall.

"Billy!" The male officer halted the Sheriff by the shoulder. "You have no choice. You must come with us."

The Sheriff sighed. Just another annoyance he didn't have time for. He turned and faced the two officers. The female officer remained apprehensive. She was the smart one. She sensed this situation was about to turn very, very bad.

The male officer, on the other hand, was a whole different story. His ego had grown to the size of Hell itself.

The Sheriff sighed again. He needed to make up time, not lose it because of irritants such as these two. So he did what came naturally to him, and punched out. His fist smashed through the rib cage of the male officer until it hit air on the other side. The female officer reached for a device on her belt, but the Sheriff seized her by the neck and lifted her off the ground. Her hands gripped his, and she clawed to free the hold he had on her. Unlike the lifeless male, she moved in a violent way. Her body squirmed and wriggled. Her legs kicked for balance. Her hand reached back for her belt, and then a jolt penetrated the Sheriff's body. The initial shock turned into a tingle, but defiance remained in the female's eyes. She pressed the taser against him again. The Sheriff squeezed his fingers until her neck snapped. Quick, silent, painless. He dropped her body, and pulled his other hand free from her colleague. Both bodies landed beside each other. The old woman reappeared at her door. She stared at the officers lying on the floor, and then at the Sheriff. He hated to leave a witness, but he was way behind on time as it was. So, he bid good day and walked away, leaving the nosey neighbour to admire his work.

Outside, the smouldering car again reminded him of how he'd let Roman and the girl slip through his fingers. He suppressed the building irritation, and closed his eyes. When he opened them, he saw the police car.

From inside the building, the old neighbour's screams hollered out.

The Sheriff climbed in to the car and grabbed the radio. "This is Officer Hamilton. I need to locate a stolen motorcycle."

CHAPTER SEVENTEEN

Roman stopped the bike and cut the engine.

Eliza unhooked the tight grasp she held around his waist, yawned, and stretched. "Why are we stopping?"

"We need to ditch the bike."

"Why?"

"Because the Sheriff knows we're riding it."

"So? You said he can only find us when Jacob is here."

"He's also taken your brother's form. He can use police resources and hunt us down."

"How would he know to do that? You said he's from Purgatory. How would he know what technology we have here?"

"This ain't the first time he's been here. Now just get off the bike."

Eliza swung her leg over the seat. "I'm serious. We have a perfectly suitable vehicle here. It also happens to be bloody fast. We could be in Scotland by tonight."

"And then what? Jacob will eventually arrive, and the Sheriff soon after that."

"But this is Billy's bike."

Roman kicked out the stand. "Like he's ever gonna be riding it again."

Eliza's eyes turned hard. Her nostrils flared. "You're a cold-hearted bastard."

"So I've been told." Roman nodded towards the café across the street. "If you need the toilet..."

"Don't you dare change the subject."

"Then don't give me a belly-full of your shit."

Her legs planted wide, and her hands found her hips. "I'll—"

"Eliza. Just go to the toilet if you need to."

"This conversation isn't over."

Roman watched her storm across the road, Billy's boots looking like a pair of flippers on the end of her delicate legs. The singer Max Wall came to mind. "See if you can grab us a couple of sausage rolls as well while you're at it."

"With what?" Eliza turned. She lifted the oversized shirt and pulled the shorts' pockets inside out. "We don't have any money."

"Use that overactive imagination of yours."

"You mean steal them?"

"I mean, find another way."

"You find another way." She turned on her heel.

An old shop bell jingled when Eliza opened the café door. Roman heard it again as the door closed behind her. What in the hell was it about her that he liked so much? She possessed strength and independence – two attributes he hated in a woman. Or maybe he liked it? He'd never met anyone like her before. She argued every single decision he made. Disobeyed every order. She never did as he asked. She had a body he would happily die for... That had to be it. Led by his dick again.

He turned his attention back to the few cars parked along the small high street. A couple of nice vehicles – a BMW and an Audi – but they'd be locked and alarmed, and he couldn't afford to draw attention to himself. Shit. Maybe Eliza was right. Maybe he was better off keeping the bike and just switching plates the first chance he got.

He went to reach for the cigarettes in his shirt pocket. Then realised he wore Billy's jumper. For fuck's sake. Now he was hungry and nicotine-deprived. He drummed his fingers against the bike. Thought about taking a wander down the road to see if he could find a Co-Op or a Spar, or anywhere that sold fags and food.

Then thought about not being here when Eliza came out.

Shit. Not only could he not go and hunt down a smoke and a bite to eat, he also had to tell Eliza that she was right about keeping the bike. It made sense. The bike was the fastest ride to Scotland.

And, he had an idea of what to do when they got there.

CHAPTER EIGHTEEN

Eliza had lost all feeling in her bare legs.

In fact, the Northern cold had numbed pretty much every part of her body. She hadn't realised it at the time, but she'd spent most of the journey with her head buried in Roman's shoulder, her eyes clasped tight shut.

Early evening had long since arrived, and tarmac and grass verges brightened under the flashing indicator light. Roman turned left. A grubby neon sign, nearing the end of its usefulness, lit up a seedy, paint-faded motel. Roman eased off the accelerator, and the bike crawled forward. No illuminated room windows and, other than a young Indian man behind the reception desk, the place looked deserted. Situated next door was a less-than-desirable truck-stop diner, where passing truckers looked to be responsible for ninety percent of its takings. Roman drove to the rear of the motel and parked in an unlit corner, out of sight.

"Are we here?" Eliza sat straight. Her arms slackened, and she reluctantly loosened her grip from around his waist. Her stiffened back ached worse than the time she'd slept on Billy's lounge floor.

"If by here you mean Aberdeen, then yes. We're here."

"Aberdeen? My father's property is in Inverness."

"Plans have changed."

"Plans? What plans? You haven't mentioned any plans to me."

He nodded towards the motel. "It's not the Ritz, but it's a bed for the night."

"Does Norman Bates come with it?" Eliza got off the bike. Red blotches covered her cold legs, and her hair felt like it nested the carcasses of a hundred insects. Was this really the only place they could find to stay? "What time is it?"

"No idea. Half-four. Five?"

"Is it wise to stop? Shouldn't we go further up?"

"No. We're gonna get a boat over to Lerwick."

"Lerwick? What's in Lerwick?"

"Another boat to Bergen."

"Norway?"

"Yep. We run. The Sheriff chases. I've done this before remember. We need to find a way to get Jacob out of you. Until then, we need to keep as much distance between us and the Sheriff as possible."

"How are we going to get a boat with no money?"

Roman glanced at her. "Like I said, I've done this before."

"Then why aren't we at some port somewhere now?"

"I need to make a phone call first."

"So make the call. I don't see why we need to stay here."

"The boat will take a couple of hours to arrange. We can rest up till then."

Eliza glanced at the rooms behind her. "Not in there?"

"Yes, in there."

He stared at her, his blue eyes looking more beautiful than ever. Warmth flooded her body and she looked away, suddenly unable to hold his gaze. She quietened. Scratched her neck, purely for something to do.

"Well?"

"Well, what?"

"I'm waiting for the argument."

"Stop over-exaggerating, I don't argue everything."

"You should stand in my shoes."

She ignored him. "How are we supposed to pay for this?"

Roman got off the bike, and flashed his pearly whites. "We're not." He started walking towards the motel.

"What do you mean, we're not?"

Roman disappeared between two trucks. Eliza saw drawn cab curtains and, she presumed, sleeping occupants. She caught up with Roman and stuck close, manoeuvring around the many lorries also parked up for the evening. She had no idea what Roman planned until he'd reached the far side of the motel. Dustbins congregated in a huddle outside the end room, the nearest bin overturned. Its mouldy contents splayed across the ground. The stench was overwhelming, but Roman seemed unbothered by it. He pulled on the window, annoyed when he couldn't open it. "Can you undo that lock?"

Eliza frowned.

"With your mind." He tapped his head. "Can you open it?"

"You want me to break in?"

"Like you said, we don't have the money to pay for it."

"You're the criminal. You do it."

"If I do it, it'll involve smashing a window."

"So?"

"So, it will make a noise. A loud one."

"Well, can't you go around front and pick the lock?"

"Of course I can, but the oink sitting in reception will see me."

Eliza stared at him. Her chest tightened, and she closed her eyes.

"Are you doing it?"

Eliza opened her eyes again. "Doing what?"

"Your telepathy?"

"No. I'm trying to calm down. What if somebody's asleep in there?"

"Honestly, who the hell's gonna want to stay here?"

"Well, we are."

Roman ran his tongue across his teeth. Casual as you like, he knocked on the window. Eliza readied herself to run, but when nobody answered, Roman turned to her and smiled.

"Maybe they're in a deep sleep."

Roman banged his fist against the glass. This time he didn't seem to care who heard. "See, nobody inside."

"What if somebody checks in later?"

"It's five o'clock in the afternoon. Trust me, the only arrivals are going to be truckers."

"So? Truckers do book into motels late at night."

"You're right. I mean, why would they want the comfort of their cab when luxurious rooms like this are on their doorstep?" He took a deep breath. His chest inflated, and his pecs stretched his jumper. "It's either break in here, where there's a bed and a shower, or sleep on the bike."

Eliza glanced back towards the lorries. Somewhere beyond was her brother's motorcycle, which could take her to a Premier Inn, or even a Travelodge. Thing was, she had no idea how to ride a motorbike. She sighed. Cursed. And turned to the window. "How the hell am I supposed to do this?"

"Just concentrate. Remember how you did it before."

"I don't know how I did it before."

"Something must have set it off."

"Yeah, I was being tortured."

"So, what are you saying? It'd help if I tortured you now?"

Eliza threw Roman a look she was sure would turn him to stone. She mumbled a string of obscenities, all aimed towards him, and focused on the inside of the window. Thick grime, dead insects, and age-old cobwebs covered the small ledge. Buried somewhere in the midst of it all was the latch. She stared. Hard. But as she predicted, it didn't move. "This is pointless. Even if I do open the window, look how small it is."

Roman spun her back to the window. "Just calm down, and try."

"Calm down? I said I did it before while under extreme duress."

"Then don't calm down. Stay wound up. I don't give a shit. Just concentrate on opening the bloody lock."

If only she could concentrate. She rolled her shoulders, feeling the immediate effect of the stretch, and wished she had the time to give the rest of her body the same attention. She glanced back through the window, just making out the latch, and focused. *Twist the latch to open. Twist the latch to open.*

Nothing happened.

She opened her eyes.

Roman raised a brow. "Is that it?"

"I told you, I don't know how to do it."

He rubbed his brow. Finally, he threw his hands up. "Step back." He lifted an elbow and smashed the glass. He'd been right. The noise was loud. Like, really loud.

He bashed away loose shards, opened the latch, and quickly raised the wooden frame to its fullest extent – which wasn't much. "Can you squeeze through that?"

"You're serious?" Eliza glared at him.

Roman interlocked his fingers. "Hey, I sure as hell can't fit."

Eliza sighed and planted a foot in his cupped hands. In one swift lift, she was up and squeezing her way through the tiny opening.

She landed on the other side, the threadbare carpet not cushioning her fall whatsoever. The bathroom door was ajar, the room beyond in darkness. She lay still for a moment, listening for sounds of people sleeping. A lorry pulled off the road, its headlights sweeping across the room and highlighting the cigarette-stained walls and 1970's décor. Then, darkness came again. Eliza stood. Roman was right: there wasn't a person alive who would pay to stay in a room like this.

She turned back to the window and jutted her head out as far as she could get it. "Roman?"

But Roman was gone.

Behind her, a hurried knock tapped on the motel door. Eliza rushed across the room. Took a quick glance through the spy hole, a habit she'd adopted since moving into her gran's place. Roman smiled and waved, as though aware of what she was doing. "Bloody man."

She opened the door. As soon as Roman was inside, she closed it again.

Eliza reached for the lamp, but Roman stopped her. "You don't want to draw attention to us being here."

"Great, so we just have to sit here in the dark."

"You don't need the lights on to sleep." Roman checked the interconnecting door. It was locked. "You take the bed. I'm good with the chair."

"And they say chivalry is dead."

Roman ignored her. "I'd grab a quick shower if I was you. You probably won't get the chance again for a couple of days."

Eliza wanted to argue, but Roman was right. Beneath her clothes, Eddie's dried blood caked her body. She'd tried to freshen up in the café toilet, but it was no good. She still felt the blood there. In her hair. Underneath her fingernails. A shower would be good. She breezed past Roman into the bathroom, slamming the door behind her.

A cord hung from a broken light fitting, and she pulled it. She immediately wished she hadn't. The bathroom was in a worse state than the bedroom: mould, missing tiles, a broken toilet seat. Water trickled from the shower when she turned it on. It never warmed. She undressed anyway, and stepped under.

It was the greatest-worst shower she'd ever taken. Cold water washed a newness into her hair. That was the great bit. The worst was the rest of her shivering body having to endure the icy temperature.

She finished up as quickly as she could, and got out. With no towels available, she stood shivering in the cold, drip-drying as much as she could before re-dressing. Billy's shirt, now damp, clung to her skin. The shorts didn't cover her legs, let alone warm them. She hastily left the bathroom, and dashed for the bed covers.

Roman didn't speak to her. Instead, he headed to the bathroom. He closed the door, and Eliza heard the shower turn on again. She lay back against the pillow, wanting to be asleep before he returned. But, she couldn't sleep. Instead, she stared up into the dark. After everything she'd been through today she expected sleep to take her quickly, but the fear of not knowing what tomorrow or the day after may bring kept her wide awake. Her body shuddered, and she pulled the covers up tight under her chin.

The shower stopped, and Eliza rolled onto her side, ready to feign sleep the moment Roman emerged. A minute must have passed, and she opened her eyes again. A slither of light escaped under the bathroom door, its beam broken only when Roman moved on the other side. Had he watched that light while she'd been in the bathroom? Eliza couldn't deny Roman had a good body. In fact, she couldn't deny that she found him extremely attractive – in a rugged kind of way. But, his demeanour confused her. And some of the things he said hurt her.

A few minutes passed before the bathroom door opened. Roman, also dressed again, made his way across the bedroom. He grabbed a pillow from the bed, and settled in what Eliza presumed was the armchair.

She gave him a moment to relax, then said, "How long are we staying here?"

"I just need to rest. Grab a couple of hours, and then we'll head off again."

"To where? We can't keep running like this."

"Trust me. The more distance we put between us and the Sheriff the better."

"Why? Jacob is always going to give away our location. We could arm ourselves at my father's. He has hunting rifles and animal traps."

"Because the moment Sheriff senses Jacob, he will be able to…" Roman struggled for the word. "Teleport, if you like, within a certain distance of his location."

"How much of a distance are we talking about?"

"From the moment Jacob appears? Teleportation – God, I hate that word – takes about seven minutes for every hundred miles travelled. After that, he will be within twenty miles of us. Give or take half a mile."

"Okay, so we run. For how long?"

Roman punched some life into the pillow. It was clear he didn't want to encourage the discussion by answering.

"And what about getting Billy back?"

"Oh God, not the Billy question again." She heard him turn to her. "I already told you, Billy is gone. He'll be in the depths of Purgatory by now, along with your father. There is no escaping that."

"I can't just leave him there."

"Yes, you can."

"But he can get out. The same way you did. The same way this Jacob has."

"Eliza. I am going to say this one last time, and then I refuse to speak of it again. First, Billy would have to escape the torture chamber, and that is no easy feat, believe me. Secondly, he needs to escape Purgatory. To do that, he needs to navigate hundreds of tunnels. That is near impossible – even if you know what tunnels to take. Thirdly, he needs to reach the waiting room. Again, with hundreds of guards chasing him, the odds for success are a billion to one. Lastly, you need to know which waiting soul is destined to be returned, and nobody knows that."

Eliza's body tightened. A badly painted Constable reproduction hung on the far wall. It started to shake. Beneath it, a brown chair toppled over.

"Great. Now you use your magic."

Eliza closed her eyes. She didn't want to use her telekinesis. She didn't even understand how she was able to use it. All she knew was she wanted Billy back more than surviving the Sheriff herself. And Roman was stopping her.

The picture fell to the floor.

"Eliza. Enough."

"I will not leave Billy there."

"Fine. Don't. All I'm saying is that I can't help you get him out."

The bulb in the bedside lamp exploded.

"Do you want someone to hear us?"

He was right. Goddamn it. Eliza inhaled, deeply, and held it. The picture reel inside her head faded and, slowly, thoughts changed from Billy to a life before all this horror began. The room quietened, and only then did she exhale.

Roman never spoke, but Eliza was damned if she was letting the subject drop. "So who does qualify for being returned?"

"Shit. I said nobody knows."

"You knew. You are here after all."

"That was down to Jacob."

"So how did he know?"

"Oh hell, I don't know. Maybe someone told him, or maybe he's just one hell of a lucky son of a bitch."

"Is it random? Any soul can be chosen?"

"For return? No. Only those taken before their time." Roman shifted position. "Now, for fuck's sake, shut up and let me sleep."

With a lack of conversation to keep her awake, Eliza rolled onto her side. The duvet still pulled up to her chin. A lorry pulled off the main road, and the bedside lamp rattled under the vibration. The ceiling brightened for a second, its outdated aertex reminding her how much of a dump the room really was. Then the lorry passed, and obscurity retook the place.

"What is Purgatory like?"

Roman exhaled a sigh of agitation, his gruff reply oozing out along with it. "Not very nice."

"That doesn't tell me much."

Another sigh. "I'm trying to sleep."

"But I'm not tired."

She heard Roman shift in the chair, but he remained quiet. Just when she thought he wouldn't answer, he said, "You remember what seeing that dead cop at Billy's did to you? What it looked like?"

How could Eliza forget? The images of Eddie slumped in a pool of his own blood with his intestines hanging out. "Every time I close my eyes."

"Well, I saw that in Purgatory on an hourly basis – only ten times more severe."

"You had it done to you?"

"More than once."

A lump caught in Eliza's throat. She clenched the duvet until her knuckles ached, suddenly feeling claustrophobic. Another lorry pulled in off the main road, momentarily shedding light on Roman. He sat staring out the window. "I didn't mean to bring up the past."

"You're worried about your brother. I get it."

"Then you get more than anyone why I can't leave him there."

Roman's head lowered and his shoulders curled his chest.

"How could you not die from all that torture?"

Roman snorted a laugh. "It's Purgatory. You can't die if you're technically already dead."

The lorry passed by, taking its light with it. "Is Billy going through the same torture?"

"Don't think about it. We have enough on our plate."

"How am I not supposed to think about it?" Eliza wanted to push the subject, to argue the importance of Billy's life. But this wasn't the time. Roman didn't need to describe in detail the horror he'd endured in Purgatory. The image of Eddie said it enough. And, as much as she wanted her brother back, Roman reliving his days there was not going to help her cause. If she had to be totally honest with herself, she was also too damn scared to know.

She sat there, listening to Roman's breathing. She could tell he'd turned back to the window, and wondered what thoughts now consumed him. Was it

Purgatory? Was it the Sheriff? "How did you end up like this?"

Roman's breathing quietened.

"I mean, you said you were once human."

"Yes."

Again, she heard him shift position. "Then what happened?"

"It was a long time ago, and I don't wish to talk about it."

"Did the Sheriff take you?"

"No. The Sheriff isn't a Reaper. He's just a jailer."

"Then how did you end up in Purgatory?"

"It doesn't matter."

Eliza rolled on to all fours and crawled to the end of the bed. Gradually her eyes accustomed to the dull moonlight, which filtered through the dusty nets – its blue haze defining Roman's face, his jaw, his neck. "Please tell me. I want to understand." She asked the question, again expecting him to tell her to shut up and get some sleep.

"I'm seven hundred years old – give or take a decade or two." The outline of Roman's chest inflated, and he sighed, only this time it was different than before: one of embarrassment rather than anger and irritation. "I had a father who loved God more than my mother, and a brother who deserved more loyalty from me than what I gave."

"How did you die?"

"Black Death in 1349. Took my brother first."

"And your family?"

Roman took a while to answer, and Eliza wondered if she'd pushed too hard with her questions.

"No family."

"I mean your son and his mother."

He quietened for a second, then said, "My son died during childbirth."

"I'm sorry."

"Don't be. I was a bastard who got my brother's wife pregnant."

His uncaring tone didn't fool Eliza. "You loved her, though?"

Roman rubbed his eyes, and shifted position once more. "Very much. But I abandoned them both, and she killed herself when she lost our son."

Eliza got up off the bed and crouched beside his chair. When she reached for his hand, he didn't move it away. She didn't speak because she didn't feel the need to. Holding his hand seemed enough.

"I am not a good person, Eliza."

"I know. Look where you're making me sleep." She heard him scoff, and for a moment they were friends again. "You know, I can help you fight the Sheriff."

Roman slipped his hand away from hers, taking their moment with him. "We've already discussed this. The answer is no."

"You know, your male chauvinistic caveman approach is beginning to aggravate me. I have a power that can help you."

Roman got up out of the chair. "You have a power that you don't know how to control properly."

"Well, it's more than you have at the moment." She stood. Roman's outline towered over her. She felt his eyes bore into her, his breathing erratic and desperate to hold back the argument she knew he wanted to have.

"We cannot argue," he said, fighting to keep his voice low and controlled. "You need to stay calm. Jacob will—"

"I am calm."

"I don't need no girl fighting my battles for me."

"I'm related to Jesus! Surely that counts for something?"

"That just means you're a mind mover. And, again, it's a power you cannot control." He turned for the door and yanked it open, not caring if anyone saw him. Two lorries pulled in to the truck stop. A third pulled out. The scene outside the motel seemed busier than sale day at Harrods.

"Where are you going?"

"The diner. I'm hungry."

"And how're you going to pay for it with no money?"

"I'll kill the waitress and cook something myself."

Eliza chased him to the door. Anger bubbled up from the pit of her stomach. "You're pathetic. Where's yesterday's guy who didn't have 'surrender' in his vocabulary?"

Roman stopped dead, and Eliza collided into the back of him. He turned to face her. "You should calm down."

"What is it about the Sheriff that scares you so much?"

Roman's eyes hardened. "I just told you that Purgatory is worse than Hell. I will not go back there. I can't survive that again."

"Then we make sure we beat him."

"He is not your fight."

"He became my fight the moment you brought me back."

"You could get hurt!"

"And you could get dead!"

Roman stood silent, his eyes locked on hers, his chest expanding and deflating with every heavy breath he took.

"Why can't you just admit that you need me?"

Without warning, Roman's body was against hers. He grabbed her arms and pulled her close, his lips urgent to find hers. She hadn't expected it. Truth be told, she hadn't even thought he liked her all that much.

He pulled back slightly, every warm and hurried breath breezing across her face. "I'm sorry. I didn't mean to do that," he whispered.

Eliza didn't care for his apologies. This time it was her lips that found his – and this surprised her even more. The attraction she felt towards him overwhelmed her, and the buried desire to feel his touch couldn't be ignored. Slowly, he responded. His arms slid around her waist. He pulled her tight against him, lifting her until she balanced on the tips of her toes. His hands caressed their way up along her back until they cupped her neck, where they held her closer while his kisses warmed every part of her mouth.

The strength of his body seduced her. His fingers stroked her hair, her face, her neck. Slowly, he walked her back towards the room. His lips never left hers, his hands holding and guiding her back into the room. Eliza heard him kick the door shut, and then his arms embraced her tighter, their urgency to keep her close obvious. He cupped her face, his fingers entwining her hair, his lips trailing her jawline and across her neck.

Eliza closed her eyes, and a subtle groan caught in the back of her throat. She felt Roman's excitement. Top two buttons undone, he swiftly hugged her waist. He reached for her oversized shirt. For a split second, his lips left her skin. The shirt lifted over her head in one swift motion, and then his lips tasted her again. How had she gotten here? A couple of days ago this man had imprisoned her in the boot of his car. She should hate him. But she didn't hate him. Quite the contrary.

His hands tenderly cupped her face, his touch caressing every inch of her neck. Giddiness swam inside her head. Her legs weakened, and she wanted nothing more than for Roman to take her now, where she stood. She slid her hands beneath his jumper, needing to explore every part of his body, needing to feel his body against hers; his toned stomach, the hardness of his muscles, the power in his shoulders. His hands covered hers, and he hastily removed his top. It fell to the floor, and his hands instantly returned to her, the bareness of his chest pressed against hers, his hands stroking and discovering every bump and ripple along her spine.

Eliza's hands wandered over the bulk that shaped his biceps. His skin was hot to the touch. She pressed her lips against his chest. Trailed her fingers down over his pecs, planting little kisses down his torso. Her hands lingered, soaking up every crevice and chink that defined his body. She heard Roman's intake of breath, pleased that her touch excited him. Then, he cupped her face and pulled her close so he could kiss her once more.

Effortlessly, he lowered her onto the bed. Eliza moved her mouth to his neck, her tongue eager to taste and explore, nibble and kiss. Roman's head arched, and his breathing quickened—

"Stop." Roman leapt off the bed. "We can't do this."

"Why?"

He searched the floor for his jumper. "It isn't a good idea."

"I think it's just what we both need."

"You are not you. Jacob is too close." He hastily dressed, and rushed to the door. "I need a drink."

CHAPTER NINETEEN

Billy opened his eyes.

The stalagmite had gone.

The hole in his torso hadn't.

His heart – did he still have one of those? He must have. He felt its fastened beat pound inside his chest. At any moment he expected it to burst right through what skin he had left. He closed his eyes. This had to be a dream. Or a nightmare. Or some wacked-out emotion brought to the surface because Eliza's murder was on his mind. Yes. That was it.

He opened his eyes again. Saw the hole in his torso. No shirt – remembered that had gone. Just bloodied skin and severed flesh.

More panic. The pounding fastened and vibrated throughout his body. Sweat leaked from every pore. Back to his torso. He tried to reach for the hole to cover it, to feel it was real, but his arms wouldn't move. He lifted his head. An ache in his neck protested the movement and he lowered it again. Took a breath, which was too rushed to calm him down. He started to laugh. He had to be dreaming.

His laughter died.

The hole in his stomach remained.

His arms still wouldn't move.

Now the tears came. His body, what was left of it, trembled. He clenched his fists and desperately pulled against the restraints – out of his view, but they felt hard and cold like iron shackles.

He tried to think. To remember. First the police station, then his father's house and the beach. Then the white light that turned dark. The endless caverns, the climbing, his father, the falling, the stalagmite. *Shit.* He recalled everything.

He raised his head again, and prayed to see the four walls of his bedroom apartment. Instead, he saw cave walls. Not dissimilar to those he'd fled through in the corridors – only these flickered under torch flames and surrounded devices and instruments of a horrifying nature.

From the ceiling hung a metal cage, its narrowness not allowing the decaying man slumped inside to fully collapse. Rats scampered alongside the far wall, navigating three pairs of metal shoes that all had cranks projecting from them. A wooden stake balanced against a circle of stones. On a table lay slim cylindrical barrels, their insides covered with iron spikes. Another barrel, this one larger with a metal clamp surrounding the hole at the top, sat only metres to his right. Then there was the axe, which rested against a grooved block. Even Billy knew it was used for beheading.

He frantically pulled again at his restraints. His knees weakened, but his body wouldn't fall. Bloody images of decapitation flashed through his mind. Perspiration drenched his shoulders and trickled his neckline. Pain pierced his chest with every heartbeat.

"Somebody help me." His cries echoed around him. "Is anybody else there?"

Then screams – his – at the mere thought of falling victim to one of the torture devices. "Help me." He tugged at the restraints with frenzied determination, until he felt a flow of blood trickle his arm.

"Be quiet. They'll hear you."

Billy quietened. He waited for the hushed voice to speak again. It didn't.

"Where are you?"

"Be quiet. You'll bring them back in here." It sounded female.

"Who are you? Can you get me out?"

"No."

"I'm hurt." He glanced back at the gaping hole that had taken the best part of his upper body. "How can I be alive?"

"Because you can't die."

"What do you mean, I can't die? What is this place?"

"That's all I'm saying. Shut up now."

"But I'm trapped."

A different voice. This one male and older. "We all are. Now be quiet."

"How many of you are there?"

"I said be quiet."

"Is my father with you?" Billy tugged at the restraints again. "I have to get out of here."

"You'll never get out."

The words repeated over and over. *You'll never get out.* Billy pulled harder. His wrists were clamped tight against the rock wall. He was going nowhere.

Drained of energy, he collapsed and hung from his restraints. Probably didn't look too dissimilar from the person in the metal cage above him.

He waited. Rasping breaths didn't calm, and his body tremors magnified. He shook his arms, the only movement being around his elbows. "Somebody help me."

A key scratched inside a lock. He heard murmurs from the unseen voices he'd spoken to. Whispered words that hurriedly ceased as the oversized wooden door to his left swung open.

Three robed people entered, hoods draped over their heads, their faces hidden in shadow. They walked single file, the last one closing the door behind him. Neither spoke to each other, nor did they acknowledge Billy as they passed. Silence hung in the air. Then a man's scream. Billy's muscles tensed and his body tightened. Out of his sight, he heard chains rattle. Then the screaming stopped. A man was dragged into view, and the blubbering began.

"Please, not again." Matted black hair covered most of the man's face. His body – nothing but skin and bone – could hardly walk. "It's not my turn."

The figures ignored him. Half-dragged, half-carried him towards the stake – set at a forty-five degree angle.

"No. No." The man's pleas for mercy grew more urgent. His eyes widened, and his heels dug into the ground. Their skid marks trailed the dirt all the way to the pole.

One robed figure held the stake steady. The other two lifted the struggling man off the ground.

"No. No." The man thrashed, tried to kick free. Unsuccessfully.

The stake impaled his body with surprising ease. Screams gurgled from his throat as the robed figures pushed him further down the pole. Billy closed his eyes, but the man's cries echoed inside his head. He opened them again in time to see the blood. Everywhere. It held Billy's focus for longer than he wanted. It didn't distract from the screams, though. They continued. On and on. Never ending. The guy should be dead. Why wasn't the guy dead? Then again, shouldn't Billy be dead?

The cloaked duo released the body. It was going nowhere, skewered into position on the stake. They took hold of the wooden pole and tilted it upright towards the stone circle. The man cried in agony, his body arced forward. Limbs hung limp. The third robed man removed a torch from the wall. The flame danced erratically as he stood before the staked man. Yellow-stained teeth broke through the shadow of his hood when he smiled, and he lowered the flame towards the circular pit. Fire immediately engulfed the area.

The man squirmed and writhed on the wooden pole. "Not again. Not again."

The robed men tilted the stake forward.

Billy couldn't watch. Yet he couldn't look away, either.

The man's screams worsened as flames licked his skin. His body convulsed against the heat. His hair caught light. His screams spat blood.

"Stop it." The words were out – and Billy immediately regretted it.

The robed men turned their attention towards him.

Billy froze.

The men removed their hoods. Now Billy saw them. Faces scarred and disfigured. Two of the men walked towards him. Billy pulled against his restraints. The men reached above him and Billy felt the clamps free their hold around his wrists. He collapsed on to all fours. When he tried to get up, he collapsed again.

The staked man still screamed, his flesh melting from his skin. But Billy had bigger problems.

The men stood either side of him. Each grabbed an arm and hoisted him off the ground.

"Get the hell off me." Billy tried to kick free, but his legs wouldn't do what his brain ordered. He struggled and fought, all to no avail.

The men tightened their grips. Billy kept resisting. He thrashed and writhed and wriggled, and finally collapsed, exhausted. He raised his head, just long enough to see the chair they carried him to. A simple chair. Wooden. High backed. Nothing torturous about it. Maybe they were going to question him. Maybe they were still searching for his father. Maybe the next half an hour of his life wasn't going to be as bad as he imagined.

They sat him down. "What the hell do you want?"

No answer, and Billy had to surrender while they clamped his ankles and wrists to the chair's arms and legs.

"I don't know where my father is," Billy offered.

They seemed uninterested.

The spiked man no longer screamed. Instead, only cries of self-pity and acceptance whimpered through the flames, his body now fully engulfed by the fire. How could he still be alive?

A robed man pushed Billy's head back against the chair, and an iron clamp wrapped his neck. Billy's attention moved from the burning man. "I shouldn't even be here. I'm not the one you want."

The robed men now had another agenda. Two of them headed out of sight, and Billy heard the unseen prisoners cry and beg for mercy once again. One, though, remained beside him. Billy tried to twist his head to see what he was doing, but the iron that clamped his neck allowed no movement.

Then he heard the crank of a lever.

His legs felt it first. Hundreds of nails stabbing his skin. He cried out. Tried to move, but the clamps pinned him to the chair.

Another crank of the lever.

The nails embedded deeper. Pain exploded in the back of his neck. Fists clenched. His body stiffened.

Another crank

Iron rods pierced his spine, his shoulder blades. He screamed, drowning out the cries from both the burning man and the unseen inmates now under attack.

Another crank.

The nails pushed further through his neck, and his voice disappeared.

Another crank.

Nails embedded further into his legs. Blood covered the chair. He wanted to move, but it wasn't the clamps pinning him down anymore.

He'd lost all power over his body.

CHAPTER TWENTY

Roman hadn't had a drink.

Instead, he'd phoned his contact. In a few hours, both he and Eliza would be on their way to Lerwick.

He opened the motel door. Readied himself for the abuse Eliza would no doubt throw at him, but none came. Darkness blocked both her and the bed from sight. Maybe she was asleep. Maybe she was just pretending so she wouldn't have to speak to him.

The two bottles of Bud he'd swiped from the cooler in the diner clanked together. Still Eliza didn't move. But he heard her breathing. She was awake.

He placed one of the bottles down on the bedside table. "I got you a beer." Didn't wait for a reply, and plopped down on the uncomfortable chair beside the window.

He heard Eliza move, but didn't turn to look at her. He didn't want to. Looking at her was too tempting. She had a hold over him, and he couldn't decide whether he liked it or not. Without thinking, he went to remove the bottle cap, then realised he didn't have an opener. Silently, he counted to ten. Waited for the building irritation to calm. Then, he got up, jammed the neck of the bottle into the bathroom door's hinge, closed the door tight, and twisted the cap off.

He settled back in the chair. Gulped back three or four sips. It tasted flat, even though it wasn't, and he sat the bottle on the narrow windowsill. Eliza still hadn't uttered a word, and he contemplated whether he should speak first. But to say what? *Sorry for leaving you hanging?*

He reached for the beer, decided against it, and closed his eyes. Conversations could wait until tomorrow. Right now, he needed sleep.

SUNDAY

Roman jolted awake and stared into the darkness. Seconds ticked by while he waited for his eyes to adjust to the room around him. The motel...Eliza... He turned. Saw nothing but darkness. She was in bed, although he couldn't see her. If fact, he couldn't hear her either. An uneasy feeling swept over him. He reached for the lamp. The room brightened, and he saw the vacant mattress.

He sat up. "Eliza?"

Waited for a response. Got none, and panic set in. He got up out of the chair. The bathroom was void of any light, but he checked the room anyway. How could he be so stupid as to fall asleep and let Eliza out of his sight? And now she'd gone.

Had she ditched him? Or had Jacob arrived and taken her off somewhere?

Roman pulled back the net curtain. A truck pulled out of the exit. At the other end of the car park, the diner seemed to have closed for the evening.

Where in the hell was Eliza?

Roman opened the door and stepped outside. Aside from the lorry's taillights disappearing in the distance, the main road was empty. He glanced at the row of rooms adjacent to the one he and Eliza had broken into. No lights. No flicker of TVs. Could Eliza or Jacob be inside one of them?

Roman turned his attention towards the reception area. A low light – maybe from a desk lamp. Perhaps whoever was working had seen her leave. He pulled the motel door shut, still unsure if it wasn't the rooms he should be checking instead, and headed towards the reception. He'd almost reached it when he heard glass smash. He spun towards the diner in time to see a female body fall through the glass door and hit the ground.

Eliza.

Dread curled Roman's heart. He wanted to race to her, but his feet would only move at a slow pace. He was halfway between the motel reception and the diner when he realized it wasn't Eliza lying there.

He swallowed back the sigh of relief and eyed the girl lying across the broken doorway. Skewered on a piece of glass that nearly severed her at the waist. Scratches lacerated her arms and legs. Blood soaked her pale blue uniform. It was the waitress he'd sweet-talked into giving him two free beers earlier. She must have only been eighteen, if a day. Roman glanced through the open doorway. He wanted to call out for Eliza, but the blooming obvious told him it wasn't Eliza inside – at least not an Eliza who was in control. He stepped over the girl. Glass crunched beneath his boots, and he entered the diner.

A jukebox sat in the corner of the room. Its rainbow of colour lit the inside of the diner. Food dried on plates. Spilt drinks and blobs of ketchup smeared table surfaces. Napkins pulled from their holders lay discarded across the floor. Roman ignored it all. Instead he waited, and listened.

Deathly quiet.

What were the odds a second psychopath – not Jacob – had chosen tonight to enter this diner and cut up the waitress? Probably a lot bloody lower than two people escaping Purgatory. No. Jacob was here. Roman would bet his life on it.

On the counter, beside the till, a cigarette smouldered in an ashtray. Roman glanced back at the dead waitress lying by his feet. Even he had to admit it was in poor taste, but he walked across the room – quiet and careful like – and picked it up. He inhaled, long and slow. The brand was cheap, and smoking it was like sucking in thin air. Still, he was on a forty-eight-hour withdrawal. At this moment in time, even this shit tasted like heaven. The melodic introduction of Frank Sinatra's "Witchcraft" broke the silence.

Roman turned to the jukebox. Such a beautiful machine looked completely out of place in a dump like this.

Something moved inside the kitchen. Roman saw it through the serving hatch. A clatter of copper pans and utensils swung from hooks on the far wall.

"Eliza?" Cigarette still in hand, Roman bolted around the counter.

He pushed open the two-way door. A dinner fork flew past him and embedded the wooden frame inches from his shoulder. A second piece of metal hurtled towards him. Too quick for him to stop. It slashed his earlobe and lodged into the frame just above its predecessor. A flash of silver in the air, and a knife nicked his shoulder, pinning his jumper to the door. Roman yanked it free.

"Jacob, you piece of shit." Roman threw the knife to the floor. "Get your arse out here where I can see you."

Eliza stepped out from the shadows. Still dressed in her brother's clothes, her hair un-brushed and hanging loose around her shoulders. Roman wanted to reach for her hand, but he didn't. He could see she wasn't right. The cold eyes staring back at him didn't belong to her. "Jacob. Long time, no see."

"What gave it away? The drinking? The dead bodies?" Jacob glanced down at the blood-drenched shirt. "This?"

"Actually, it was that crappy tune you used to whistle day-in day-out. Thought it was going to make my fucking ears bleed."

Jacob laughed. "I see you're still the same cantankerous old fool with an ego the size of Hertfordshire."

"And you're still a demented, psychopathic nut-job." Roman scanned the room, what he could see of it. He needed a plan. "So, now we both know that neither of us has changed much over the years, why don't you get out of the girl's body and go find someone else to fuck off?"

Jacob smiled. He slowly ran his hands down Eliza's sides. "I quite like her. She feels nice. But you know that already, don't you?"

Roman tensed. He wanted to charge that little bastard and rip his fucking head off. Instead, he walked to the nearby counter and perched against it. "What about you? I thought you'd be halfway to Brazil by now?"

"Where?"

Roman didn't have time to explain the last geographic millennium. A stream of police sirens wailed in the distance. Guess he hadn't been the only one to hear the waitress nosedive through the glass door. "You're still here because of me, right?"

"Obviously."

Blue and red neon glowed through the window. The cops had arrived.

"Because of what I did to you?"

Jacob smiled. "I did plan on killing you."

"Then why didn't you?"

"Because it was too easy. It would be over too quickly. I want to make you suffer like you made me suffer."

"And what makes you think you could do that?" Outside, car doors opened and closed. Time was running out.

"Maybe I've picked up a trick or two since our Purgatory days."

"I doubt it'll be enough to take me down."

"It will be."

"I did nothing you wouldn't have done if our roles had been reversed, and you know it." Roman glanced through the serving hatch.

Outside, several police cars parked in a disorganised mess around the car park, and at least fifteen police officers scattered the immediate area. A tall officer, older than the rest, jogged over to the reception.

"Point is, you did do it…and you did it to me."

Roman turned and looked at Jacob. "Quick question. How did you escape?"

Jacob seemed surprised. "You know how I escaped."

"No, I mean, how did you know who to hook on to?"

Jacob smiled. "Let's just say, you weren't my only friend down there."

"So who was my completion?"

"Just someone."

Roman thought back to their time shared in Purgatory. It couldn't have been another prisoner. A guard, maybe? "I hate to break it to you, Jacob, but I was never your friend down there. In fact, this is the first time I've even given you a seconds thought since I left."

Anger flared in Jacob's eyes. He banged the counter. "Do you have any idea what I went through after you escaped?"

"I expect pretty much the same as before I escaped. Torture, pain, unthinkable punishment, hideous maltreatment and abuse, blah, blah, blah." Roman turned back to the window. His lack of empathy seemed only to rile Jacob.

"Yes. And all of it made bearable by one thought. That one day an opportunity to escape would appear again. Then I would find you and bestow payback, tenfold."

Roman looked at him. He had no time left for small talk. He'd never hit a woman in his life, but if the only way to take control of Jacob and get Eliza out of this room was to knock her out cold, then so be it. The thought did not sit well with him. "And if you lose?"

"You're not understanding me, are you? Let me see if I can make this clearer." Jacob stepped a little closer. "I don't need to hurt you. I can just torture the girl."

"I will never let you do that."

Jacob laughed. "You can't stop me?"

Roman charged towards his enemy. Jacob flicked his hand. Roman flew backwards across the room, crashing against the chrome counter. Plates fell and smashed around him, and he fell to his knees.

Shit. Jacob had harnessed Eliza's telekinesis. And, unlike Eliza, he seemed to know exactly how to use it.

"I was going to make you watch while I played with her." Jacob stood over him. "But not knowing what I am doing to her will torture you more."

One by one, the saucepans launched from the meat hooks. Roman ducked and dodged some. Others hit him head-on.

Outside, hurried footsteps scampered over the potholed tarmac.

"This is the police. You have one minute to come out with your hands up or we will be forced to enter."

Roman got to his feet. He had seconds before they stormed the place. He shook the broken ceramic from his hair. When he searched for Jacob, he caught him heading towards the back door. "Jacob, you want your revenge, you can have it. Just don't you dare hurt her."

Jacob paused. He winked and flashed a smirk that looked out of place on Eliza. "Don't worry, she'll be in good hands." Then he kicked the door open, and raced outside.

Roman raced after him. No way in hell was he about to let Jacob go. Behind him, police shouted their last warning and entered the diner. Out back, it was three cops against one Jacob.

Against one Eliza.

All three officers blocked Jacob's path, Asps extended. One frowned. Another raised the Asp when Roman appeared, yet looked hesitant to use it. Confusion stalled all of them. And who could blame them. They saw Eliza, covered in the waitress's blood. She looked as though she'd survived the massacre – not caused it. "Miss, stay right there."

"Please, help me." Jacob's words pleaded in Eliza's voice. "He's trying to kill me."

The three officers turned their attention towards Roman.

"He killed a woman. Inside. He's a madman." Jacob played along, clearly enjoying every manipulative minute of his charade.

An officer stepped forward and hesitantly ushered Eliza behind him. He never took his eyes off Roman. "Get down on your knees. Hands behind your head."

"Whoa," Roman raised his hands. "I am not the threat."

He took a careful step forward. "Listen to me. She is not what she seems. You need to get away from her right now."

Jacob backed up behind the officers.

Roman continued. "For fuck's sake, listen to me. Get her back in front of you where you can see her."

Police footsteps reached the kitchen behind him. It would be less than sixty seconds before they arrived at the back door.

It was too late. Jacob made his move. He slapped his palms against the officer's ears. A glint of satisfaction brightened Eliza's expression, and Jacob twisted the cop's head. The sickening crack was instantaneous. Life darkened from the officer's eyes, and he hit the deck. Jacob licked Eliza's lips. He turned to the next officer. Flashed a grin that stretched from ear to ear. Without glancing back, he waved his hand. The Asp flew out of the dead officer's hand and speared the second officer. The cop screamed, and his colleague rushed to help him.

Roman also lunged towards them. But it was too late. The Asp gouged on through the officer's stomach and tore straight into the chest of the last surviving cop.

Eliza laughed – Jacob's way. She looked at Roman. "Good luck explaining all this." Then she turned and ran.

Roman followed. He could not lose Eliza.

Police piled out from the back of the diner.

Roman ran faster.

Jacob was even faster than that. He darted around a lorry and vanished from sight. When Roman reached the same lorry, he'd lost all sight of Eliza.

"Jacob?" He ran to the next lorry. Nothing.

Behind him, he heard police orders to spread out and search the car park. Roman ran to the next lorry. Still nothing.

He cursed. He heard the police closing in around him. His choices had just been reduced to one option.

Run.

CHAPTER TWENTY-ONE

Roman ran like hell.

He didn't check to see if any police officers chased him. He just fled. He couldn't see it yet, but the motorbike would be where he left it. He scooted through the lorries as fast as he could, until he reached the edge of the park. The bike was gone. That was impossible. Jacob couldn't drive, let alone jumpstart a bike like that. Could he?

He stepped back, taking cover again among the lorries. *Shit.* The police were closing in around him. Going back towards the motel was out of the question. Only one direction appeared clear of police. The moors. If he didn't hurry and use it, he'd be left with no option but to fight his way out of the car park. The moors surrounded the area for as far as the eye could see in daylight. If he started running now, maybe he'd gain enough distance before the police helicopter, with its heat-seeking crap equipment, arrived. Shit. Who was he kidding? His body heat would stick out on the radar like a nudist in a convent.

A lorry engine revved to life, its headlights blinding him. He had to think. And fast. Jacob already had a head start in a direction that was unknown to Roman. And soon, more police would arrive with dogs and helicopters. Shit. Those mutts would go crazy for his scent.

The lorry revved its engine again, and Roman fought to keep the cloud of exhaust fumes from assaulting his nasal cavity. He watched the lorry pull away, and waited until it disappeared to the front of the motel. Moments later, he saw its taillights riding off into the distance that was the main road.

Roman had just thought of a second option.

A male police officer screamed through the commotion for somebody to block the bloody exit. Time was running out. Roman zig-zagged back through the parked lorries as quickly as he could. Few cab curtains remained closed; most were open. Finally, he found a driver standing by an open door, his skew-whiff hair hanging around sleepy eyes. He puffed on a cigarette, then sipped from the orange flask he held in his hand.

Roman slowed his run to a moderate walk, and sauntered up to him. "Hey, mate. Any idea what the hell's going on round there?"

The driver shrugged. "Woke you too, eh?"

"Yeah. I got a ten-hour drive in front of me."

"You and me both, pal. Fucking yokel cops. Don't know their arses from their elbows."

A second lorry engine rumbled to life and began to pull out of the truck stop.

"Another one bites the dust," the driver said, and drained the last of the nicotine from his cigarette.

Roman glanced inside the cab. "You alone in there?"

"Yeah, unfortunately. If I'd known I weren't gonna get no sleep tonight, I'd have prepared better, if you know what I mean."

"I do, mate. I do." Roman checked around him. Four police officers moved in a crouching position along the back wall of the motel. From the front, he heard the same male voice scream that he was still waiting for somebody to block the exit.

The driver stomped out the cigarette. "Well, that's me done. I'm off. See if I can get some shut-eye down the road."

In the distance, the sky illuminated red and blue. The cavalry was on its way.

Roman grabbed the driver's arm. "I need you to take me with you."

The driver looked alarmed. "Hey, man. I'm into kinky shit as much as the next guy, but I sure as hell ain't into no dick-on-dick action."

"Then that's unlucky for you mate, 'cause you are going to get shafted tonight, just not in the way you think." Roman punched the driver out cold. Harder than he meant to. The poor sod had just taken a punch for Jacob.

The driver's legs buckled, his eyes rolled to the back of his head, and Roman caught him before he hit the floor. A vehicle pulled in from the main road, the distinct sound of barking announcing Roman's worst fear. Time had just run out. He glanced around the car park, glad nobody around had seen the assault he'd just committed, and turned back to the driver limp in his arms. What to do with him? Leave him behind? No, that would just notify the police he'd stolen a lorry. Whether he liked it or not, the driver had to go with him.

Roman hoisted him over his shoulder and fireman carried him up into the cab. He flopped the driver down in the back and out of sight. A quick body search located the keys in the back pocket of the guy's jeans, and within minutes Roman had the engine started.

The baseball cap he found hanging on a hook behind the driver's chair fitted perfectly. Thank God for small mercies.

Roman pulled the lorry forward and headed around to the front of the motel. Three or four police dogs yapped and pulled on their leads, eager to get to work. The door to the diner lay wide open, and inside numerous officers surrounded the dead waitress.

Roman had to get away, and quick.

He looked forward. Fuck. A police officer blocked the exit.

Roman edged forward. He could always ram the guy. Although, in hindsight, probably not the best idea he'd come up with that evening.

The officer held up a hand and motioned for Roman to stop. Christ, he didn't look a day over eighteen. Roman obliged, his foot hovering near the accelerator in case things went south.

The officer approached his cab and stared up at the window. "Can you switch off the engine and step out of the vehicle please, sir?"

"What's the problem, Officer?"

"I'd like you to switch off the engine and get out of the vehicle please, sir."

Shit. Roman felt the accelerator beneath his foot. He had a split second to make a decision. Go, or stay? He switched off the engine, and opened the cab door.

Yells of horror screamed through the air, and Roman could only imagine who else Jacob had mutilated before making his escape. Simultaneously, every officer turned and raced to the back of the motel. Every officer, bar one. He glared at Roman through anxious eyes. Now it was he who had the decision to make: stay at his post and guard the exit, or go and join his colleagues and witness the mutilation of whoever Jacob had undoubtedly left for them to find.

The officer glanced over his shoulder. "What the hell is going on back there?"

A good minute passed before a colleague staggered into view. He retched, the colour completely draining from his face, and vomited. The officer turned to Roman, unsure what to do, then rushed to his colleague's side. Roman closed the cab door.

The lorry engine started and he pulled away, now no longer a priority for the police.

CHAPTER TWENTY-TWO

Like an idiot, the occupant pulled the car over to the side of the road and stopped.

Jacob smiled, and approached the driver's side. An older woman, maybe fifty or so – it was hard to tell the real age of anyone anymore – rolled down her window.

"Oh, my dear girl. Are you alright? Are you hurt?" The words rushed from her mouth.

Jacob glanced back at the motorbike, its front end crumpled against the trunk of a tree. The blast of steam that had earlier billowed out from the exhaust was now nothing more than a light mist. When he'd run from Roman back at the diner, Eliza's powers had directed him to it. Those same powers had also worked wonders in starting the mechanical contraption. However, mastering the art to manoeuvre it had been a whole different story. In fact, everything he'd experienced since escaping purgatory had been unbelievable. But, this travel malarkey? He came from a time where travel involved riding horseback – and that was if you were lucky enough to own a horse. Needless to say, he'd walked pretty much everywhere.

He glanced back at the vehicle the woman used. Much bigger than the bike. Looked more comfortable, too. He could get her to operate it for him. He looked up. Horror still filled her eyes — eyes that were no longer looking at the bike behind him. He followed her gaze, and stared down at the bloody shirt he wore. "It's not my blood."

"Whose is it?"

"A lady. Some way back now."

Shock replaced horror. "Your friend?" Now her words were slow.

Jacob shook his head.

"I think I should phone the police."

Jacob reached through the open window. The contraption she held to her ear seemed familiar to him — or to Eliza, who was buried deep inside him. He himself hadn't a clue what it was. But that feeling of needing to stop the woman from using it surfaced. Whatever the signal he was picking up from Eliza was, he knew it hadn't done him wrong yet. He slapped the phone from the woman's hand.

Startled, the woman reached for a button on the car door. The window between them began to rise. Jacob grabbed the glass and tried to hold it down, but it kept rising until the top crushed his fingers. He whipped his hands clear and punched the glass. It hurt — more than he had given any thought to — but shattered nonetheless. Tyres squealed and the car shot forward, leaving a trail of black marks on the road and a disgusting odour in the air.

Well, that hadn't gone quite to plan. Jacob watched the red taillights disappear into the darkness. One thing was certain: the women of the twenty-first century – no matter how old they were – were proving to be a pain in his backside.

He shuddered, the chill in the air being too much for the short trouser things and flimsy shirt. He pulled the sleeves down over his hands, grateful for the little warmth it provided, and started off along the road on foot. He didn't understand much of this century. Not the dress code. Nor the vehicles people used for travel. Certainly not the devices people used to speak to each other. Even the massive growth in population over the last couple hundred years or so, and the alarming rate at which the small towns had developed, baffled him.

And that was a problem.

Roman had the upper hand. He knew this land. He knew this whole world that was so new and confusing to Jacob. But one thing Jacob knew for sure. Roman would come for him. And even with the girl's powers, if Jacob didn't understand his surroundings, he didn't stand a chance of winning.

He reckoned he'd walked just over a mile when he heard the rumble of another engine some way behind him. He needed one of these vehicles if he wanted to put as much distance as possible between himself and Roman before dawn. The glow of the headlights hit him, gradually brightening the road ahead. He glanced over his shoulder. Looked to be a similar vehicle to that which had stopped before. He squinted, but couldn't see who or how many people were inside. He shielded his eyes from the lights, still unable to see, and waved the vehicle down. Two youngsters stared out at him as they passed by. Then, fifteen metres ahead of him, brake lights illuminated, and the car stopped.

A fair-haired lad stuck his head out of the open window. He noticed the blood-soaked clothes immediately. "Hey, lady, you okay?

Jacob changed tactic. He jogged the distance between them. "Please help me. I've been attacked."

Now the boy looked nervous. He quickly checked the darkened road. "What? Who by? Is he still around?" Now he searched the woods running parallel with the road.

"Just help me." Jacob reached for the door handle, but it was locked.

The two boys glanced at one another. "You have a lot of blood on you. You need a hospital?"

Jacob shook his head.

"I think we should call the cops."

Christ. People of this time certainly asked a lot of questions. Jacob reached through the window and grabbed the passenger by the scruff of his neck. He wasn't risking this ride, that was for damn sure.

The driver yelled dond made a grab for his friend. He tugged on his mate with all his might, and put up an above-average fight to keep his friend inside the car. But, even with Eliza's petite frame, Jacob maintained his strength. He yanked the kid hard, and pulled him clean out of the window. In one swoop, Jacob's hands circled the boy's head. He gripped his chin, savouring the rush of excitement that always came the split second before taking a life, and twisted diagonal with a sharp flick. The boy's eyes widened, and his body went limp.

The engine revved, drowning out the driver's cries for help. The car accelerated forward, jerking and hopping several metres. Then stalled. Jacob dropped the passenger. He strolled towards the car, its engine repeatedly groaning for life. The driver glanced up at him through the window. He looked like an animal snared in a trap with no way of escape. It fascinated Jacob that, even when a human's – and animal's – fate was sealed, instinct dictated they continue to fight for survival.

Jacob reached for the door handle. The boy reached for the lock.

Jacob released the handle and took a step back. He eyed the boy for a second and weighed up his options of entry. Then he stepped forward and whacked the driver's window.

"You crazy bitch. Get the hell away from me," the boy twisted the key in the ignition again.

The engine revved, and this time Jacob punched the window. His fist penetrated the glass, and he grabbed hold of the boy's clothes. The boy leaned away, the neckline of his jumper stretched to its capacity, and he floored the accelerator. The car sped forward, its engine screaming for second gear. Jacob tightened his grip, sprinting alongside the vehicle to keep up. The car swerved across the road, and Jacob released his hold, clinging hold of the window frame instead. This second attempt to steal a vehicle wasn't all it was cracked up to be, either. The boy punched out, and Jacob fell to the ground. The back wheels missed his legs by inches.

Jacob smacked his fist against the road. How stupid of him. He channelled his anger until he felt Eliza's power electrify his whole body. As he wanted, the car's back end skated across the tarmac, veering across the white lines until it mounted the grass verge. It rolled into a road sign, one that looked to have a picture of a deer on it, and came to a halt.

The engine continued to purr. Smoke pumped from the exhaust. God, Jacob loved this newfound power. He just had to remember to use it more. He stood up and swept Eliza's hair from his face. Her body held up well, considering she was of the weaker sex. He felt a discomfort in his hand and glanced down to see a dislocation bent her little finger at an odd angle. He shook his head, snapped it back straight, and walked over to the car.

The boy still held the steering wheel. He glanced up at Jacob, his cheeks wet from tears. "Please don't kill me."

Jacob tutted. He shook his head. Folk of today admitted defeat far too easily. He walked around the car and opened the passenger door. "What is this thing called?"

The boy looked confused.

Jacob whacked the car roof. "This. What is it?"

"A…a…car."
"Good. You will operate it for me."

CHAPTER TWENTY–THREE

The only difference between police vehicles was the county badge.

And the police were far too busy with the massacre around them to notice something so insignificant.

The Sheriff pulled up the handbrake, but didn't get out of the car. Instead, he watched. Lots of activity surrounding the far-end motel room. Even more around the diner next door. He opened the door, still not getting out. Jacob's scent, along with Roman's, and a reek of death emanating from at least seven or eight people, filled the air.

So, where would Jacob have gone?

The Sheriff got out of the car, straightened down his uniform, which, like the county badges, was slightly different from the other uniforms around him, and surveyed the scene. Jacob's scent was fainter here – he must have first holed up in the motel. The Sheriff headed across the parking lot to room fourteen. As expected, nobody bothered him when he entered. Guys in white overalls photographed the bed, the bathroom, a chair. And towards the back, others dusted for prints on the small window and the bathroom door.

The Sheriff inhaled. Jacob's scent hung heavy in the air – and so did Roman's. They were still together. The Sheriff sniffed again. He could smell them everywhere, which made it somewhat difficult to determine where they'd gone next.

Back outside. The Sheriff glanced around. His attention settled on the diner. From this angle an ambulance blocked the view inside, but the stench of death was everywhere. The Sheriff strolled past the reception area, making a mental note to return later and question the Indian guy behind the desk, and continued towards the tiny restaurant. He tipped his hat at the paramedics who attended to a police officer in the back of the ambulance, and resumed his pace.

He saw the girl, almost dismembered, lying just inside the door. Definitely Jacob's work and, going by the state of her, Jacob was making up for lost time. Tape cordoned off the diner entrance with a five-meter circumference, and the blood-spattered area around the waitress's body was void of all police and paramedics while the crime scene guys did their job.

Which made getting past them and into the diner very tricky for the Sheriff.

He turned, and again gave a quick check of the area. Looked for a solution to his problem. Found it. Everywhere had a back door. And the diner would be no different.

Round back, three more corpses – these being police officers. Another circumference of tape. More guys in white overalls.

Jacob and Roman had also spent time out here. And by the smell of it, it was after they'd been inside the diner. The Sheriff strolled past, unbothered by the police, and followed Jacob's scent towards the lorry park. Officers were present here, too. Searching lorries and questioning their drivers. Not one acknowledged the Sheriff as he passed by.

The scent of both Roman and Jacob led him to an empty bay in the far corner of the car park. Jacob had arrived first. His scent was fainter than Roman's.

Then their scent became two, with Jacob's heading off to his right, and Roman's appearing to head back the way he'd just walked.

Now the Sheriff faced a dilemma.

A yearning need to pursue Roman gnawed inside his brain. He had searched for him for so many decades. Yet his orders to apprehend Jacob were just that: orders. To break them would be sentencing himself to the torture chamber, or worse – death. How would he ever achieve vengeance if he was a prisoner himself?

Damn it.

Not trusting himself to look back, he glanced to his right.

Jacob it was.

CHAPTER TWENTY–FOUR

Roman headed south along the A90.

He'd been driving for little under an hour – different fields, but the same monotonous scenery passing him by. He had absolutely no idea where Jacob may have taken Eliza. Had he turned off somewhere? Had he headed west, or north? Had he doubled back, or was he – as Roman assumed – on his way back down to Cornwall? Roman whacked the steering wheel. Every minute that ticked by was a minute lost. The Sheriff, even if he'd still been down on the south coast when Jacob appeared, would be here by now. Possibly even already at the motel. He eased off the accelerator and pulled to the side of the road. Options were running thin, and as much as he didn't want to admit it, locating Eliza on his own looked to be an impossibility.

He needed help.

Behind him, he heard the groggy mumblings as the lorry driver began to stir. The man sat up, and it crossed Roman's mind that it would be a whole lot easier if he just chucked the man's arse out on to the roadside. The driver felt the side of his face, probably still sore after the punch he'd received. It took him a good ten or twelve seconds to realise his surroundings.

His gaze met Roman's in the rear-view mirror, and panic overshadowed his confusion. "Who the hell are you? Where am I?"

"Shh. I'm trying to think."

Misplaced bravery flared in the driver's eyes, and he raised his fists and propelled forward. Roman predicted the move, probably even before the driver had thought of it himself. He twisted in his seat and caught the man's punch in the palm of his hand. His fingers clenched tight over the guy's knuckles, and the driver buckled and cried out. In one swoop, Roman released him and socked him in the side of the face for the second time that night. The driver's eyelids drooped and, although he raised his hands to block any further assault, Roman hit him again. The driver collapsed backwards and sprawled the back seat, mimicking pretty much the same position as before.

Too much time had been wasted producing no results whatsoever. Roman banged the steering wheel again. Only one option seemed available to him, and it frightened him to his core. Roman sat forward. His hand hovered on the key, but the fear held him back from turning it. His hands again clenched the steering wheel, and he closed his eyes. Slowly, Eliza's image found him. He had to stay focused on her if he was to go through with this idiotic plan of his. Eliza danced in his mind, and Roman calmed a little. If he was to stand any chance of finding her, he had to return to the motel. Because that was where he would undoubtedly find the Sheriff.

Roman reached the motel in just under twenty minutes.

The heavy presence of Scottish police remained and, although on any normal day he'd pray against it, right now Roman hoped the Sheriff hadn't already been and gone. A crazy thing to hope for considering the horrors the Sheriff could do to him, but Roman needed the Sheriff. He needed the Sheriff to follow Jacob's scent. Then, all Roman needed to do was follow the Sheriff.

Seemed simple really.

So, why did this gut-clenching fear gnaw inside Roman's stomach? Perhaps it had something to do with being caught and taken back to Purgatory again. Because the reality was, the Sheriff would probably spot Roman – if he hadn't already sensed him – and more than likely kill him on sight.

Roman rolled up to the motel entrance. Still no sign of the Sheriff – or Billy. An officer, different from the one who'd stopped him from leaving, blocked the way. Roman continued to search the array of people: police, ambulance crew, the coroner. The Sheriff may not even be Billy anymore. He could have adopted any one of their personas, and Roman wouldn't know it until it was too late. Dogs barked some way off in the distance, and an illuminated funnel from the search helicopter circling the sky above shone down across the moors like a spotlight from heaven itself.

Suddenly, Roman's plan seemed stupid. Really stupid. If the Sheriff didn't spot him, one of the police he'd fled from surely would.

Roman looked at the unconscious man in the back of the cab. Maybe driving into the lion's den wasn't such a good idea after all. The officer waved Roman on, and Roman complied with the order. He tilted his baseball cap, didn't bother to play the game of asking what was going on in the motel, and pulled away from the truck stop. In his side mirror, he watched the officer turn from his direction, no longer bothered by him, and retake his stance to guard the entrance.

Several lorries had parked up ahead on the grass verge in what looked to be a self-made lay-by, and Roman pulled in behind them and cut the engine. Police scattered the motel like ants around a sticky sweet. In the distance, the dogs' yapping turned into hysterical barking. They sounded close, much closer than before. *Shit*. He kept saying it. This was a ludicrous plan. Roman would never get on site and locate the Sheriff without being detected. And, what if the Sheriff had already been and gone? Roman's only chance to find Eliza would have vanished along with it.

He sat back in the cab, inhaled a deep breath, and held it. It did nothing to lessen the anxiety. Nor did picking at his thumbnail; in particular, the dry piece of skin around it, which had chosen this precise moment to irritate the hell out of him.

His mind again drifted to Eliza. The Sheriff could be so close to her. Maybe he'd already found her. Then again, maybe Jacob no longer had control. Maybe the Sheriff wouldn't be able to locate her just yet. Shit. Way too many maybes, and that worry agitated him further. He checked his watch. 3.30 a.m. Stretched, and watched the police go about dealing with the aftermath Jacob had left behind. Maybe one of them was the Sheriff? Fuck. Another fucking maybe.

Roman looked harder. Quickly dismissed the cops that were actively working, which was a good seventy percent of the workforce. But the others? They could be potentials. The young copper guarding the motel entrance, for example. However, he'd seen Roman and hadn't batted an eyelid, so definitely not the Sheriff.

What about the others? The police officer who strolled between the motel and the diner. The three officers huddled together talking. The two paramedics smoking cigarettes beside one of the ambulances.

Roman visually examined each and every one of them. Twice. Looking for an unusual mannerism. An unwarranted smirk. An out-of-place glint in an eye.

Nothing.

Maybe the Sheriff hadn't arrived here yet. Or, maybe the Sheriff was around back somewhere. Or maybe the Sheriff, as Roman feared, had been and gone.

"Fuck." He was just going over old ground. Just when had he lost those big brass balls of his? Because they sure as hell weren't hanging between his legs anymore. He needed to man the fuck up and get the job done. Too much thinking was screwing with his head. He needed to do what he did best: action.

He reached for the door handle, pushed open the door, and jumped down from the cab. Screw the Sheriff. He'd deal with him if and when the time came.

He just wasn't expecting it to come this soon.

Billy emerged from the side of the diner. Everything about him perfect: his walk, his stance, his look. Everything, that was, except the coldness in those eyes. The Sheriff couldn't disguise that. He walked into full view and headed towards the motel reception.

Roman's heartbeat fastened. A layer of sweat dampened his skin. He wanted to turn and run. Instead, he waited. The Sheriff hadn't appeared to notice him, nor sensed that he was nearby, which wasn't totally unexpected. After all, Roman's earlier scent also remained heavily in the air. And he wanted to keep it that way, at least for the time being. The Sheriff passed the reception, ignored the other officers standing nearby, and marched towards a police car parked just inside the entrance.

Roman climbed back into the cab and started the engine. The Sheriff looked to be leaving, which meant he must have tracked Jacob. In the wing mirror, Roman watched the officer shift the temporary barricade to one side, and then the Sheriff pulled out onto the main road. He took a quick glance in Roman's direction – probably looking at the road, but still enough to put the fear of God into Roman – and then headed off in the opposite direction.

Roman whacked the lorry into reverse. He backed up to the motel and spun hard-left on the steering. The rear of the lorry swung into the entrance, the front of the cab swung right and mounted the grass verge on the opposite side of the road. The cop shouted for Roman to stop. Roman didn't, and the makeshift barricade buckled underneath the lorry's back wheels.

Several police officers rushed from the motel room. Others joined them, all looking confused as to what was happening. Roman turned hard-right until the steering wouldn't rotate anymore. Ahead, the darkened road had swallowed the Sheriff's cop car. If Roman didn't get this lorry moving soon, he'd lose the Sheriff for good.

He pushed the gear into first and punched the accelerator. The lorry juddered forward, slow to pick up speed. The cab remounted the grass verge for a second time. Roman found second gear. The tyres found tarmac, and then the lorry found the open road.

In the wing mirror, Roman watched the police hover around the demolished barricade. He half expected them to dash for their cars and give chase, but they didn't. Instead, they stood and watched him put distance between them.

Maybe he was just lucky.

Who was he kidding?

The fields surrounding the motel smouldered under a flicker of blue and pink neon. Then, sirens shattered the silence. Two police cars accelerated out of the truck stop and reached the lorry within seconds. Roman pressed the accelerator to the floor, and the lorry gained further speed. Neither cop car tried to overtake, instead staying a comfortable couple of meters behind. Up ahead, a bend loomed. Roman hit the brakes and dropped a gear. Wheels locked, and tyres screeched. The smell of burning rubber quickly filled the cab.

Roman lifted the brake. Tyres momentarily gripped the road, but it was short lived. He hit the brake again and tried to manoeuvre the lorry around the corner. The steering fought back, pulling in the opposite direction. Roman yelled in frustration, and gripped the wheel harder.

The lorry barely held the road, and Roman was thankful when he finally straightened up. The police cars still followed. He'd never outrun them like this. He had to get rid of them – and quick. He flicked on the full beam. No sign of the Sheriff ahead. Just ashen trees racing past under headlight.

The man in the back of the cab sat up and rubbed his head.

Crap. Roman had forgotten all about him. "If you know what's good for you, you'll stay put." Regardless of the warning, he readied himself for an incoming attack – although how he imagined he could ever hold it off while keeping the pursuing police at bay was anyone's guess.

The attack never came. "Man, please stop and let me go."

Roman's lips twitched a smile. That was not a bad idea. He reached for the handbrake and yanked it up. Simultaneously, he slammed both feet down on the brake. The wheels locked. The lorry skidded. The guy in the back slammed forward into Roman's seat. In the wing mirrors, smoke billowed from the back wheels.

The police car to his left smashed into the back of the lorry. Its back end spun out and veered into the middle of the road. It collided with the second car, sending it spinning off into the trees alongside the road.

Roman put the lorry back into first gear. He glanced into the rear-view mirror. "If you want out, do it now."

The man in the back clambered over the seat and reached for the passenger door handle. It opened, and he threw himself out. He didn't glance back at Roman. Instead, he took off back along the road towards the crashed police cars.

Roman leaned across the seat. Cursed when he couldn't reach the door to pull it shut. Fuck it. He started off along the road again. When the lorry found second gear, he accelerated and the door slammed shut on its own. He checked his watch. Just under ten minutes had passed.

He still had time to catch up with the Sheriff.

CHAPTER TWENTY-FIVE

He glanced at the smooth, peachy tone of Billy's hands, and watched them morph back into the ashen, spindle-like bones he admired so very much.

The Sheriff smiled, and rubbed his neck. It felt good to stretch his legs after being cooped up in the cop's body. His black coat hung loose around his sides. Much more comfortable than the starch-hardened uniform the cop was forced to wear, and he felt for his hat – just to make sure it sat on his head where it should be. He cracked his fingers. Savoured the relief in his knuckles. Then turned towards the motorbike that lay crumpled beside the tree. Jacob's stench surrounded him. No longer a strong odour, but, like the diner, Jacob had definitely been here.

The Sheriff glanced up. He sniffed the air, then turned in the direction that Jacob had continued his journey. By the Sheriff's reckoning, he was trailing by an hour or so. He walked back to the police car. Went to get in, and stopped.

Another familiar smell found him. Roman.

He stared into the night until two headlights blasted though the darkness some way back. The Sheriff smiled and sniffed the air again. Roman's smell was overpowering, but Jacob definitely wasn't with him. Or maybe Jacob was with him and just hidden inside the girl at present. If that was case, and Roman had the girl, surely they'd be fleeing for pastures new?

The Sheriff waited – for what, he wasn't quite sure. The headlights brightened until their full beam erased the distance between himself and the lorry, and, hard as he tried, he couldn't confirm who or how many bodies were in the cab behind. He half expected the lorry to accelerate. To maybe attempt to mow the Sheriff down in pursuit of freedom. Instead, it did something the Sheriff had not expected. It stopped.

The Sheriff contemplated his next move. Orders were to locate and return Jacob to Purgatory. However, there was a slim chance Jacob could be in the vehicle with Roman.

The Sheriff started towards the lorry. His focus remained on the cab. Still, no sign of anybody inside.

He had covered half the distance when the finger whistle echoed through the air. The Sheriff stopped. He knew who it was, even before he glanced over his shoulder. Anger rose in his throat when he spotted Roman leaning against the police car. His brashness aggravated the Sheriff even further when he saluted his greeting.

The Sheriff marched back towards Roman, his strides long and powerful. "How the hell did you get there?"

"Maybe you're just getting slow, old man."

The Sheriff clenched his fist and swung.

He connected, and Roman air-lifted over the boot of the car and landed on the grass verge.

Roman lifted his head. Spat the grit from his bloodied mouth. "Jesus, what happened to that intoxicating sense of humour of yours?"

The Sheriff grabbed Roman around the neck and yanked him up until his feet dangled a foot above the ground.

"Okay. Okay. I used the woods for cover."

Underneath the brave exterior and all the bullshit, Roman was scared. The Sheriff sensed it. "Is Jacob with you?"

"Jacob? Isn't he a short guy? Wooden leg. Irish accent?"

The Sheriff squeezed tighter.

Roman punched out. He elbowed the Sheriff in the side of the face time and time again. It was both desperate and time consuming.

Roman's neck began to crush between the Sheriff's fingers. "Last chance. Is Jacob with you?"

Roman fought to loosen the Sheriff's bony hand "No," Roman wheezed.

"Then, I will settle for you."

"I want to make a deal

The Sheriff laughed. "I don't do deals. You should know that more than anyone."

"You can take me back."

"I plan on doing that anyway."

"But I'll go willingly."

"As if you have a choice."

Roman raised his knee. It connected with the Sheriff's groin. Not too painful, but the Sheriff released his grip.

Roman fell to the floor. The Sheriff rearranged himself. He looked down at Roman. God, he had missed the feistiness Holbrook delivered. He reached for him again.

Roman backed away. "I want to help you find Jacob."

The Sheriff stopped. He narrowed his eyes. "I can do that on my own."

"Correct. But you also want me back in Purgatory." Roman massaged his neck.

"Again, I can do that without your help."

"Correct again, although without my cooperation, it may take you a while. How long's it been since my escape?"

The Sheriff pursed his lips.

"And, you can't transport two souls at a time. Your mission right now is to return with Jacob Witenie."

"So?"

"If you take me back first, you would have disobeyed direct orders and given Jacob the chance to run again. It doesn't matter how much of a prize I am, you'll be damned for it."

"You underestimate my importance in Purgatory."

Roman smiled. "Then take me back now."

The Sheriff hesitated. Roman's pulse pumped way too fast in his neck, but his body language? That was surprisingly solid.

"I have some unfinished business with Jacob. Once I take care of that, you can have him."

"And what exactly do I get out of this?"

"You can return Jacob with the comfort of knowing I won't run."

"You expect me to believe you'll wait for me?"

"Yes."

The Sheriff laughed. "You must think me stupid."

"I don't see you have any other choice. If you don't make the deal, I'll be long gone by the time you get back, and you can spend another century or two searching for me."

The Sheriff stepped back and rubbed his chin. "Why would you sacrifice yourself?"

"That is of no concern to you."

"It is if I am to consider what you ask."

Roman got to his feet.

"Ah, you don't want the host hurt."

"She has nothing to do with this."

The Sheriff laughed. "You care about her?"

Roman's body tensed. "Do we have a deal or not?"

"Never thought I'd see the day where you'd care about another human more than yourself." The Sheriff continued to laugh. It was exaggerated and he knew it would annoy Roman, but it sent the point home. "Thing is, I don't need you in Purgatory. I can just torture the girl. You'd suffer enough with that alone."

"But, wouldn't you rather see me suffer than just know it was happening somewhere?"

The Sheriff's laugh slowly died until it was little more than a smirk on his lips. Roman was right. The

Sheriff wanted to see this maggot suffer every day for the next century. "If you double cross me, I will come after the girl and take her back in your place. She will not be as hard to find."

"I understand."

"Do you? Because I plan on breaking every bone you possess. I plan on burning the skin from your body. I plan on letting the rats nibble on your flesh. I plan on digging out your teeth and fingernails with a spoon… And then the next day, I'll do it all over again. That is the place she will take."

"Jesus Christ. I get it." Roman looked away. He paced the small distance between the Sheriff and the police car. His body was rigid and anxious. Finally, he stopped and turned his attention towards the motorcycle. "Jacob took that from the motel."

"It would appear so."

He turned to the wooded area. "So, where did he go?"

The Sheriff waited. He didn't trust Roman. There wasn't a human alive who'd willingly go to Purgatory. Especially one who'd already been there.

"And, how the hell'd he know how to start the thing in the first place, let alone ride it?" Roman continued.

"You've inhabited a body before. You must remember."

Roman's lips tightened.

The Sheriff smiled. "You don't like being compared to him, do you?"

Roman glared. "That's because we are nothing alike."

"You both ended up in Purgatory for a reason."

"I don't kill people."

"No? Or maybe you just don't think the bad ones count."

Roman looked away. He knelt beside the bike. Started to examine the footprints around it.

"Seen your brother lately?"

Roman leapt up. He grabbed the Sheriff. The first punch landed the side of his face. The second, the Sheriff stopped in its tracks. He hauled Roman close. Roman tried to pull free. Raised his fist to lash out again, but the Sheriff pinned his arms down. Roman wriggled, but he wasn't going anywhere. Finally, he gave up.

The Sheriff stroked the side of Roman's face. "I know it was he who sent you to me – to save the Salem girl."

"You know nothing."

The Sheriff extended his index finger until the tip of his grimy talon brushed Roman's eyelashes.

Roman's pupils contracted to the size of pin holes. It was a look Roman had given him many times in the past.

"You're angry."

Roman's glare hardened.

The Sheriff smiled. It was brief. He dug his nail into Roman's skin until it split apart. Blood flooded Roman's eyeball, finally overflowing into a single trickle down his cheek.

Roman stiffened, but he made no attempt to move.

The Sheriff smiled. He dragged his nail under Roman's eye. "Remember when I scooped out your eye?"

Blood ran down the side of Roman's face and soaked into the neckline of his jumper. He winced. Clenched his fists. But, still, his pupils didn't dilate.

The Sheriff stopped when he reached Roman's tear duct. He patted Roman's face. "Be careful that anger doesn't become your downfall."

Roman glared at him. The Sheriff released him and strolled to police car. Teaming up with Roman did not sit right with him. Killing him and dragging his overdue arse back to Purgatory, however, did.

But, Roman had been right about one thing.

After his escape, the Sheriff had taken the best part of a century searching for him. That long search had turned up nothing other than a lot of wasted hours. And, such an abysmal result had caused immense problems with his Purgatory elders. It had taken the Sheriff almost the whole of that time again to rebuild his standing in Purgatory.

He opened the car door. Looked at the cramped space inside. He'd never fit. He removed his hat and stroked his balding head. Felt the scars on his scalp – scars he'd received for not returning Roman. He owed Roman dearly for that humiliation.

He glanced in Roman's direction. The cocky shite. Back examining the footprints around the bike. The wound beneath his eye already healed.

Roman took a couple of steps forward. Now he looked at the loose dirt along the roadside. "Looks like a car stopped here."

The Sheriff fought the building urge to rip Roman's throat out. He had to remain focused. Returning Roman now would prove him disobedient. And he would certainly receive the death penalty if he had to explain to his elders that, while retuning Jacob, Roman had once again fled.

Roman hurried past the Sheriff. Lying in the undergrowth was the body of a young teenager.

The Sheriff would keep Roman close. Let him believe their deal was honoured. Then, when the time came, the Sheriff would secure Roman while he returned Jacob. Roman would not run this time. And, the best part – the Sheriff would also come back for the girl.

Roman stood. "The kid's dead. Jacob must have his car."

This information was of little interest to the Sheriff. Whether in a car or on foot, the Sheriff had already determined how much of a lead Jacob had on him. He glanced back at the car. Sighed. Listened as his bones shrunk and reshaped, and morphed back into the cop's form.

Roman walked up to him. "So, do we have a deal?" He held out his hand.

The Sheriff glanced at the waiting hand. Desperation oozed from Roman. The Sheriff didn't shake straight away. Torturing Roman – no matter how small and insignificant the method – was always pleasurable. Finally, the Sheriff smiled. "I guess we have a deal."

He slapped Roman's palm, and shook.

Roman wrapped his fingers and yanked the Sheriff close. "If you decide to double-cross me and hurt the girl, I will kill you with my bare hands."

The Sheriff smiled. "I've missed you, Roman."

CHAPTER TWENTY-SIX

The boy's blubbering irritated Jacob to his core.

So much so, that having him dead by brutal means nearly topped having the use of his navigational knowledge. "What year is this?"

The boy flicked a hurried glance towards Jacob.

"Keep your eye on the road, boy, and answer me."

The boy whipped his head forward, and Jacob waited for an answer.

"T…T…Twenty E…Eighteen." The boy glanced his way again.

"Watch where you're going, boy. I won't be telling you no more."

Ahead, the early-morning sun began its daily climb over the distant hills, and the boy's tearstained cheeks glistened under the new day's orange glow. It didn't take the boy long before he slowly turned to eye Jacob again.

His staring irritated Jacob more than the incessant crying he'd been forced to endure the past half an hour. Enough was enough. Jacob whacked the dash. "I'll dig your goddamn eyes out with my own fingernails if you look this way again."

The boy's sobbing restarted.

Jacob sighed. He was damned if he killed the boy, and damned if he didn't. "How long till we get to Cornwall?"

The boy struggled to speak.

"I won't ask a second time."

The boy tried hard to answer, but the words caught behind uncontrollable sobs.

Jacob gave up. The youth of today were nothing more than snivelling little insects. At the first sign of Cornwall, he'd gut the boy clean open. Jacob smiled to himself, and said, "Are we at least *nearly* there?"

"No. I...I don't know."

"You're utterly useless, you know that?"

"I'm sorry." The boy blotted his face with the sleeve of his coat. "We're in Scotland."

The car veered left, and the wheel-hubs scrapped the mud verge. Jacob reached for the steering wheel but the boy beat him to it, and the car regained composure.

"Do that again, and you won't live to see morning.

"But I... I... can't s... see."

"And you'll see less dead. Got it?"

Other than an unsure nod, the boy said nothing. Jacob sat back, although far from relaxed, and watched the waking colour of the day unfold around him. He had never been to Scotland. In fact, he had never been anywhere that wasn't south of England. Places looked the same, though. Identical fields, and what would have been ramshackle villages back in his time were now filled with two or three storey dwellings. Even the roads were pre-routed using a black river of tar.

It wasn't long before his mind drifted to Roman. They'd been friends once, or at least that's what Jacob had believed. Enduring Purgatory, and the endless torture, had only been made bearable because Roman had been by his side, urging him not to give up hope. Jacob had never been a big believer in hope. He'd certainly never given any to the victims he murdered, and he certainly wasn't going to give any now. It was only during his years in Purgatory with Roman that he had let hope in. And then Roman stole it away again.

Tyres screeched across the tarmac. The car dipped, and Jacob propelled forward, whacking his head against the dash. Blood trickled the bridge of his nose, and a green mist clouded his eyes.

Eliza watched the deer hit the car and mount the bonnet. She screamed a warning to the young kid beside her, but the deer whacked the windscreen. Its head slammed through, halting inches from her own face. The car skidded towards the trees and left the road, spiralling into the air. Eliza's body left the seat. Bashed against the side door, the ceiling, the driver. Broken glass showered her. Leaves and branches whipped her arms and face. The dead eyes of the deer disappeared.

And then the car stopped, and Eliza felt nothing.

CHAPTER TWENTY-SEVEN

Roman sat in the passenger seat, nervous as hell.

The Sheriff drove. Although mirroring Billy again, Roman still imagined the hands wrapping the wheel as spindle-like fingers hanging from arms longer than any human's should be.

Roman picked at his thumb. He hated the thought of making conversation with his torturer. But he hated the silence even more. He stretched his neck. Heard it crack, although it did little to relieve the stiffness or build-up of tension, and took a deep breath. "Since when did you learn how to drive?"

"You know, for all your faults, you do amuse me."

"And why's that?"

The Sheriff grinned, but an answer never came.

"So, where are we? Are we close?"

"I can only follow the trail Jacob has left behind."

"But you sense him, right? Is it strong? Are we close to catching up with him?"

The Sheriff sighed. "Tell me, why are you so desperate to protect the girl?"

"Because she's an innocent in all this."

"And for that reason you'd sacrifice your own freedom?"

Roman bit down on his lip. He wanted to tell the Sheriff to go to hell. He glanced down at his hands. The skin around his thumb was raw. "Yeah."

The Sheriff laughed.

"I'm glad that amuses you."

"I've witnessed your selfishness with my own eyes, Roman. I witnessed the poor bastards you screwed over just to lessen your own torture."

"That was a long time ago."

"Not that long ago." The Sheriff tutted. He wagged his index finger. "And to think, I did everything I could to break you, and all I needed was the girl."

"You're mistaken."

"Am I?"

"Yes. I'm still the sociopathic bastard I always was."

The Sheriff laughed harder. "Ah, Roman. I did tell you how much I missed our banter, didn't I?"

Roman clenched his fists. If he didn't need the Sheriff to find Eliza, he'd start a war with him right now. "I wish I could say the feeling was mutual."

"Remember the consequences of double-crossing me, Roman."

"And you remember mine. The girl isn't to be harmed."

The car abruptly plunged forward, and screeched to a halt. Roman braced himself against the dash. The Sheriff had the driver's door open before the car had completely stopped. He didn't wait for Roman, and climbed out.

"What is it? What's wrong?" Roman got out, too.

"The scent's gone."

"What do you mean, it's gone? Just like that?" Roman glanced about the road. Early morning was well into the sky, and the autumn foliage gave a vintage look to the surroundings. "So, what now?"

"So, now we drive on a little further and I see if I can pick it up again." The Sheriff walked back to the car, but Roman stayed put. Something wasn't right.

"Get in the car, Roman. You're wasting time."

Roman motioned for him to wait. Fury glared back, but Roman ignored him. He knelt, and examined the black tyre marks coating the road. "There's been an accident."

"So?"

"So, Jacob disappears when he feels vulnerable." Roman stood. By the side of the road, he saw the deer, its neck broken and the animal lying at an angle that, if nothing else, confirmed it hadn't survived the impact. The feeling of dread Roman hated so much when he didn't want to be right knotted his stomach. He walked towards the decaying carcass, and felt its stomach.

Still warm-ish. Maybe killed no more than half an hour ago.

Roman turned back to the Sheriff, but he seemed neither intrigued by Roman's notion, nor even interested in it. Roman looked back at the road. The tyre marks swerved on another twenty metres or so. A buckled bumper lying not much further on from that.

Roman stiffened with anxiety, but followed the wreckage. Fragments of broken lights: amber glass, red glass, clear glass no doubt from a car window. "This vehicle's rolled."

He heard the Sheriff close the car door, unsure whether his unlikely partner in crime was preparing to leave him, or about to join in with the search.

It turned out to be the latter. "This means nothing. Anybody could have done that."

"It'll take five minutes to check it out."

"If you're jerking me about, our deal is off and the girl becomes fair game."

"And if I'm right?"

"Then I guess I've found Jacob." The Sheriff pushed past Roman. He jogged on a couple of steps. "Here. The foliage is broken."

Roman caught up with him. Past the mass of wrecked branches and bushes, a drop of maybe fifty feet. "Hear that?"

"What?"

"Listen."

Both men quietened. The distant hum of an engine – hard to hear, and muffled by the trees, but below them nonetheless.

"Eliza!" Roman shouted down, but no reply came. He turned to the Sheriff. "See if that police car has a rope in it?"

But the Sheriff had already started back towards the car. When he returned, he held a rope.

"You can lower me down." Roman reached for it, but the Sheriff withdrew it from his grasp.

"We both go down."

"Then I'll go first."

The Sheriff glared at him. "You think I'm stupid?"

"I don't know. Are you?" If Eliza was down there and the Sheriff got to her first, Roman could kiss her life away. "We made a deal. I'll hold up my end."

"And you think I believe that?"

"I won't risk the girl's life." Roman reached for the rope again, but the Sheriff turned his back and walked to the car.

He knotted the rope through the tow hook, and turned to Roman. "If you give me reason to, I'll inflict twice as much pain on this girl of yours than you ever felt."

The Sheriff took the other end of the rope. Tugged it, and leaned back over the cliff edge. A small smile found his lips, and he winked. "Keep that thought with you once you arrive down."

Roman hardened his stare, but this was not the time to pick a fight. He didn't know if he was going to find Eliza in the car, or if there even was a car down there, but he also couldn't chance the Sheriff reaching her if she was. He'd made a deal with the Devil, and now he needed to sever it before it was too late.

The Sheriff started his descent.

Roman rushed to the boot of the car. He searched the tools. Found a tyre iron, and ran back to the edge.

The Sheriff had lowered himself no more than ten feet. "I'll start with her navel first, Roman. Remember how that felt."

Roman watched Billy's full head of hair – different from the Sheriff's bald skull he'd been used to seeing in Purgatory – and tried to muster up some sort of plan. He gripped the tyre iron. If the Sheriff took Eliza to Purgatory to use against Roman, it would be the worst kind of torture the Sheriff could wreak. He wouldn't have to lay a finger on Roman, all he'd have to do was lay a finger on Eliza. And Roman would never allow that while he still had a breath in his body.

He speared the tyre iron downwards. It smashed through the top of the Sheriff's head, cracking Billy's skull into two. The Sheriff yelled out – more from frustration than pain. His hold of the rope released, and he plunged into the trees and vanished from sight.

Roman grabbed the rope and quickly lowered over the edge. Broken branches ripped his clothes, and when he glanced below, he saw nothing but a sea of further branches and foliage. He couldn't hear the Sheriff, and hoped to God he'd put him out of action long enough to reach Eliza.

Another broken tree tried and failed to hinder his journey down. And then the car came into view. It lay on its roof, two tyres dislocated from the axle, the exhaust pipe bent out over the left-hand side.

Roman searched the area for the Sheriff. Relief overwhelmed him when he located Billy's motionless body slumped over a boulder. The tyre iron still protruded his skull.

Roman released the rope and dropped the last five metres. The area reeked with petrol. Roman clambered over jagged rock and pushed his way through a swarm of branches. The vehicle lay on its roof. Petrol dribbled down its paintwork. An arm, bloodied and unmoving, lay visible by the driver's window. Roman stopped in his tracks. He couldn't deal with seeing Eliza dead again, because this time he was alone with no other living human to sacrifice for her. He swallowed, readied himself for the worse, and slowly approached the car.

Roman rounded the car. The occupant, a young lad, lay crumpled in a heap on the underside of the roof. Crimson coated his face, and although Roman felt for a pulse, he could sense the boy had died some time ago. Relief that it wasn't Eliza lying there consumed him, but it was short lived. Quickly, fear reared its ugly head as he begged the question, *Where in the hell was Eliza?*

He peered inside the car again, lower this time. Eliza hung upside down in the passenger seat, held up only by the seatbelt. Roman raced around the car. The dented door was wedged against a tree. It had the only window that hadn't been shattered by the accident. He pushed the car. Tried to make as little room as possible to open the door and get inside.

He glanced at Eliza, strung upside down, her arms hanging lifeless, her long hair partly covering her face. Other than the tiny twitch of a pulse in her neck, every ounce of her looked dead.

"Eliza, can you hear me?"

Eliza didn't move.

Roman got to his feet and rushed back to the driver's side. A quick glance in the Sheriff's direction. He hadn't moved, but how long his unconsciousness would last was anybody's guess.

Roman dropped to his knees. "Eliza, can you hear me?"

When she didn't reply, he dragged the boy's body clear and crawled inside the car. He reached out for her arm, and shook her. "Eliza?"

Eliza stirred. Semi-conscious was better than unconscious, and slowly her eyes flickered open. She coughed and hauled in new breath, and then the inevitable look of fear as she searched her unknown surroundings. Finally, her eyes settled on Roman, and she calmed. "Roman?"

Was it Eliza or Jacob? Roman didn't have time to find out. "Let's get you out of here, shall we? Are you hurt? Can you move?"

But Eliza wasn't listening. She stared past Roman, and her look of fear increased. She had spotted the Sheriff – or Jacob had. Roman still wasn't sure who he was freeing. Eliza grasped for the belt clip, only to cry out in pain. Tears filled panicked eyes, and she grappled for it again. Again, pain consumed her. She reached for her shoulder.

Roman grabbed her hand and stopped her.

"But we have to get out of here. I have to get out of here." She reached for the clip again.

"You need to calm down."

"He's here. That thing is here." Her voice wavered, and her eyes glazed over.

Roman glanced behind him. Saw Billy, still lying on the boulder. Of course, Jacob wouldn't have seen the Sheriff. He turned back towards Eliza. She teetered dangerously on the verge of passing out.

"Eliza. Look at me."

Eliza's eyes opened, but struggled to focus on him again. "Don't let him get me."

"Eliza, look at me. I need you to put your hands on the roof of the car, okay? I'm going to unclip your belt."

Eliza nodded. She weakly felt for the roof below her.

Roman reached for the clip. "Ready?"

Eliza nodded.

"On three... One...Two...Three." Roman pressed the button. The belt sprang back across Eliza's body, and released her into Roman's waiting arms. "Okay, I'm going to pull you out, but I need you to help me."

He dragged her in to the open, and helped her to her feet. She swayed, tottering on the edge of unconsciousness, and Roman knew he didn't have long until she passed out again. He felt her dislocated shoulder. Brushed his hands over the rest of her body, checking for other breaks and injuries. When he'd finished, his hands lingered against her arms. "Are you hurt anywhere else?"

Eliza reached for her arm.

"Your shoulder's dislocated. I need to know if you feel pain anywhere else."

"The... the boy..."

Roman glanced at the young driver, then back at the Sheriff. He reached into his trouser pocket and felt for his lighter. One flick of the wheel, and a flame magically appeared. He propelled it towards the car. It landed in the undergrowth, quickly igniting the fuel-soaked ground around it.

He heard Eliza gasp as he wrapped her shoulder. "Time's just run out. We need to move. Now." He guided her around the car to an undergrowth of trees and foliage that stretched, what? A mile? Maybe two? Would it be enough to cover his tracks long enough to escape?

Eliza's head started to bow.

"No, no. no. Honey, I need you to stay with me, okay?"

Eliza nodded, but her head drooped forward.

Flames popped and crackled, and the fire quickly spread to the belly of the undercarriage. In less than a minute it would consume the car and the people around it. And, what he hoped would buy him some time – the petrol tank.

Eliza's eyes closed, and her legs buckled beneath her. Roman caught her before she hit the floor.

The fire in the undercarriage intensified. Metal twisted and buckled under extreme heat, and something in the engine exploded. Any other day, carrying Eliza through this terrain wouldn't have caused a problem. But today, right now, he needed to move fast. He needed her to run.

Flames engulfed the inside of the car, and thick black smoke bellowed through the trees and up into the sky. He'd made his decision to flee, and although he didn't think for one minute he'd make it more than a couple of miles before the Sheriff awoke and hunted them down, he lifted Eliza ungraciously into his arms, and disappeared among the trees.

The car exploded, and Roman stumbled as the force ripped apart the trees behind him. He collected his breath, repositioned Eliza, and got back onto his feet.

He could only hope that the blast had also sent the Sheriff straight back to Purgatory.

CHAPTER TWENTY-EIGHT

The second eruption came from the engine.

The intensity of it flipped the car into the air and back onto its rims. Inside, leather seats melted and withered away as the fire ate through anything that blocked its route to the outside. Flames engulfed the trees, licking the foliage and disintegrating all they touched.

The Sheriff remained behind the safety of the boulder and surveyed the sight before him. Humiliation and anger consumed him – and Roman would suffer dearly for it. Still a little dizzy, he felt his head. Found what felt like an iron rod still piercing it, and pulled it free. He threw it to the ground and stood. He brushed himself down. Tiny burn holes singed the right-hand side of the police uniform, and he'd lost a shoe. This wouldn't do at all. He closed his eyes and took a deep breath. As he exhaled, he heard the splintering of his spine stretch and arched forward. A smile found his lips, and when he opened his eyes again and glanced down at his attire, he saw it was again his own pale skin that covered his hands. He felt the pleasing roughness of his long black coat, flicked his overgrown fringe from his face, and straightened the top hat that now donned his head. Now he felt better. Now he could think a little more clearly.

The smell of burning flesh, an aroma he knew so well but which offered little comfort to him now, consumed the smoke-filled air. He got to his feet and brushed down his clothes. Lying beside the car, he saw the scorched remains of a person. Roman? The Sheriff sniffed the air. Smoke filled his nostrils, making it hard to pick up any scent. But he knew it wasn't Roman. Just like he knew it wasn't Jacob or the girl.

"Roman!"

But the double-crossing desperado had fled. Until Jacob showed himself, the Sheriff was powerless to pick up a scent, especially while this smoke surrounded him. And without a scent to follow, he was incapable of tracking down Roman.

"Roman! You'd better hide good, because I will hunt you down!"

The Sheriff kicked the back end of the car. His boot caught light, and he quickly stamped it out. The Sheriff's breathing calmed. He'd rip Jacob out through the young girl's eye sockets – and make Roman watch every scream-filled moment of it.

The Sheriff smiled. He had to admit, he adored his torturous imagination – as did his elders. Couldn't say the same about his prisoners, though. And Roman sure as hell hadn't enjoyed his time at the Sheriff's hand.

Not seeing an obvious route Roman may have taken, he turned and looked up at the climb he had ahead of him. The rope was alight. The trees were alight. It certainly made things a little tricky.

Nevertheless, he grabbed the rope. Tugged to be sure it remained tied to the car, and that the flames hadn't burned completely through just yet. All was good. He hoisted himself off the ground. It wouldn't be long until Jacob showed himself again, and the Sheriff would waste no time in hunting him down.

He reached the top with ease. Brushed the loose dust and dirt from his clothes, and headed towards the police car.

Suddenly, he stopped. His superior appeared in front of him. "Why are you here?"

His superior stepped forward. "You are to return to Purgatory immediately.'

"But I have found Jacob Witenie."

"And you will find him again." The Sheriff's superior lowered his hood. Similar in looks to the Sheriff, only much, much older. "I suggest you return now."

The Sheriff waited for his superior to disappear, and then he cursed.

Roman was so close. At any moment, Jacob could reveal their whereabouts.

He paced alongside the car. Thought about ignoring this unexpected call to return back. But he couldn't. His Elders would know. And if they'd summoned him back, it would be for good reason.

The Sheriff clasped his hands together. He closed his eyes. Took a deep breath. "Reditum."

CHAPTER TWENTY-NINE

About an hour before, Roman had started to limp.

Now the pain had become so unbearable, he knew he had to hurry and find somewhere safe to stop while he could still walk. Eliza had roused twice while he carried her. Both times a mixture of bewilderment and panic had clouded those brown eyes of hers before she passed out again. And both times Roman hadn't been sure which one of the souls inside had looked at him: Eliza or Jacob.

It was one more problem to add to the ever-growing list of shit that troubled him.

Top of that list was Eliza's unconsciousness. She should have awakened by now, and as much as Roman wanted to drag her from the oblivion that held her captive, he decided to leave her be. In his haste to escape the Sheriff, he hadn't been too careful in covering his tracks when fleeing the crash site. In fact, he'd been downright clumsy, and may just as well have left a trail of breadcrumbs for the Purgatory freak to follow. If he woke Eliza now and it was Jacob who greeted him, the Sheriff would hone in on his scent immediately. Eliza sleeping, although worrying, held Jacob at bay, and that gave Roman the time he needed to gain as much distance as possible. And he needed that time, because for all he knew, the Sheriff was already hot on their trail.

Roman glanced up at the sky and hoped stretching his neck would alleviate the ache in his shoulders. This autumn had been an unusually warm one. The sun had already taken the sky, and any clouds remaining when dawn first broke had long since burned away. That was a good thing. Roman needed to find somewhere safe to rest up, and since holing up in a motel was clearly out of the question after the Boys in Blue had located them so quickly the night before, the likelihood they'd be spending today – and tonight if they lived long enough – being at one with nature seemed almost evident.

Some distance ahead, Roman heard the growl of a motor. He glanced behind him. Still no sign of the Sheriff, and the black smoke from Eliza's burning car, which at first had soiled the sky for as far as the eye could see, had now completely depleted. Back in front of him, at the far end of the field, he saw a weathered and decrepit fence. He'd just about given up hope of ever finding a road again when, through the gaps of the trees, a shiny red tractor trudged past, closely followed by a short convoy of cars. Eliza slipped in his arms. He grimaced and repositioned his hold under her. Just a little further, and then he would have to wake her.

The trek across the field felt endless, a carpet of uninterrupted grass and a horizon that kept its distance no matter how long he marched towards it. Roman concentrated on the fence. The tractor had gone, as had the procession behind it. A man walking along a country lane while carrying an unconscious woman in his arms didn't look good to those with even the most limited of imaginations. And the last thing Roman needed was a confrontation with a do-gooder, or worse, the police.

Eliza slipped in his arms again, and he looked down at her. Blood dried into her hairline, and smoke grit smeared across her face. Nevertheless, beauty didn't elude her. He reached the fence, and stopped. He couldn't carry her anymore. Even the lightness of her body now felt heavy, and his arms shook under her weight. He could do nothing other than drop to the ground. Dew had already saturated the bottoms of his trousers, and it wasted no time in soaking through to his knees. He propped Eliza on his thigh.

"Eliza?" He gently shook her shoulder.

She stirred and opened her eyes.

"Hey." He searched for any flicker of green. "How're you feeling?"

Eliza felt her head and immediately cried out in agony.

Roman watched her clasp her arm, still unsure of to whom he spoke. "You've dislocated your shoulder."

Tears filled Eliza's eyes, and it took all of a minute for her to calm. Then, her eyes left his, and she frantically searched her surroundings. "Where are we? Where's Jacob?"

Roman held her tight, thankful he didn't have Jacob to deal with. "Don't worry. We're safe for now."

"There was a boy in the car."

Roman could have lied and said the boy hadn't died. But really, what was the point? He shook his head and hoped he didn't have to spell out the kid's death.

"What happened to him?"

"Forget the boy. I need to pop your arm back in."

"No." Eliza attempted to stand. "Not yet. I need a minute."

"I hate to say this, but it's going to hurt just as much in a minute."

Eliza felt her head again. "I can't stomach it yet." She gazed up at him with a look that desperately pleaded for some kind of reassurance.

"You're a nurse. You know you're gonna struggle with a dislocated shoulder more than one that just hurts. It has to be done."

"That's what my dad said."

Roman paused. She looked totally helpless, almost childlike. "What's your father got to do with this?"

It took a moment, but her weakness eventually dissolved, and although Roman still sensed it simmering beneath the surface, Eliza got off his knee and lay flat onto her back. "Okay, do it."

"Are you sure?"

"Just hurry up before I change my mind." She looked at him, her eyelashes wet with tears.

Roman straightened out her arm. He didn't take pleasure in what he was about to do. He didn't want to hurt her, to cause her any more pain than he already had, but she couldn't continue with such an injury. He knew it and, thank God, so did she. He shifted position and placed his foot just below her armpit. "Close your eyes," he said.

A single tear washed its way down Eliza's muddied cheek, and she closed her eyes. Roman watched her for a second, then tightened his grip. Slowly, he pulled. Eliza's brow creased, and a buried shriek emerged past her lips. She tried to pull her arm away, but Roman continued to pull, slow and steady. His boot pressed into her torso, and he longed for this torture to be over already.

Eliza's back arched, and her eyes opened. She cried out again and reached for her shoulder. "Stop, please stop."

But Roman continued to pull, shutting out her pleas for him to cease hurting her until he felt her shoulder pop back into place. Only then did he release his grip and allow Eliza to crawl into a ball. Roman could do nothing other than sit back and watch her. Pangs of guilt swept over him. He felt ashamed of what he'd just done, even though he knew it to be the right thing. Again, he wondered when exactly these feelings of compassion had started to consume him. Questioned why had he not slammed the door on his godforsaken conscience the second it had come knocking. But the truth was, it didn't matter anymore. What he felt for Eliza was firmly rooted inside him, and there was nothing he could do about it.

He shook his head. Cleared his thoughts. He used to be a man in control, a man who did what he pleased and took what he wanted. A man who got on with the job at hand. Now look at him. Empathy and remorse flooded his veins; feelings he hadn't experienced since learning of the deaths of his son and Jane.

He wiped his eyes, surprised and angry that tears threatened him. Fuck this new weakness. It was going to get them both killed. He looked for something to support Eliza's arm. His belt would have to do, and he whipped it free from the trouser loops.

He shifted closer to her. Her cries were no more than whimpers now. "Eliza?" He paused briefly. He wanted to give her a moment, but the truth was, time just wasn't on their side. "Sit up."

Eliza rolled over and looked at him. He expected a look of hatred or disgust for what he'd done to her. He expected her to shrug away from his touch. He received neither, and it threw him off guard.

Without thinking, he slipped his hand beneath her and helped her up. "I need to support your arm."

Eliza complied. She made no attempt to pull free, and voiced none of the predicted verbal requests for him to leave her be.

He slipped the belt around her arm and buckled it around her neck. Now she had a sling. It worked better than he could have hoped. "We need to find shelter. Can you walk?"

Eliza nodded. Roman loosened his hold around her waist. Her eyes clouded over, and it was obvious that, on top of everything else she had to contend with, she probably also had a severe concussion. When she showed no signs of collapsing, Roman motioned for her to wait where she was while he headed towards the fence.

"Where're you going?"

He paused mid-straddle, grateful for the chance to compose himself. "Stay here. I'll be back in a minute."

He swung his leg over the fence and landed the grass verge on the other side. No traffic, and no sign of anyone else. Just a narrow lane that headed uphill to the south, and downhill to the north. He and his brother had played in similar surroundings as lads in Cornwall, and later, when testosterone had kicked in as a teenager, he'd seduced many a young woman in places like this with promises of love and marriage. Yet, as with most places nowadays, landscapes had become so overcrowded with housing estates and retail parks, that it was impossible to see any further than half a mile.

He went back to Eliza. "Okay, it's safe."

Eliza reached one handed for the fence and Roman helped her over, feeling every cry of pain she suppressed. But there was no time to mollycoddle her. He'd put them both in danger by deceiving the Sheriff. Any feelings of concern he felt for her well-being had to be channelled into finding somewhere safe for them to hole up until he could figure out where to go from here.

Once Eliza stood beside him, he forced his gaze from her. He searched up and down the road. Instinct told him to head up. Higher ground would be better.

"Where are we going?"

"We need to find somewhere to lay low for a bit until I can work out what the hell to do next." He started up the narrow lane but stopped when he realised Eliza hadn't followed him. "What's wrong? Can you not walk? Is it your shoulder?"

Eliza nodded, but her eyes told a different story. Her shoulder wasn't the only problem. Her concussion was. "What happened to the boat?"

"We'll never make it in time."

"Can't we catch the next one?"

Roman shook his head.

"Then let's head back to my father's. He has money there. Cars. We could get far away from here. Catch a flight somewhere."

"Scotland was your idea."

"When the Sheriff was in Cornwall, yes. But now he's here."

"We can't go back to your father's."

"Then let's just go to the police. Explain what happened."

"Are you nuts? I'm wanted for multiple murders."

"Multiple? As in more than one? Who else have you killed?"

Roman glanced at his fingers. "Well, there's McKenzie, for one. Then there's everyone in the hospital. Your neighbour you already know about. And who knows what they'll make of the young cop and his girlfriend at your brother's."

"Eddie is on me."

"Lot of good that confession will do me. They'll probably think I've done away with you, too. And it won't be long before they pin Billy and your father's disappearances on me. And there's the matter of the waitress and three policemen at the motel. The kid's body lying not too far from the lorry I stole—"

"What waitress? What policemen?"

Roman paused. Silently cursed. Thought about his answer. The best he came up with was, "Never mind."

Eliza eyed him.

Like hell she'd let it lie. Shit. Why had he mentioned the police? He could kick himself for being so stupid.

How could he tell her Jacob had killed again? That she'd killed again? The lie left his mouth before he knew what he was saying. "Jacob had you. I had to escape, and they were in my way."

"You hurt them?"

Roman stared at her, unable to look away.

Her bottom lip quivered, something he hadn't seen before. "You killed them?"

"Like I said, they were in my way."

"So you killed them? Couldn't you have just knocked them out a bit?"

"Look, what's done is done. Talking about it isn't going to bring them back, so get over it. Right now, we need to move."

"I'm not going anywhere with you." Eliza turned from him.

Roman grabbed her by the shoulders and spun her back to face him. She bit back the pain, but he ignored it. "Where the hell are you going?"

"Let go of me!"

"You're not safe on your own."

She pushed him away, and gripped her shoulder. "Maybe not, but I can't be near someone who can kill as easily as you."

"You don't understand—"

"They were innocent men just doing their jobs."

"Eliza, listen—"

"No. I won't listen. You keep killing people."

"You need to calm down."

"Clam down?"

"Think of Jacob."

"Oh, screw Jacob." Hatred clouded her eyes. "You've killed. I could pretend to understand Mr. McKenzie's death because you were trying to save me. Even Mrs. McKenzie I coerced myself into believing you had no choice, and it was self-defence. But the police?"

She turned from him, and Roman watched her do her best to march off down the lane – one arm held by his belt, Billy's boots slopping up and down on her feet, and her legs unsteady at best.

"Eliza, it's not what you think."

"I don't care anymore. I'm turning myself in."

"For what?"

"For killing Eddie."

"Jacob killed Eddie. Not you."

"I'm not listening to you."

"Eliza. Stop walking."

"No."

Roman's body ached from head to foot, and he had neither the time nor the patience to jog alongside this woman while trying to convince her to stay with him.

The female species could stay mad for days if you gave them reason to, and he knew if he opened his mouth and spoke again, he'd further add to that reason. He did, however, hold much affection for Eliza. He didn't know why. She was far from his type. For a start she had a career, and a good one at that. She was clearly educated, and confident enough not to have to show off her body and rely on her looks for attention. She wasn't frightened to speak her mind, which actually irritated the shit out of him, and unlike the desperate chicks he usually picked up in bars, she showed zero desire to hang on his every word. But most surprising of all, she only occupied a B cup as opposed to the usual D he enjoyed so much. Roman scratched his chin as, for the first time in his lifetime, the obvious question begged... What in the hell did *she* see in *him?*
"Jacob killed the fucking policemen."

Eliza stopped walking, but she didn't turn to face him. Roman waited, staring silently at the back of her head for what seemed a lifetime. This definitely was not a good time to have this conversation.

"You're lying." Her voice was a mere whisper.

"Now? Or before?"

"Now."

Roman shook his head, even though he knew she couldn't see him.

"You just want me to go with you."

"No."

"Then why would you lie to me and say you'd done it?"

"Would you have felt better if you'd known it was Jacob?"

"I killed the three policemen?" Eliza turned to face him, her eyes glistening with tears. "Did I kill the waitress, too?"

"No. Jacob killed her. Remember that."

"Is that supposed to make me feel better?" She held out her hands, palms up, and winced when the movement jarred her shoulder. "I've killed so many people. And those poor kids in the car."

Roman stepped towards her. He took her hands in his. "You are not a killer."

"I have a mountain of dead bodies piling up around me, I have a psychopath inside me, and I have some creature from the Black Lagoon chasing me."

"So you're having a bit of a bad day. Worry about it later. Right now, we need to move."

"No. I need to hand myself in."

"Are you insane?"

"I need to find the nearest police station and get them to lock me up."

"What you need is to stick with me until I can find a way out of this mess."

"And where're we going to go? Off for another disastrous night in a seedy motel?"

Roman looked her in the eye. Did she mean disastrous as in them nearly sleeping together? Or was she referring to the arrival of the police, and Jacob's early-morning killing spree? He wanted to ask, but instead half-urged, half-pulled her up the lane. "We're on the edge of Cairngorms National Park."

"Where Balmoral is?"

"We'll find somewhere to hide. You just have to trust me."

"Trust?" Eliza stood fast. "This has nothing to do with trust. Look at you. You can't help me. You're only going to get yourself slaughtered."

"In case you haven't noticed, I'm very hard to kill."

"Okay, so you don't die for very long. But Jacob escaped you once. He'll do it again. And when he does, more people will pay for that mistake with their lives."

"And you think the police will be able to help you? Because they won't. They can't."

"Maybe not. But if I'm locked in a cell, Jacob can't hurt anyone else."

She had a point. Roman knew that while Jacob inhabited Eliza's body he'd never be able to fight him, let alone win. "I can do it. Lock you up, I mean."

"And how're you going to do that when we don't even have anywhere to hide? Tie me to a tree?"

"I'll find us somewhere."

"Where?"

"Somewhere."

"For how long? The day? The night?"

"Can we deal with one problem at a time?"

"You haven't a clue, have you? You've got us knee deep in shit, and even though you're drowning, you're still trying to swim."

Roman paused. Every word that left his mouth gave her ammunition to use against him. Maybe a few cold hard truths would restore a little balance. "Fine. Then let me put it another way. Go to the cops. Have them stick you in a cell. Then what? You wait for Jacob to show himself. Do you really want to be responsible for the death of all those officers when the Sheriff arrives? Because he will arrive. And those officers will try and stop him from getting to who they see as you – a sweet young woman. And by trying to save you, they will pay dearly for it with their lives. What's more, while this mutilation is going on, you'll be able to sit back and watch the whole show from the comfort of your own cell—"

Eliza slapped him across the face.

"What's the matter? Truth hurt?"

Eliza went to slap him again, but Roman caught her wrist. He didn't know what else to do. Had he gone too far? He had no back-up plan. No other peril to threaten her with. The only thing left to do was throw her kicking and screaming body – which it would no doubt become the moment he picked her up – over his shoulder, and carry her to wherever the hell he was heading.

A single tear toppled down Eliza's cheek and, instantaneously, regret extinguished the fire. "I'm so sorry. I appreciate everything you're doing. Really."

Roman released her hand, resisting the urge to rub the soreness in his cheek. He'd been slapped many times in his lifetime, but none had stung as much as this one.

"How long will we have to hide for?"

Roman shrugged, and held out his hand. "Like I said, one problem at a time. Let's find somewhere to hole up first."

Eliza looked away from him, her hand hesitant to take his.

Nevertheless, he kept it outstretched towards her, his aching arm relieved when she finally interlocked her fingers with his. He stared down into her eyes. "We can beat him, but we have to stick together."

Eliza nodded. Roman waited for her to turn away, but instead she reached for his cheek. Soft skin lightly caressed the side of his face. "I am sorry I slapped you. I just don't know what I'm doing anymore."

Roman didn't know how to respond. Eliza's gaze held his. She didn't turn from him. Showed no signs of lowering her hand. He covered her hand with his and pressed it closer, her fingertips like electricity against his skin. Whatever the hell this thing was that he felt for her, he wanted it. He needed it.

Eliza leaned in closer. "I just want this moment. No running. No fighting."

Roman inhaled the warmth of her breath. Her gentle lips found his, and he wrapped her waist and held her close. He also needed this moment, because, contrary to what he told Eliza – they'd probably never have another one.

CHAPTER THIRTY

The stalagmites didn't slow him.

Neither did the stalactites.

At times, the low ceiling caused him to duck, but the Sheriff navigated the tunnels like a man who knew what he was doing. And rightly so. These tunnels had been his life – and home – for centuries. Nobody knew these tunnels like he knew them.

Finally, the faint cries of those being brutalised found him. Shadowy screams echoed through the passageway. The Sheriff neared the torture chamber, the closed doors the only thing muffling them. The Sheriff quickened his pace. Dealing with two unauthorised captures – although intriguing – wasn't something he had time to sort out now. Jacob and Roman were at the forefront of his mind, and still his top priority.

He pushed the doors open. The screaming now at full volume. A whip cracked, and a naked man strung up on the far side of the cavern screamed again. Before his voice had a chance to die, the whip cracked against his lacerated skin for what looked to be the hundredth time. As much as the Sheriff would like to stay and watch – even soak up the atmosphere and participate a little – he stepped inside and released the doors. They slammed shut behind him. The noise of the closure bounced from wall to wall, terrorising the prisoners even more.

The Sheriff smiled. Then remembered he wanted to get out of there and back to Scotland as quickly as possible.

He passed the fire pit. Flames licked the top – not too hot for the Sheriff, but any human who walked the earth would class the heat as blistering. The Sheriff smirked at the thought. Hell's fire. Now *that* had been hot, although an unjust punishment, he thought, for his crimes as a human. Nevertheless, Hell is what greeted him in his afterlife, and Hell is what he'd endured for the first one hundred and fifty-eight years of it.

One of the guards approached him. Humbly bowed.

He held that position until the Sheriff said, "Who are they?"

The guard looked up, still hesitant to make eye contact. "We are not sure. One appears to be the other's father."

"Did they escape the waiting room?"

"No. They are in full form."

"Who sent them here?"

"So far, it appears nobody did."

"So how did they get here?"

The guard shifted position. "We are in the process of finding that out."

"They've talked?"

"One hasn't"

"So the other has?"

The guard stiffened. "We have yet to locate the second intruder."

"You've only caught one of them?"

"Yes. But it's only a matter of time until we have both."

"Time is something I don't have." The Sheriff sighed.

The guard took a step back. Even under the cover of the robe's hood, the Sheriff could see perspiration beading the guard's forehead. He was nervous – and with good reason. Bringing notification of a prisoner's early death during torture was not a heinous crime – yet it still resulted in the messenger spending a day inside the brazen bull. But, bringing news as serious as an unlawful entry and a missing person – this would end with the messenger's death.

"Take me to the one you do have."

The guard turned and hurried through the chamber. A recently severed body lay on the rack. Not a stranger to the Sheriff, so not the person he sought now. On the wall to the Sheriff's left, a woman hung upside down. Not dead, yet. Her blood dripped into a bucket beneath her – one drip every five seconds. A nice, slow death. The Sheriff continued to follow the guard. Flame light flickered off the cavern walls, giving an almost dreamy feel to the horror taking place inside. The Sheriff passed the rack. Ran his finger over the limp body.

Licked the blood from his fingers. The sweet taste almost made it worth being called back.

"The man is here." The guard pointed to a man strung up by his hands. His head tilted slightly back. A strap tied his neck, a heretics fork jammed underneath his chin.

"How long has he been like that?"

"Eighteen hours."

The Sheriff grabbed the man's chin between finger and thumb and pulled it downwards. Fork prongs impaled the man's skin, and he screamed out. The Sheriff held the man's head steady. After all, if he pulled any further the man would be skewered before the Sheriff had a chance to question him. "Get this thing off his neck."

The guard hurriedly removed the leather strap. Now free from restriction, the man's head immediately lulled forward. The Sheriff grabbed him by the hair. Lifted his head up. Blood soaked his face, but the Sheriff still saw the familiarity.

A smile formed. For the Sheriff looked directly at the cop.

"Sire, would you like me to prepare another torture device?"

"No. You may leave me now."

The guard quickly retreated.

The Sheriff stared at Billy. "There are two of you here, yes?"

A chuckle exhaled past blood-stained teeth. Nothing like a full-bellied laugh. In fact, it was a show of strength that really was quite pathetic.

"Billy, isn't it?"

Confusion filled Billy's eyes.

"You know, your sister shows the same heroism."

"She's here?" Billy's words were weak.

"No. But she will be soon. I understand your father has also graced us with his presence." The Sheriff turned away. "Pray tell...where is he?"

Billy remained quiet.

"He will be found. And when he is, I will force you to watch while I rip his body apart."

Again, that chuckle. This time, not so pathetic. "Be my guest."

The Sheriff turned back to face him. "Maybe you would feel differently watching the same pain inflicted on your sister?"

Billy's body tensed. "Don't you—"

The Sheriff raised his hand. "I really don't have time for small talk. How did you and your father get here?"

Billy said nothing.

"Okay. Let's speed this up a little." The Sheriff gripped Billy's head. "Everything I do to you from this point on, I will also do to your sister. Think about that while you act the hero. Now. How did you and your father get here?"

Billy remained silent.

The Sheriff sighed. He forced his claws into Billy's mouth. "Last chance."

Horror filled Billy's eyes.

The Sheriff forced open Billy's mouth.

Billy cried out. Unformed words tried to leave his mouth. The Sheriff relaxed his grip. Listened.

Still, Billy's words were muffled, and the Sheriff removed his hand completely.

"I'll tell you. Just don't hurt my sister."

"Better make it good then."

"My father sacrificed my sister on the Cross."

"The True Cross?"

Billy nodded.

"That doesn't explain how you got here."

"A guy did it. I don't know who he is. He used his blood."

So, Roman had tainted the route to Heaven. Nice. The Sheriff reached for Billy's face again. Then stopped. "That would make your witch sister a Mind Mover."

"I don't know what that is."

It meant the witch wasn't any ordinary witch. "You know when I said everything that happened to you from here on in would also be inflicted on your sister?"

Realisation dawned on Billy. He tried to pull from the Sheriff's grip but, of course, couldn't. The Sheriff forced his hands back inside Billy's mouth. Slowly, he pulled Billy's mouth open to its fullest capacity. Billy thrust and twisted for freedom. Chains clanged and stretched taut, holding back Billy's kicks. The Sheriff smiled. A feeling of calm warmed his blood.

Then, he ripped Billy's jaw clean away.

CHAPTER THIRTY-ONE

Eliza was tired.

At the top of the hill, a small stone monument separated a fork in the road. Roman stopped. It was eroded and worn to within an inch of resembling a disfigured rock.

"Why are we stopping?" Eliza stood beside him.

"This looks vaguely familiar."

"You've been here before?"

"I've been everywhere before."

Eliza turned back to the statue. "What is it?"

"A shrine. Erected centuries before I even graced this fair old land." Roman glanced at her and smiled. "A praying angel, if I remember correctly."

"But you can't be sure?"

"Can't be certain of anything anymore."

He turned from her, and worry reared its ugly head. He looked lost. Not lost as in where the hell was he going – he'd just told her that. But he looked as though he'd lost his direction in life. For the first time, he look vulnerable.

He glanced at her again. "Maybe I should have trusted the Sheriff would make good on our agreement."

"What agreement?"

Roman hesitated. He seemed reluctant to answer.

When he tried to continue walking, Eliza stood fast. "What agreement?"

Roman turned to her, but didn't make eye contact. "That you would be unharmed if I went to Purgatory."

"And you believed him?"

Now he looked at her. "Obviously not, but it was the only way I could find you."

Eliza wiped her forehead, and let out a long sigh.

"Your arm hurting?"

"It's fine." She wanted to smile, but just didn't have the energy. "Are we close to a hideout?"

"Honestly? I have no idea. I don't even know where we are."

"I thought you'd been here before. Had a vague idea?"

"A few hundred years ago, yeah. Things have changed a bit since then."

"So..." She stared at the two roads ahead of her. "Pick a way. Left or Right?"

"Left."

"You sure?"

"Fifty percent."

He was desperately trying to make light of the shit they were in. She loved him for that. Eliza sighed again. "Left it is then." She stepped past him and started up the hill.

The further they walked, the steeper the lane became. Trees grew on either side of the road, the branches stretching out high above them. In the distance, Eliza heard the whirl of bicycle wheels, and before she could act, Roman tugged her across to the boundary. She ducked alongside him, letting the bushes hide their position. It was the second time he'd done it. The first time being roughly thirty minutes prior, when an old lady trundled past in a car so small, Roman had annoyingly commented that it couldn't possibly be classed as a car at all.

Roman wrapped his arm around her, and Eliza nestled into his chest. She liked the feel of him around her. Even though they were in a heap of trouble, when Roman was beside her she felt safe. As they had half an hour prior, they remained crouched together, waiting for the coast to clear once again.

A cyclist raced past. It didn't take long for him to disappear. Roman stood and checked the road. He motioned to Eliza, and she stood. The cyclist's yellow jersey now a blur in the distance.

"Your sling..." Roman repositioned his belt around her arm. "Better?"

Eliza nodded.

"Good. Let's get moving."

Roman walked on, but immediately Eliza started to lag. Her arm throbbed more than she wanted to let on. Her head ached. She thought about calling out for him to slow a little, but her pride wouldn't allow it. She didn't want her weakness to be the reason they didn't find shelter tonight. On top of that, neither of them had eaten anything for the best part of eighteen hours. Roman had to be feeling the fatigue as well.

He glanced over his shoulder. Saw her following a little way behind, but said nothing. He just turned forward again, and continued walking.

It was subtle, but Eliza noticed he slowed his pace. And she was thankful for it. Within fifteen minutes, she was back walking alongside him. She turned to face him. Winced mid-movement, but stopped short of reaching for her shoulder. "Do you hear that? Sounds like a waterfall."

"I don't remember there being any waterfalls around here."

"There must be. I can hear it."

"I'm pretty sure a thing as large as a waterfall would've caught my eye."

"Well, whatever. It sounds like there's one there now." Eliza turned from him. This was a good thing. Finally, she felt a little optimistic.

Roman, on the other hand, didn't look as though he shared her positivity. "What am I supposed to do with a waterfall?"

"It's a tourist spot."

"Are you fucking kidding me?" Roman swept his fringe back from his face. "We need to find somewhere to hide for the afternoon. Possibly the night. We need to rest up if we're to stand even the slimmest of fighting chances against the Sheriff. But instead, you want to dilly-dally around with tourist spots and scenic views?"

Eliza glanced up at him. He sounded angry, but he looked frustrated. She waited until his irritation simmered slightly. He could hardly miss how she looked. If her face was as pale as her hands, then she didn't look good. She continued to watch him, and although he stared back at her, his eyes didn't seem to connect. He took a deep breath and glanced up at the hill again.

He didn't seem to hurry the long exhalation as it left his lungs. "Let's say you're right, and a waterfall has magically appeared in the last four hundred years or so. How is that going to help us now?"

Eliza ignored his sarcasm. "It means we must have reached that park place you mentioned."

"I don't need a waterfall to tell me that." He sighed and, again, looked to bury his anger. He swept out his hand and stepped aside. "Fine, you lead the way."

"And go where?"

"I thought you had it all figured out? I mean, I was hoping to find shelter in the form of an abandoned cabin somewhere on the moors. But hey, you think a waterfall is our salvation? Then be my guest. I'm just too damn tired to argue the toss with you anymore, Eliza."

"You don't have to be an arse about it."

"If me trying to save your life makes me an arse, then fine, you're right again. I'm an arse."

Eliza held his arrogant stare. She didn't feel like she'd make it another twenty yards, let alone trudge across the moors for what could end up being miles and miles while he searched for a cabin that may or may not be there. She brushed past him. "You're definitely an arse."

She knew he watched her climb the hill. She also couldn't hear him follow her. But, she refused to turn and give him the satisfaction of checking on him.

Ten yards. Fifteen. Twenty. Christ. He was being such an arsehole.

"Eliza?"

Eliza didn't stop. She didn't slow down, and she didn't glance back over her shoulder. Roman also didn't call out a second time.

She glanced up at the sky, hard to see through the trees, but paled to near white no matter how hard the sun tried to warm it. She hated the back end of the year, regardless of how mild these past few months had been. The cold dried out her skin, she hated having to dress in layers, and most of all, she bloody hated the festive holiday and all the pompous bullshit it stood for. It had, after all, also taken her mother's life.

"Will you at least let me help you?" Roman had started to follow her again.

"I don't need any help."

"You clearly do."

"How would you know?"

"I don't have to be Einstein to see how much you're struggling."

Eliza glanced over her shoulder. She threw him one of her off-handed glares she was so good at. "Are you surprised? I've just been in a car accident. I have a dislocated shoulder. I am hungry. I am tired. My head is killing me—"

"Yeah, and not letting me help you is just cutting your nose off to spite your face."

"God, you infuriate me."

"And you infuriate me." He smiled. "But I'm like a drug you love to hate, right?"

Eliza stopped and turned to him. "Why would you say that?"

"I'm right, aren't I?"

She felt her cheeks flush. She couldn't deny the attraction she felt for him. When he stared at her, even while angry, and those blue eyes of his twinkled, she felt like she'd do anything he asked.

Roman also stopped. The space of fifteen yards measured between them seemed like miles. Eliza wanted to hold out her hand to him. She wanted him to take it, to pull her close. She waited for him to close the gap, but he just looked at her. Eventually, she turned and continued along the path. Gradually the tarmac disintegrated, and Billy's massive boots found the soggy mud of an uneven track.

She'd taken the wrong route, it would seem. And she could just feel Roman's gloating behind her. The path led down into a wooded area below. It was not a good choice of direction, and she was certain Roman would stop her before she attempted to descend it. But to her surprise, he didn't. Probably his way of teaching her a lesson.

Fine. If that was how he wanted to play it...

Her boots slid and skated through the mud, and she fought what felt like a steadily losing battle to hold her balance. Several times, she was forced to pause for breath. She glanced up at Roman, expecting him to still be at the top of the path – that cocky smile spread across his face. Truth was, he'd started to follow her down.

Could she swallow her pride enough to reach out for his hand? Could she ask for his help to hold her steady? What was wrong with her? Playing along with the false show of strength she so obviously wanted to portray was downright stupid.

"Are you okay? Do you want to take five?"

"No. I'm fine." There. Again. He'd offered her the chance to accept his help without having to ask for it. And what did she do? Exactly what he'd accused her of. She cut her nose off to spite her face. She over-stretched for a nearby branch, not even looking at him anymore, and continued onwards. Each carefully placed step still managed to slide a further, uncontrolled inch than she wanted to go.

"Then can we stop for me?"

This time she did look at him. "I told you, I'm fine." The branch snapped under her weight.

Instinctively, Roman reached out to grab her, but there was far too much distance between them. Eliza's feet slipped from under her, and she fell to the ground with a thud. She cried out, and seized her shoulder. It served her right. Roman scrambled down the twenty or so feet that separated them, clasping at every branch he could get his hands on. Eliza rolled onto her side. Congealed mud coated her legs and stuck to her shirt like glue. And now, even with all the other problems she had to face, she had the added insult of doing it with her clothes wet through.

Roman dropped beside her, one hand quick to gently lift her head while the other felt her arm. "This is all my fault."

Eliza cringed with embarrassment. "No. It isn't. I was being pig-headed."

Roman helped her to her feet. "Let's get off this path and find a different route."

When she didn't raise any objections, he glanced around. Eliza also searched for an alternative method that didn't include so much mud. Their options were limited. Brambles blocked their left, and although the forest to their right was easily accessible, she had no idea where it would lead them.

Nevertheless, Roman pointed towards the trees. "I reckon we go through there."

Again, Eliza didn't voice any objection. Her choice had led them into mud. Let him lead them. He'd done a better job than her so far.

Roman threw her a wary glance.

"What's wrong?"

Roman shrugged.

"Why are you staring at me like that?"

"Why aren't you arguing with me?"

Eliza looked almost stunned by his out-of-the-blue interrogation. "Why would I argue?"

"You always argue." Roman studied her harder.

"Maybe I just agree with you."

"You never agree with me."

"Stop this! What's wrong with you?"

He seemed relieved at her sudden outburst. "Just keep bloody arguing the toss with me. I thought you were Jacob."

"You think I'm Jacob now?"

"Not right now, no. But I keep waiting for you to lick your bloody lips or wipe your mouth with the back of your hand. Hell, I'm even constantly looking for your eyes to turn green."

"Is that what he does?"

"Yes."

Eliza reached for Roman's hand. "Would Jacob do this?" She leaned closer. Just having him this near roused an excitement within her that she'd never felt with anyone else. She lightly pressed her lips against his. Felt the prickliness of his stubble around her mouth as he responded. Maybe the feelings she felt for him were real. Maybe they were the outcome of a stressful couple of days. Whichever, she liked them.

Roman pulled away and glanced at her fingers interlocked with his. His shoulders relaxed. "Come on, let's head this way."

He led her through the forest, the fallen leaves making the mud much easier to combat. Birds sung in the trees above, and a startled squirrel dropped an acorn and scampered off into hiding. On any other day, this walk would have been romantic. Ahead, rays of sunlight filtered down through a clearing in the trees. An old wooden bridge arched from the ground, and the faint trickle of water could be heard.

"Guess you were right about that waterfall," Roman said.

Eliza squeezed his hand. No argument, but enough for him to know that Jacob hadn't resurfaced. Roman reached the bridge, and stopped. Decades of having the water filter down through the forest floor had allowed nature to form a fall.

"Come on. Let's carry on this way."

Again, no argument from Eliza. Just that squeeze of the hand she was beginning to enjoy giving.

CHAPTER THIRTY-TWO

The temperature had dropped.

The promise of the sun holding off the crisp autumn morning had fallen short of delivery, and now greying clouds accumulated with the threat of rain. Roman reached for the collars of his jacket before remembering he didn't wear it. *Shit.* He pulled back a tree branch, and waited for Eliza to pass through. She hadn't really strung a sentence together since they'd left the bridge. Just the odd mumbled answer in reply to his questions, and even those sounded forced. But, she still held his hand. And she still gave it a squeeze every now and again.

And he loved it.

She looked beat to the point of collapsing. If he didn't find somewhere to hide soon, he feared neither of them would get out of this mess alive.

"Tell me about your brother," Eliza unexpectedly asked.

"There isn't much to tell."

There was a short silence, and Roman released the branch. It pinged free like a catapult, and he hoped Eliza wouldn't press him further.

"I'm struggling here."

"I know you are."

"And your talking distracts me from the pain."

A lump caught in the back of Roman's throat. He sighed, although not so Eliza heard. Roman had briefly mentioned his brother when telling Eliza about his son and Jane. But, apart from the Sheriff bringing up the subject earlier that morning to goad him, it had been a long time since he'd allowed himself to even think about him, or their past. To be forced to remember now would be worse than sticking pins in his eyes, and he neither wanted nor needed the extra aggravation. Instead, he needed to stay focused.

And yet, even knowing this, he still answered her question. "We used to be best friends."

"When was that?"

"A long time ago."

"Did he know about you and his wife?"

Roman bowed his head. Why did he allow her to ask these questions? Anyone else would've been shouted down with the threat of immense pain or death for invading his privacy like this. "Not at first."

"Then when?"

"I don't know. Later? After I left? Why does it even matter?"

"I could ask you the same thing."

"You analysing me, doctor? Do I look like a charity case to you?" Anger bubbled inside him. Not from

Eliza's questions, but from the fear that he would actually answer them…honestly.

"I'm a nurse, not a doctor."

He pressed on for an argument, the perfect distraction. "My past is my past, and that's where it's staying. Okay?"

He waited for her to retaliate and give him the fight he craved, but it never came. Instead, she continued to trudge along the overgrown path as if she hadn't even heard him. Roman followed behind like a lap dog. He'd never met anyone like her before. She wasn't afraid of him like most people were, and if she was then she sure as hell knew how to hide it. "Am I getting the silent treatment now?"

"No."

"So you've just chosen now to finally shut up when I ask you to."

"Nope."

"Then what?"

"I'm just wondering."

"Wondering? Wondering what?"

"Whether your inability to discuss your past is down to your own insecurities, or because you think I may disapprove."

"Hey, I don't need that psychoanalyst bullshit from you."

"Then talk to me."

"What do you want me to say? That I spent the last six months of my life on this fucking planet mourning my brother's death? That I was so riddled with guilt over what I'd done that I thought about killing myself?

That I battled my demons swallowing gallons of ale, and taking the virtue of every stupid and naïve woman willing to give it up? And still am?" He paused. *Shit.* He'd given her what she wanted.

Eliza stopped walking and turned to him. "My intention was not to upset you. I just want to know you more."

"Know, or understand?"

Her fingers lightly stroked the back of his hand, her touch soft and strong at the same time. "I already understand."

God, he loved her. He continued to watch her stroke his hand. He didn't want to tell her any more about himself. He hated himself. He hated everything he stood for. Hated the thought of her seeing him for what he really was – a good-for-nothing arsehole. "After the news of my son's death reached me, I returned home and found Jane had taken her own life. I don't know if my own guilt betrayed me or if my brother already knew of our infidelity, but we never spoke after that."

"Never?"

"Well, not while we were alive."

"You saw him after you'd died?"

Roman nodded. "We were both chosen to serve God."

"Your brother's like you?"

"Uh-huh. All down to my father's prayers being answered, if you can believe that crap." Roman cocked a grin. "Bit of a sick joke, if you ask me. Our partnership in the afterlife was strained to say the least."

"So, there are others like you out there?" It didn't really seem like a question. More her thinking out loud. "Wow. How many?"

"Too many to count."

"I had no idea." Eliza started to walk on again, this time at a much slower pace. "And do they walk among us like you do?"

"Some do. Others don't."

"Does your brother?"

He could tell where her line of questioning was leading. "Yes."

"But you don't see him?"

"Not for a long time, since he sent me to Purgatory."

She paused again, only briefly to snap a bare twig from its branch. Then continued on. "Why?"

It was Roman who halted her. "Eliza. I have told you things I have never told anyone. My brother and I worked alongside each other for nearly three centuries and, although I repeatedly tried, we were never able to find the relationship we'd shared as young men. I don't blame him for that, just as I don't blame him for sending me to Purgatory. However, his reason for the latter will die with me. Please don't ask me that again."

Eliza studied him for a moment, then flashed a fleeting smile. "You know saying that makes me want to know even more, right?"

"Eliza—"

"I only have one other question."

Roman sighed. He'd already revealed so much of himself to her. He thought about changing the subject, but knew she wouldn't let it rest until she got what she wanted. "What is it?"

"Does your brother have a name?"

Roman felt the tension drain from his body. He tightened his grip around her hand, and passed her. Now it was he who led her through the forest. "Nathaniel. His name is Nathaniel."

For the twenty-some minutes that passed afterwards, Eliza had asked nothing more about his family, or his past.

Then he saw it. Through the trees. A dark grey – could be black – felt roof, partially covered in dead leaves and clumps of moss. "Down there, a shed." He released Eliza's hand, and quickened his pace along the path until he stood looking down upon the small building.

"Wait here. Let me check it out first." Of course, he didn't think for one moment that Eliza would actually listen to him. He looked back and threw her a glare that reiterated his order. Who was he kidding? Eliza would do whatever the hell she wanted.

Roman stared back at the drop he had to climb. *Shit.* How the hell was Eliza supposed to get down that?

Thorny nettles snaked across the ground, and tree branches congested nearly every trail he could see. Finally, he found what looked to be his best chance to reach the shed. He stretched out for the first branch, and gave it a tug. It felt sturdy, although he doubted it would hold his weight if he fell. He stepped down, digging his heels into the soft mud to gain what little control he could.

He took another step, and had no choice but to let go of the branch and reach for another. The incline was way steeper than he'd first anticipated, and no matter how hard he tried to make this feat look easy, he knew it would probably end with him falling on his arse. He took another step, grasped for a third branch, and prayed to whatever God was listening that he stayed on his feet.

Miraculously, he reached the shed whilst still standing. He turned, expecting to see Eliza struggling down behind him. To say he was surprised that she remained where he'd left her was an understatement. He started to comment on the fact, but stopped short of letting the words pass his lips. She didn't need his wisecracks right now, she needed his support. *Support.* How the hell could he do that? He'd just barely gotten himself down here unscathed. How was he supposed to help her?

"Are you okay?" Eliza called down.

"I'm fine. Wait there. I'll check the place out." Roman rounded the shed. It was older than he'd first assumed. A hefty brass padlock secured the door, and he rattled it. Yep. Definitely locked. Other than a small log pile stacked against a nearby tree and an empty gas bottle lying beside the door, there seemed nothing out of place. He continued around the shed. A single window, boarded up with wood that had seen much better days. It easily pulled free from the nails. Roman wiped away nesting spiders, and peered in. Darkness thwarted his view, but he could see nobody was inside.

He walked back to the front of the shed. Stepped back. Then planted his boot as close to the hasp as he could.

The door burst inwards.

Shaded light flooded the tiny room. Various saws and tools hung from the walls, and a tangle of old sheets piled two feet high in the far corner. Once happy it was safe, he returned to Eliza.

Although propped against a tree, she still waited at the top of the slope.

She saw him, and straightened. "Shall I come down?"

"Yeah." Roman started up the hill. "Watch your step, though."

He watched her carefully as she descended towards him. Every step she took mimicked those he had taken. She reached for the same branches, and slipped at the exact same points he had.

He reached her mid-way, and she immediately grabbed hold of him. "You okay? You need to rest?"

She shook her head. "Do you?"

He didn't know if her reply was said to lift the mood, to demonstrate general concern about his well-being, or if her sarcastic tongue had found its voice again. Either way, he smiled, and started back down the trail he'd already conquered once. When he reached the shed for a second time without landing on his backside, he allowed his relief to have a couple of seconds centre stage.

"What's in there?" Eliza said, walking around to the front of the shack.

"A place to rest up."

She stepped inside. "Just like the first cabin you took me to, only smaller." She lifted one of the sheets. "It's definitely not the Ritz, but it'll do for the time being."

He reached for the chainsaw – bright yellow, and looking almost brand new – and pulled the sleeve off the bar and chain. "Looks like it's out of petrol. See if you can find some for me."

"Does it work?"

"Only one way to find out." Roman stepped outside. He tried a drop start. Nothing. He tried again, but still the saw failed to start. "Found any fuel in there yet?"

"None that I can see." Eliza appeared at the door. "We have a whole shed of tools in here. Won't any of them do for weapons?"

"Looks like they'll have to." He returned to the shed. Sooner or later, the damp, wooden walls would feel like they imprisoned him. And the hard, grime-infested floor would eventually cause his back to stiffen so much that even a vigorous stretch wouldn't cure it. He placed the saw back on the small wooden ledge where he'd found it. "Maybe you should get some rest."

"What about Jacob?"

She was right. He glanced at the wooden roof above him. Two newly replaced planks, much cleaner than the rest, and not the leaking, corrugated crap that had been the cabin roof on Bodmin. He had to come up with a plan, because once Jacob surfaced – and he would inevitably surface – the Sheriff wouldn't be far behind. And they just hadn't put enough distance between themselves and the Sheriff yet to allow that to happen.

Eliza grabbed some jars from the small, handmade work unit. She emptied out the nails and other small odds and sods that filled them. "I'll go and get us some water from the fall."

Roman stopped her. "You are not to leave this shed."

"What?"

"I mean it. You are to stay here until I figure out what we're gonna do."

"For how long?"

"For as long as it takes."

"What am I supposed to do?"

"Anything you want – as long as you do it in here."

"Fancy a game of hide and seek?"

"Jesus Christ. This ain't the time for sarcasm." He turned back to the open door. Although the trees prevented the majority of sunlight to reach the depths of the forest floor, the brightness outside still filled the doorway with such light that it momentarily blinded him. Damn. The cabin was darker than he'd first realised.

"You need to let me be useful, otherwise I am going to go mad in here…"

He paused, trying to rush his vision to adjust.

"And, in case you have forgotten, I have also saved your life from the Sheriff – not once, but twice."

Outside, somewhere off to his left, the fallen forest crunched under weighty footsteps. The hairs on the back of his neck spiked, and he turned back to the dimness of the shed. Silhouetted shapes hung on the walls. They were hard to match to a familiar tool. He reached for the nearest implement, and only once his hand gripped the wooden handle did he realise it to be that of a small axe.

"What is it?"

He motioned to Eliza to quieten and get as far from the door as possible.

On the other side of the shed wall, heavy footsteps approached.

Roman tightened his grip around the handle. He backed against the side of the shed, his shoulder just shy of the doorframe. He so wanted to believe the Sheriff would never make such a clumsy mistake, and therefore it couldn't possibly be him. But, if he'd learned only one thing over these last couple of days, it was to always expect the unexpected. A shadow crept across the open entrance.

It paused.

Roman raised the axe above his head, and took a deep breath. If the Sheriff had found them, then Roman had one shot at striking him dead long enough to flee again. If he missed or buggered it up, however, the Sheriff had the chance to end his life in the blink of an eye.

The shadow moved again, its length growing across the dirty floor until a figure silhouetted the doorway.

Roman paused. The Sheriff was a crazy-shaped bastard, but unless he'd grown a couple of extra legs in the last couple of hours, that was no human outside.

Roman lowered the axe, and stepped out from behind the wall.

The stag looked up at him. Seemed disinterested in the axe he held, and returned to the foliage.

Stupidity danced all around him. "I'm going out to check the perimeter. Do not leave this shed."

If Eliza pulled a face, he didn't see it.

CHAPTER THIRTY-THREE

Roman had only been gone five minutes.

And that was being generous.

He reached the shed. Eliza wasn't inside. He took a more thorough look, but there was little place else she could hide in the small hut. "Eliza?" Goddamn it. Where the hell had she gone? He whacked the wooden doorframe. Noticed the missing jam jars.

"Roman?"

The sound of her voice did not calm him. He spun to face her. "What the hell are you doing out there? I specifically told you to stay inside this shed."

"And I told you I needed water. There's a waterfall just—"

Roman stopped listening. He dragged her inside, then went back to the door. Apart from the usual forest sounds, there didn't appear to be any signs of unwanted company. If he had the time and the energy, he'd walk the perimeter again to satisfy his need to know they were safe.

"If I tell you to do something, you'd better bloody well do it." He booted the shed door. It slammed shut, didn't catch the lock, and bounced back open. Embarrassment was an emotion he very rarely felt. Why should he? Every action he'd ever taken had been because he'd planned it. He was strong, always had been. Control came as easy to him as the bored housewives he picked up. But now? Now, when he really needed to pull something out of the bag, he had nothing to give. Hell, he couldn't even control Eliza.

"We needed water." She thrust a glass jam jar at him. Held his glare a moment longer than was necessary. Oh, her eyes were clear in telling him that, as much as he hated it, they both knew she'd been right in getting them something to drink. She slumped down on the blanket, and didn't utter another word.

Roman considered the jar. The more he looked at the water inside, the more his mouth dried up. He wanted to gulp down every last drop, but wouldn't that make him the biggest hypocritical arsehole of all time? Fuck it. He owned that title already.

He unscrewed the lid, eyed a sulking Eliza, and said, "Don't suppose you managed to spear a fish or two to go with it?"

"I don't find you funny."

"I am a little funny." Roman swigged down the water, only stopping when half was gone. He handed the rest to Eliza.

"I've had some."

"So, have some more."

She turned her head, unamused.

"Jesus Christ, woman. A couple of hours ago you were kissing me. Now, over some fucking water, you're giving me this crap?"

Anger flared in her eyes. "A couple of hours ago, I was traumatised."

"Of course you were." Roman re-screwed the lid, made a tiny space on the work surface, and put the jar down. This girl could have an argument in an empty room. "Would you like me to make a better sling?"

"No."

Roman laughed. "What the hell do you want from me?"

Eliza stared up at him. "For you to admit I was right about the water."

"I already did."

"No. You made a joke about fish."

"Same thing."

"It's not!" She glared at him. Her mouth tightened and her chest expanded with what he could only imagine to be the torrent of abuse she readied to hurl at him. "You undermine every good thing I bring to this shit-fest."

Roman stopped and paused for breath. Saying what he was about to say was going to kill him, but if it resulted in an easier life, so-be-it. "Eliza, I am sorry. Although it was stupid and dangerous, you were right to get the water. Please accept my apology."

The anger remained in her eyes. "No."

He looked at her. The stream of daylight, which filtered in, still warmed her dirt-smeared skin with a golden glow. God, she was beautiful. He blinked, remembering she was also a fucking argumentative bitch. "Whatever. You want me, I'll be outside."

Roman left the shed, grabbing the axe as he went. He picked up a log. Balanced it on a larger stump, and swung down. The wood split into two. He reached for another. Fucking Eliza. Didn't she see he was trying to keep her alive? He hammered the axe down upon the log. Like the first, it split in two.

"Hey."

Roman turned.

Eliza stood in the shed doorway. "I'm sorry. I don't mean to argue with you. I guess I'm just rebelling against decades of living with a controlling father."

If this was her olive branch, it was too bloody late. Roman reached for another log and placed it on the stump.

"I'm so tired. I don't think I can keep Jacob at bay any longer. Can't you just drag the son of a bitch out of me so I can get some sleep?"

He swung the axe down upon the log. "Doing that will kill you. He has to leave of his own accord."

"And that's your plan?"

"Until I think of another one." Roman placed another log.

Eliza grabbed his arm. "Why are we not running? Get to that port. Arrange another boat to stow away on."

Roman shrugged from her. "I came outside to be alone so I could think."

Eliza stepped back. Roman swung the axe. When he glanced over his shoulder, Eliza had returned to the shed.

Shit. Roman lowered the axe. Tilted his head back and watched the way the sunlight sparkled like diamonds through the trees.

He sighed, and walked back to the shed. Eliza stood by the counter. She rolled the glass of water between her palms.

"You're better off without me."

"And maybe I'm not."

"Look at the mess I've gotten you into. You shouldn't even like me. I'm not a good person to have around, Eliza."

"And when Jacob reappears and goes on a killing spree, will that be a better person for me to have around?"

Roman turned his attention to the floor.

"He will kill and I'll be arrested—"

Roman glanced up. "That won't happen."

"Of course it will happen. You think the cops, or the judge for that matter, are going to believe my cock n' bull story about being possessed by a Purgatory escapee? Jesus Christ, they'll lock me up and throw away the key."

Shit. She had a point.

"And I hate to think what body count Jacob'll rack up in prison in the meantime." Eliza paused. Now she stared at Roman, a quizzical expression on her face. "What is it? What's the matter?"

Roman hadn't noticed himself zone out. He still heard Eliza talk, every word of it in fact. But the other part of his brain – the part where all his ideas, good and bad, manifested – that part had gone into overdrive. He noticed the size of the chain assembled in the corner of the shed. He noticed the rolled cable hanging on the far wall behind Eliza. And he noticed the length of manila rope dangling from a hook above him. His body tightened. Not because he was scared, or anxious. No. This was pure adrenaline and excitement that coarsened his blood.

"Why are you smiling?"

Roman hadn't noticed he was. "I need you to wake Jacob up."

"What? Why would you say that?"

"Because it's how we're going to win."

"But you said the Sheriff will find us if he's awake."

"He will. But when he gets here he will find Jacob, not you." He could see Eliza didn't understand. "I have something else in mind. I want Jacob completely out of your body before the Sheriff arrives."

"You said Jacob has to leave of his own free will. Why would he do that?"

"Because I'm not going to give him any other choice."

"So the Sheriff takes Jacob?" Now Eliza seemed enthused. "And we get the hell away from here?"

Roman watched her pace the small area. He wanted to share in her excitement of a future together, but her future couldn't include him. "Eliza, the Sheriff will keep hunting me. That problem remains the same."

"So? You've managed to stay off his radar this long. You can do it again."

"I'm also wanted by the police for mass murder."

"Then we can go on the run together."

Roman laughed.

Eliza stopped pacing. "What's so funny?"

"Eliza, you're a nurse."

"Yes."

"You're not a criminal."

"What's your point?"

"You're not made for a life on the run."

"Says who? You?"

Roman sighed. "Maybe I'm tired of running."

"Then why is all this a good plan?"

"Because it keeps you alive."

"And gets you dead." She turned from him. Stormed the only three paces the room allowed.

"My mind's made up."

She swung back to face him. "What in the hell is wrong with you? Where's that fire?"

"Eliza—"

"No. I'm serious. What was the point of the last couple of days if you knew you were going to give up?"

"Do you even have on your listening ears? You were – are – the point."

"Well, what if I refuse to let Jacob through?"

"And how long d'you think you'll manage that? You're going to fall asleep sooner or later... Hell, you just said you can hardly keep your eyes open."

Eliza raised her hand to slap him.

"Or you can just lose your temper and let Jacob through that way."

Mid poise, Eliza changed her mind. She lowered her hand and looked Roman up and down. "You're a devious bastard."

"So I've been told."

"I thought we were in this together, but you haven't changed a bit, have you?"

Roman closed his eyes and tilted his head up towards the ceiling. "You still don't get it, do you? The Sheriff wants me, and after he takes Jacob back he's going to return for me. We can't stop that, but we can try to control it."

Eliza reached for him. She cupped his face in her hands. "But we're stronger together."

She was pleading, begging him not to leave her, and he was so close to caving in. He closed his eyes and, just for a moment, allowed himself to drink in the trace of her touch; the warmth of her palms against his face. His whole body ached for her. He opened his eyes and looked at her. She was oblivious to the power she held over him, and giving in would be so easy to do. But it wasn't the life he wanted for her – for them. He took her hands and pressed his lips against them. "Do you trust me to keep you safe?"

"Of course I do, but it means nothing if you don't keep yourself safe as well."

Roman nodded, but he didn't verbally respond – not right away, anyway. Anything he said now was a lie just to keep her happy.

"Okay. Let's get Jacob out, and then it's you and me, kid."

CHAPTER THIRTY-FOUR

Eliza stirred.

"Hello, Jacob." Roman folded his arms, and waited for Jacob's focus to find him.

It did, and a brief flicker of concern widened Eliza's eyes. The cockiness Jacob had shown back in the motel room was long gone. He tried to stand, but when he realised his bound hands were secured fast behind him and padlocked to a length of chain, the inevitable look of panic reared its ugly head. Roman's gut churned. Seeing Eliza look so terrified of him tested his ability to go through with this plan. But it wasn't Eliza that looked at him in that way. It was Jacob – and Roman had to remember that.

So, he waited, giving Jacob a couple of seconds. Just enough time to calm down and absorb the amount of crap he was knee-deep in. Given that the Sheriff would inevitably have sensed Jacob's arrival and would be on his way by now, it took Jacob longer than Roman wanted. A good five minutes longer, to be precise.

Jacob tugged again at the chain, pulling it taut through a newly created, boot-sized hole in the back panelling of the shed. Finally he stilled, turned to stare up at Roman, and sighed in surrender. "This is all a little juvenile, don't you think?"

Roman reached for the jar of water – anything to distract him from looking at the vile being that held Eliza hostage.

"So what exactly am I tied to?" Jacob jerked the chain again, his cockiness suddenly returning. "Let me guess. Would it be a tree?"

Roman swirled the water around the jar. Jacob's arrogant demeanour had returned, but no matter how much he tried to hide it, Roman still sensed the unease.

"How long do you expect this to hold me?"

"Not long."

"Ah, so you have another plan up your sleeve?"

Even though he wasn't thirsty, Roman sipped from the jar.

"You always were a devious devil, Roman. So come on, tell me. How do you plan on saving the girl?"

Roman kept his eyes fixed on the jar.

"That is your plan, isn't it?" Jacob sniggered. "Saving the girl? Only it's flawed. We both know you can't kill me without killing her. And she's of little help to you, not while she's buried deep inside me. She isn't strong enough."

Roman eyed him. "You should give her more credit."

Jacob studied Roman for a moment, his unemotional smile fixed like stone. Finally, it widened into a grin. "Nice try, but my first assumption is correct. I feel her inside me. She is of little threat." He licked his lips, but the restraints stopped him from wiping the back of his hand across his mouth.

Roman pushed back his cuff and checked the time. Eleven in the morning. Forty-five minutes since Eliza had drifted off to sleep, and nearly six minutes since Jacob had woken up. Wherever the Sheriff was, he couldn't be far away now. Any moment now, Roman would tell Jacob about the Sheriff. But timing was everything. First he wanted to know how the hell Jacob got out of Purgatory.

"Checking the time... Must mean reinforcements are on the way?"

Roman lowered his arm.

"No one is a match for me, not while I have control of the girl's power. Not even you."

"We'll see."

Jacob's smile weakened. The cockiness left his face. "I think you're bluffing."

Roman shrugged. "I don't need you to believe me."

Anger flared in Jacob's eyes. He turned his attention towards the shed door, which immediately flew open. It missed Roman by inches, and smashed against the counter.

Roman waited a moment, giving the daylight time to flood the tiny room and his heart time to slow. "Is this your plan? To kill me with fresh air?"

Jacob laughed, albeit cold and angry. "Let's see if you're still laughing when I undo these restraints."

For the first time since Jacob woke, Roman smiled.

"Something amusing?"

Roman shook his head. "I think I need to give you a quick lesson on telekinesis. Number one: You can only move what you can see, and by my reckoning, you can't see your hands behind you to know how I've tied them.

"Number two: You know that chain you're padlocked to? You have no idea where it goes or what it's secured to.

"And number three? You're fucked."

Eliza's eyes hardened, more than any time she'd ever been angry with Roman. Jacob held still for a moment, and when it became obvious that his hands would not magically free themselves, he began to visibly search the shed.

"I took the liberty of moving everything that could kill me out of the shed before you woke up."

Jacob's eyes narrowed. "What do you want?"

"Who told you how to get out of Purgatory?"

Jacob smiled. "That's it?"

Roman shrugged. "Call it curiosity."

Again, Jacob struggled at the restraints. Finally, he stopped. "Will you untie me if I tell you?"

"What do you think?"

Jacob eyed him. "You know that guard that used to bring the mouldy bread..."

"Yes."

"Well, it wasn't him." A pair of gardening gloves flew from the far end of the counter and slapped Roman in the face.

Roman laughed; even harder when an orange overall followed it. When a bucket and a hardhat surged his way, he sidestepped both and re-took his position against the counter. Jacob frantically searched the shed. Fear shone through, and Roman wasn't even sure if he tried to hide it anymore. But Roman had to tread carefully. He needed Jacob out of Eliza's body, not to retreat further inside her.

A folded chair toppled over. It scooted across the floor and knocked Roman off balance. "Untie me!"

"I told you. I'm waiting for somebody."

Jacob stilled. "Nobody is coming."

Roman straightened. He smiled, not too condescending, but enough to show that Jacob fought a losing battle.

"Maybe hurting you isn't a big enough incentive to make you talk. But would you hold out if it were the girl's health at stake?"

"Let me tell you a little more about possession." Roman held his smile, but inside his heart pounded against his chest. "Your host has to be alive."

"Your poker face is very convincing, Roman." A stray length of rope lifted from the floor. "But you played me back in Purgatory with that very face. Well, I've learnt a few things since then."

"Go ahead. You hurt her, you hurt yourself."

The rope flicked towards Eliza and wrapped her throat. "Difference now is that I don't believe you for a single moment."

Although Roman anticipated the move – heck, he'd steered Jacob to this very moment so Jacob would believe him when he finally mentioned the Sheriff – watching it was a whole different kettle of fish. The rope tightened around Eliza's neck until Roman could stand it no more. He rushed towards Eliza. Grabbed the ends of the rope. Struggled to pull them loose, gaining maybe an inch before they snapped tight around her neck again.

"You can't beat me, Roman," Jacob said, his voice hoarse as he struggled for air.

"Jacob, let her go. You can't use her if she's dead."

"Maybe not, but I don't really need her anymore anyway, do I?"

Eliza gasped for air. A chuckle wheezed past Jacob's lips, and Roman tugged harder to loosen the ends of the rope. He made little leeway. Eliza was slowly suffocating before his eyes.

Now, Roman could play his hand. "The Sheriff is coming for you."

The rope loosened slightly. "You're lying."

Roman collapsed back onto his arse, his breathing heavy but relieved. "You said it yourself. I'm a devious bastard. I made a deal with him to save myself."

Jacob watched him. A smile broke out, and he scoffed. "That's a good story."

"No story. That's why I'm with the girl. If I have her, then I have you."

"You have feelings for this girl, Roman. Any fool can see it."

"I'm flattered you think so. But I don't have feelings for anyone or anything. You should know that better than anybody. Her only importance to me is you. I hand you over, I get my freedom. But you kill her, you kill yourself, and I lose my deal."

"The Sheriff would never make a deal like that with you. He wants your blood more than anything else on this godforsaken earth."

"Maybe. But he has orders. You're going back before me."

Jacob's mouth parted, yet no words left his lips. His eyes stared off into the distance and for a moment, Eliza's body froze.

The rope around her neck went completely limp and dropped to the floor.

Then, Eliza started to convulse.

Her body arched, and her head slapped backwards. Beneath her skin, two hands pushed against her chest and through her shirt in a bid to get out. Her scream pierced the air, and she lashed from side to side as much as her bound body would allow.

Roman crawled beside her. "Jacob, you're going to kill her."

Blood trickled from Eliza's nose. Tears streamed from shiny green eyes.

Roman grabbed her shoulders and forced her still. "Jacob, just get the fuck out of her."

Another scream, and Eliza's green eyes faded to brown. Her body wilted, and her head drooped forward. The shed fell silent, and only the sound of Roman's heavy breath polluted the air. He lifted Eliza's head, and wiped the hair from her face. She was unconscious…but alive, and Roman wondered how much more of this shit she could possibly sustain.

A man of seemingly average build and height stepped from the shadows. Slowly, Roman placed the blade into Eliza's right hand and rose to his feet. Now, upon closer inspection, he saw the very same Jacob he'd spent all those years trussed up alongside in Purgatory: his shoulder-length mane, dirty and wet looking; his facial hair bristling through random parts of the skin that scar tissue didn't already cover; his shirtless torso showing off the torture the Sheriff had cut into him on a daily basis. And, my God, if he wasn't still wearing those same damn trousers with the same damn rips and tears in them.

"I like what you've done to yourself. Very chic."

Jacob stepped forward, his chest heaving with every enraged breath he took. His arms curled by his sides, and he narrowed his eyes the way he used to in Purgatory. The way he used to when the evil within him was about to explode. He glanced outside at the small forest. Seemed to settle his sights on the log pile, or rather the old axe propped against it. It didn't move.

"The power's hers, Jacob. Always has been, and always will be."

Jacob cursed, and turned back to Roman.

"Now you're just plain old you again."

"You tricked me?"

"No."

Jacob's lips pursed tight. His fists clenched, and Roman readied himself for attack. Instead, Jacob turned and raced into the open. Romans first impulse was to chase after him, but Jacob returned, axe in hand and raised high above his head. He charged through the doorway and swung the axe down. Roman dodged. The axe missed him by inches. Roman stumbled and fell to the floor, and Jacob swung again. Roman turned. A cool breeze passed his face and the axe head embedded the floorboard inches between himself and Eliza. Rage thundered through Roman's soul. He plunged his foot deep into Jacob's gut and booted him backwards. Jacob's grip loosened around the axe handle, and he sprawled back through the door and out in to the forest beyond.

Roman didn't glance at Eliza again. He raced towards the door to find Jacob already scrambling to his feet. Now the fight was outside, and that's where it was going to stay. Roman rushed at his intended target, his fist clenched and deliberate. He swung. Connected with the side of Jacob's temple and forced him to the ground. Roman drew back his arm, another punch prepared, but Jacob kicked his ankles out from under him. Roman's legs buckled, and he plummeted to the floor. Jacob was quick to pounce. He leapt across Roman and straddled him, seizing the chance to hammer down blow after clumsy blow. Roman blocked every one, and a split-second opening enabled him to roll onto his side. Jacob rolled with him, his punches now finding daylight between Roman's defences.

Roman felt his body tire. Jacob went low and Roman took one, two, three whacks to his kidneys. For the sixty seconds that followed, he tried to blot the pain from his mind. He caught sight of Eliza lying in the shed, and his anger returned. A frustrated yell boomed from the pit of his stomach, and he flicked Jacob aside and struggled onto his knees. He needed the upper hand. He needed to be on his feet.

A shovel smashed the back of Roman's head. He collapsed face down into the dirt. Around him, the scenery blurred and morphed. He shook his head and tried to clear his vision, but the world remained hazy.

Jacob's foot struck him in the gut. Roman felt a couple of ribs crack. He dropped to his elbow and cradled his stomach. Jacob kicked him again, this time with enough force to catapult Roman over on to his back. Roman gasped for air. He had nothing left to give.

Jacob straddled him, a smile on his face. "You were one of the strongest men I'd ever met. What happened to you?"

Roman's riffled through his options. Strength would not beat Jacob. Roman needed something else. Something—

Jacob grabbed the neck of his jumper and hauled him inches from the ground. "You've been living this life for too long, my friend."

He punched Roman in the face. "You've become weak." Another punch.

Roman spat the blood from his mouth and forced a smile, even though it hurt like fucking hell. "You don't know shit."

Jacob punched him again.

Roman's head snapped to the side, and Jacob's laughter drilled through his ears.

"Jesus Christ. Where's that fire you once had?"

Roman closed his eyes. He tried to steady his breathing, to muster some control and energy. The Sheriff would be here soon, and if Roman didn't pull his shit together, he'd end up back in Purgatory watching Eliza suffer the same way he had.

And he would rather die than let that happen.

Jacob punched him again. More blood spat from Roman's mouth, and what didn't make it to the ground dribbled over swelling lips and soaked his neckline.

"Come on, Roman. The girl's capable of giving me a better fight than this." Jacob released his grip. "Actually, that's not such a bad idea."

Jacob's attention turned to the shed. A smile found his lips, and he stepped clear of Roman.

Roman stretched after him, but his reach didn't extend far enough. "Jacob, don't you touch her." He rolled onto all fours. His body was already healing from the attack – just not fast enough.

Jacob glanced over his shoulder. He saw Roman struggling to his feet, and flashed that conceited smile. "Admitting defeat was never your strong point, was it?"

Roman grinned. Pain crippled him from head to toe, but Jacob was right: he was a fighter, not a quitter. He charged Jacob, fuelled by a venom he had never before felt. His shoulder plunged into Jacob's gut and, like a rugby player, he took him to the ground and let his own body crush him like salt. A grunt of wind exhaled Jacob's lungs, and when he tried to push Roman away, Roman swung for him. Blow after deliberate blow, the punches reigned down until his arms ached, and blood – Jacob's – covered his raw knuckles.

But Roman wanted more.

To his left, a rock the size of a basketball. He grabbed it and lifted it high above his head.

Roman stopped. Sudden. His arms raised. His fingers clenched around the small boulder. Jacob's face no longer resembled the man he'd once shared Purgatory with. Blood coughed past his lips, and although his body remained more intact that Roman's, his war was over.

Jacob looked up at him through swollen eyes, a look of surprise when Roman didn't move. "You really have gone soft."

Roman said nothing. Could do nothing. Jacob had to stay alive for the Sheriff to take him. Roman sat back and lowered his arms. The rock rolled free from his clasp. He wiped his top lip dry of sweat. Bile spat from his mouth. He got up as gingerly as he could without making it too obvious of the agony he was in. A couple of his ribs, maybe three or four, were broken for sure. And he even felt the possibility of a punctured lung – all of which his adrenalin-driven breathing was magnifying ten-fold.

"If you're not going to kill me, I must be free to leave?"

Roman stood panting but silent.

Jacob tried to sit, but Roman kicked him back to the ground. "I told you, the Sheriff's coming for you."

"That was the truth?"

"It was." Roman lifted his foot. He wanted to feel some regret about handing Jacob over to the Sheriff – after all, Jacob wouldn't have been here at all if Roman hadn't double-crossed him and stolen his ride out of Purgatory in the first place. But the simple fact was that Roman wanted Jacob dead, and the only thing that frustrated him more was that he couldn't do it himself.

He hammered his foot against the side of Jacobs's head.

Jacob's unconscious body received ten further seconds of Roman's time. Not to reflect on his actions, but to make sure the fucker was out for the count once and for all.

Roman turned to the cabin. With pained steps, he staggered towards it. His heart screamed for him to get back to Eliza more than his body screamed for him to stop and rest. He reached the entrance, the door still open, and saw Eliza lifting her head to look at him. She looked dazed and confused, and when she couldn't move her tied arms, panic set in.

Roman hurried to her. "You're tied up. It's okay."

"What happened? Where's Jacob?"

"Outside." Roman grabbed the knife out of her hand, and felt for the frayed rope. "Now hold still so I can cut you free."

"Is he dead?"

"No."

"Can't we kill him and let the Sheriff have his dead body?"

"No."

"Why?"

"Because the moment he dies, his soul goes to the waiting room. The Sheriff needs to take him back himself."

"So we're leaving now?"

Roman stopped cutting and looked at her.

"Tell me we're both leaving."

"Are you sure you want this life?"

"More than anything."

"Then I guess we're leaving."

Behind him, the sound of footsteps lumbered through the doorway. Eliza's eyes widened, but before the warning reached her lips, Roman had the axe in hand. He twisted and hurled it across the shed, watching it rotate through the air until it landed centre of Jacob's chest.

Jacob glanced down. Blood oozed around the axe head. A single river of red formed between his pecs and flowed down towards his navel. Jacob dropped to his knees, the shears still gripped in his hand. He looked at Roman. Tried to speak. But only blood gurgled past parted lips. Roman met his gaze, and his jaw tightened. A sense of vengeful satisfaction wanted to break through, but a much deeper problem shadowed the situation. If Jacob died, Roman had nothing to offer the Sheriff.

He stood, walked behind the man who'd had his ear the entire time he'd been in Purgatory, and kicked him face-down into the floor. He didn't know right from wrong anymore. In fact, he didn't care. All he knew was that he couldn't live without Eliza. He glanced up at her. "We're leaving. Now."

Relief brightened Eliza's eyes, and a small smile found the corners of her mouth. "What about him?"

Roman stamped his foot down between Jacob's shoulder blades and crushed his body hard against the floor. The axe head cracked his chest bone apart, and any life that remained inside drained away.

"He stays here."

Roman half-cut, half-yanked the last of the rope apart. "We need to leave here, now."

He pulled Eliza to her feet. "Head back the way we came in."

"You say that like I'm going on my own."

"Don't worry, I'll be right behind you."

"What?" Eliza darted in front of him and closed the shed door. She stood fast and blocked Roman from re-opening it. "I can see what you're thinking."

"Then close your eyes."

"Don't go and do something stupid. Not when we can leave."

Roman took her by the shoulders and moved her to one side. "I need to hide Jacob's body. That's all." He bent for Jacob's feet.

"Then let me help."

Jacob's legs dropped to the floor, and Roman straightened again. He took a deep breath before he spoke. "We don't have time to argue. I need you to start back for the road. I'll catch up. I promise." He didn't sound convincing, and if he expected his looks to contradict his voice, well, honestly, he just didn't have the energy. Of course he wasn't going with Eliza. The Sheriff needed to take someone back. It clearly wasn't Jacob anymore, so it had to be Roman. As long as it wasn't Eliza.

"If you're not with me by the time I reach the road, I'm heading back here."

Eliza stared at him, using those big brown eyes of hers to lure him in, and he let her. Finally, when he could put off the inevitable no longer, he spun her to face the door. "You really need to go."

He felt her shoulders tense, but nevertheless, she raised her chin, pressed back her shoulders, and reached for the handle.

She hesitated, and Roman fought the urge to pull her close and wrap her in his arms. He yearned to press his lips against hers, and then, together, leave for a place where no sod knew, nor cared, about who the hell they were. "Eliza, please, go now before it's too late."

Eliza turned the door handle and paused. "Promise me you'll catch up."

"I promise." The words came too quick to be genuine.

Nevertheless, Eliza pulled open the door. But she didn't leave.

Outside, waiting, the Sheriff smiled.

CHAPTER THIRTY-FIVE

Perspiration moistened Roman's skin.

He fought the urge to swallow the sudden rush of saliva, pulled Eliza away from the door, and placed himself between her and the Sheriff. "What took you so long? Jacob nearly escaped."

Uncertainty hardened the Sheriff's eyes. He glanced from Roman to Eliza, and then his gaze settled on Jacob's body. "You killed him?"

"Had to."

"But he wasn't yours to take."

"Way I see it, I did you a favour."

The Sheriff scoffed. "Then pray tell why does it look as though you're now leaving?"

"Not leaving. Just getting some fresh air is all. It's good for the soul. But you wouldn't know that. Never having one, I mean." He looked the Sheriff in the eye. Centuries of aging etched his skin, its paleness even more dry and grainy than those who haunted his nightmares.

The Sheriff extended his index finger, and wagged it. "I told you what would happen if you tried to back out of our arrangement, did I not?"

Roman felt Eliza's hand slip into his. She tried to tug him away from the door, but Roman stood fast. "I wasn't backing—"

The Sheriff hammered a blow into Roman's stomach.

Roman clasped his ribs, and an agonising yell spat from his mouth. Eliza reached for him again, but he forced her away. He was in deep shit. They were both in deep, deep shit. He drew in a laboured breath, and stood as best he could.

"I told you what I would do to the girl."

The Sheriff stepped forward, but Roman blocked him from entering. "I wasn't backing out of our deal. Jacob ran from the crash site. I had no choice but to follow him."

"There's always a choice." The Sheriff smiled. "Just like I'm making a choice right now."

Roman tensed, and waited for the inevitable.

"Don't you want to know what that choice is?"

"Which of my bones to break next?"

The Sheriff smiled, his razor-sharp incisors curling over his lips. "Oh, I plan on breaking them all. No. Right now I'm choosing who to take back first. You, or the girl."

"You'd be breaking orders if you take her back first."

"Orders?" The Sheriff motioned towards Jacob. "You appear to have changed those orders, have you not?"

"Goddamn it. I told you the truth. Jacob ran. She's innocen—"

The Sheriff punched Roman in the stomach again. Roman doubled over and dropped to his knees. He gasped for breath, and struggled to stand once more. To his left, he saw Jacob's body magically flip onto its back.

The axe slipped free from his chest, and its handle flew straight into Eliza's waiting palm. "Stop it. I'll go with you. Just don't hurt him anymore."

"No." Roman clambered to his feet, but he still didn't fully straighten. "Eliza, what are you doing?"

"He's going to kill you."

"No, he's not."

The Sheriff tutted. "Actually, I am."

Eliza gripped the axe. "You will not hurt him anymore."

"And you think your telekinesis can stop me? Do you have any idea how dangerous I can be, girl?"

"Girl? I'm a fucked-off, telekinetic nurse who has Jesus as her great, great grandad. Do you know how dangerous that can be?"

A belly laugh roared from the Sheriff, and for seconds it boomed around the small clearing. Then it stopped. Abruptly. "Your brother showed the same gallantry. Stupid really."

"My brother? You've seen him?"

"Seen him. Tortured him. Killed him. And tomorrow I will do it all again – to you."

"For fuck's sake," Roman pleaded with Eliza. "Will you get the hell out of here while you still have the chance?"

"But he has Billy."

"Looks like you've finally met your match, Roman." The Sheriff glanced towards Eliza, and a twinkle brightened his yellow eyes. "I'm going to have so much fun with you, my dear."

"Give it your best shot." The axe catapulted from Eliza's hand and slammed into the Sheriff's abdomen. The force knocked him backwards through the door.

The Sheriff bent over, resting his hands on his knees. He exhaled a long, slow breath. "Woo-wee. Was that supposed to kill me?"

He straightened, and focused his attention back on Eliza. When he realised the axe was back in her hand, he chuckled. "You are very quick, I'll give you that."

Roman moved to Eliza's side. "What the hell are you doing? You can't kill him."

The axe hurled towards the Sheriff again and embedded his right thigh. He moved with speed, but before he could grab it, the blade wrenched free and flew back into Eliza's waiting palm. He made a play towards her, but the axe launched at him for a third time. It scraped the side of his face and spun him off balance. He felt for his ear, saw it lying at his feet, and his face reddened. His fists clenched and he glared around the surrounding area. The axe head embedded a tree trunk. When it didn't free itself, the Sheriff's frustration turned into a faint smile.

He turned towards Eliza. "Not as strong as you thought, are you, my dear?"

He folded his arms and tapped a spindly index finger against his chin. "You know, taking the girl back first would be extremely more enjoyable."

Roman charged in front of Eliza. "If you fucking touch her, I swear—"

The Sheriff spun. Outstretched his long, lanky arm. He grabbed Roman around the throat, and stopped him dead in his tracks. "However, you are correct. You are supposed to go back first."

The Sheriff raised his arm, and Roman felt his feet leave the ground. The hand around his neck tightened, and he could do nothing other than kick and struggle in an attempt to get free. Through blurred eyesight he saw Eliza watching, horror and panic etched across her face. He just prayed that she would take this chance to run. Stupid, really. Instead, she darted towards him. He felt her arms wrap his waist, her hands desperately trying to tug him downwards. Her cries pleading the Sheriff to spare him went unheard.

Roman glanced down. The Sheriff grinned, seemingly enjoying Eliza's feeble attempts to free his prisoner. Then, he struck out. White bony knuckles slapped Eliza across the jaw. She fell back, landing two or three feet from the Sheriff's feet. "Don't worry, my dear. I'll be back for you soon."

Eliza scrambled to her knees.

"Eliza. No." The raspy order lodged in Roman's throat.

She paused and stared up at him. She knew. The look in her eyes told him that she knew. They had lost. The Sheriff had won. Again, she motioned to get up.

Roman knew what was next. He'd experienced this before. The first time the Sheriff had transported him to Purgatory. Soon, darkness would surround him, and Eliza would disappear from view. The forest would disappear. The blue sky and the green fields would all disappear. Air would rush past him so fast it would cut and slice his skin apart. This was the beginning of a horror he'd spent centuries hiding from.

He glanced down at Eliza. "Find my brother."

Then the darkness took him.

THE UNDOING

Read on for an extract from the next Hunted thriller
in the series

CHAPTER ONE

SUNDAY
Cairngorms National Park, Scotland

Everything was quiet.

The wind didn't rattle through the trees. Birds didn't chirp happy songs from high above. And Roman's voice, asking if she was okay, never came.

Eliza opened her eyes. The shed door stood open. Apart from Jacob's lifeless form, nobody was inside. She crawled to her feet, not bothering to brush the forest floor from her legs, and approached the tiny, wooden building.

Nothing inside indicated where the Sheriff could have taken Roman.

Back outside, the trees swayed in the breeze. The coolness hit Eliza's bare legs and she shivered. She had no idea what to do. She had no idea where she was. And she had no idea how the hell she was supposed to find a way back to civilisation.

She hung her head and past events resurfaced. Moments earlier, she and Roman had killed Jacob and then unsuccessfully engaged the Sheriff in battle. And now the Sheriff had Roman back in Purgatory.

Find my brother.

They'd been the last words Roman had spoken to her.

It was an impossible task. Roman had barely ever spoken about his brother. So how was she supposed to find him? She couldn't even remember his name. Heck, come to think of it, she couldn't remember Roman's full name.

She stared at her feet. Dried blood and mud darkened what had once been sand-coloured, suede boots. The blood could have belonged to any number of people. So many had died around her. The waitress at the diner. The police at the motel. The teenagers in the car. Tears filled her eyes and she crumpled onto her knees. She wanted Roman back. She *needed* him back. This was not how they'd planned their ending. She should be on the run right now – with Roman by her side and the Sheriff defeated.

The Sheriff. What if he returned for her like he'd promised?

At the rear of the shed, the narrow path she'd slid down earlier that day looked twice as hard to climb back up. She glanced around for an easier route but couldn't find one. Taking a deep breath, she dug the toe of her boot into the mud and reached for a branch.

Behind her, the shed door slammed shut.

Eliza froze. She listened as someone paced around inside the small, wooden building. Had the Sheriff returned?

Eliza forgot the hill and fled towards the trees, finding cover behind a nearby trunk. She crouched and watched through the branches.

The Sheriff stepped away from the shed door. His coat was stretched tight across his shoulders, and he was tall enough to reach the roof of the shed even with his upper body hunched over.

He sniffed the air, like he had in her father's driveway. "Eliza, I can smell you're close."

He couldn't smell her. Jacob had been the one he'd tracked. And Jacob was dead.

"Make yourself known to me, girl, and, in return, your brother shall go free."

Eliza dug her fists into the loose dirt. Tears blurred her vision. If she thought there was the slightest chance the Sheriff would keep that promise, she'd willingly give herself up to him this very second. But she'd be a fool to believe him. She clenched both handfuls of dirt, afraid that if she let go, there would be nothing to stop her from walking out into the small clearing.

The Sheriff turned and began to slowly inspect the woods. His scan reached Eliza's position in the trees and she held her breath, too frightened to move. He stared in her direction for ages. Then he moved on, completing a full 360 of the forest around them.

"Your brother will pay dearly for your betrayal."

The Sheriff grabbed a log from the pile and hurled it into the trees opposite. It smashed against a bough and splintered into pieces.

Birds scattered into the sky. A scream built in Eliza's throat and she covered her mouth. She turned her back to the trunk, both hands pressed hard against her lips. The Sheriff shouted out her name and Eliza squeezed her eyes shut. The echo had only just about died when he bellowed her name again.

Time ticked by, but Eliza didn't hear the Sheriff call out for her again. She opened her eyes and loosened the grip on her mouth. New tears replaced the dried ones and she told herself she had to move. But her paralysed body wouldn't follow her command.

Minutes ticked by like hours. Her brother and Roman had sacrificed so much for her –their very lives – and how did she repay them? By hiding pathetically behind a tree.

Nathaniel. That was the name of Roman's brother.

Okay, she had a name. But it still didn't help her any.

She grit her teeth and wiped her eyes dry on the back of her hand. If nothing else, the last few days had taught her that she was better than this...snivelling wreck. She was a fighter. The Sheriff could be anywhere – maybe back in Purgatory, maybe somewhere in the woods waiting for her. But she'd fought him – not once, but three times. And she'd survived every encounter. In fact, he was the one who should be worried about her. Because the next time she saw him, she would kill him.

She stood and peered out from behind the tree, her determination to find Roman and Billy sparking her inner strength. The clearing was empty. But wherever the Sheriff was now, Eliza was under no illusions; he would return.

She twisted round the other side of the tree and looked at the hill behind the shed. Her hands clenched into fists and she evaluated the surrounding forest – her only other option of escape. But where would that lead her? She could walk for miles and never find a way out.

A sour taste filled her mouth and she wrapped her arms around herself. It wouldn't be long before daylight faded. She needed to find help. She needed to head back up the hill.

Giving the area one last scan, she stepped out from behind the tree and crept towards the shed. Twigs snapped under foot, louder than the crack of a whip. She reached the shed window and peered inside. Jacob still lay dead on the floor. A desire to rejoice at the death of the man who had lived inside her and made her life a living hell was short-lived. She turned to the hill.

The sweat she worked up climbing soon cooled. She rubbed her legs, warding away the afternoon chill. The forest was growing darker with every passing minute. Freezing conditions would accompany the darkness, and her inadequate clothing would do nothing to keep her warm. Her brisk pace quickened to a jog. Trees and foliage passed in a blur. She had to figure out how to track down Nathaniel.

So, what did she know? She didn't know where Roman lived. Nor where he liked to hang out. Nor what his job was. Nor who his friends were, if he even had any.

Then, an idea sprang to mind.

She might not know who Roman's friends were, but she knew who his acquaintances had been…her father and Davis.

A newfound bounce in her step, she quickened her pace. Both Davis and her father were gone – one dead and the other lost in the depths of Purgatory. Asking them for information was out of the question. But her father had kept impeccable records on everything. Surely that included Roman. All she needed was a phone number or an address. Anything.

Finally, she had a plan. Now all she had to do was find that road.

CHAPTER TWO

Roman opened his eyes.

The guard's size-nines booted him in the stomach.

He rolled onto his back, stalling to give his newly cracked rib a chance to heal. The cloaked guard stood over him, his face hidden in the hood's shadow. But Roman knew who it was. The gold medallion that hung from the chain around his neck identified him clearly.

Roman raised himself onto his elbows. "Well, well, well. As I live and breathe. Thomas Blood."

Thomas removed his hood. He looked remarkably tanned considering life down here in the pit meant the sun hadn't touched his skin in centuries. He smiled but said nothing.

"Still not much of a talker, eh?"

"Words waste time."

A catch pole rested against the cave wall. Not the worst of torturous instruments to encounter while down here. More of an annoyance because once it clamped your neck it never let go. Thomas reached for it.

Roman flipped onto his front and sprang to his knees, ready to run, but Thomas booted him in the side. Using the pole, he pushed Roman onto his back again.

Roman coughed and pain exploded around his ribs.

Thomas planted a foot either side of his chest and twirled the ten-foot pole one-eighty so two iron jaws pressed against Roman's throat. Then he jammed it downwards. The arms inside the jaw detracted and slithered past the sides of Roman's neck until he felt cold iron press hard against his throat. Only then did the arms spring out, trapping his neck inside. Roman twisted, but the tip of a two-inch spike at the base of the iron jaw pressed deep beneath his chin. He had little choice but to quickly relax.

Roman had been here before and knew the drill. The arms inside the jaw clamped his throat and when Thomas lifted the pole, Roman had no option but to rise with it.

"Is this really necessary?"

Thomas gripped the middle of the pole, about five feet from Roman and well out of arm's reach. He stepped forward, forcing Roman backwards.

Roman instinctively grabbed the pole for balance. He took another step backwards, yanking the pole – and Thomas – towards him. Thomas stumbled forward and fell. The far end of the weighted pole dropped with him. At the other end, the iron jaw elevated and the spike impaled Roman's chin, its tip puncturing his mouth and finding the underneath of his tongue. Roman grabbed the pole and pulled it from Thomas's grasp. It slipped through Thomas's fingers. Its sheer length made it heavier than it needed to be, but Roman raised it as high as he could, leapt over Thomas, and bolted.

He didn't get far.

Six cloaked guards cut him off a mere fifty metres along the passageway. Roman tried to turn but the pole whacked against the cave wall and stopped him.

Roman stopped, held up his hands, and surrendered. The pole dropped and the spike elevated and pierced the underside of his mouth again. He flinched and waited for Thomas to duck beneath his arms. He waited even longer for Thomas to raise the end of pole off the ground. When he did, the spike slithered free from his chin.

Roman lowered his head – at least, as far as he could before the spike started to pierce his mouth again. He'd tried this same move once before, centuries ago. This was the second time he'd failed to pull it off.

"Use the shackles," Thomas said irritably.

A guard bent before Roman and did as he was ordered. Roman couldn't see – he couldn't look down, the spike ready to pierce his chin again if he did. But he heard the chains. And he felt their heaviness around his ankles. The guard stood, but there was no eye contact, no matter how much Roman willed it. He added two more shackles, one for each of Roman's wrists. Heck, even Houdini would struggle to escape this.

Without uttering another word, Thomas jabbed the pole forward for the second time. Roman stumbled backwards. He tried to balance, but the shackles restricted his movement. Instinctively, he reached for the pole for support again. The chain linking the cuffs to his shackles pulled tight. His hands failed to reach the stick and, powerless to do anything else, Roman toppled.

The iron jaw around his neck inevitably went with him. As did the pole. The spike stabbed the roof of his mouth and, this time, Roman cried out.

"Get him up," Thomas said.

The guards dragged Roman to his feet. Thomas's eyes sparkled with satisfaction. He pushed the pole forward, nudging Roman backwards, his tiny steps scampering along the passage to keep pace with his captor.

Deja vu.

A chill descended and Roman clenched his fists. He didn't need to be facing front to know where he was heading. The prisoners couldn't be heard – yet. But their screams lived inside his head and had woken him every single morning since his escape.

Thomas kept walking and Roman had no choice but to scurry backwards in sync with him – straight into a stalagmite. The iron jaw pressed against his throat and the spike embedded his mouth further. Blood oozed over his lips and Roman tensed.

Thomas grinned.

Roman grinned back, the pain subsiding. "I'm surprised the Sheriff isn't here to personally welcome me, seeing as it's taken the best part of a few hundred years to finally catch me."

"He has other matters to attend to first, but he'll be here. Don't you worry about that." Thomas smiled, revealing stained teeth, and the stench of centuries-old plaque polluted the air.

Roman tensed. "He's still in Cairngorms?"

The thought of the Sheriff pursuing Eliza caused adrenaline to surge through his body. His pulse pounded inside his ears and he attacked, hands stiff, fingers curled – just the right shape to squeeze around Thomas's neck and rip his head from his shoulders. The cuffs pulled the chain tight and Roman reached no further than a foot. A guttural roar bellowed past his lips and he attacked again. The same restriction stopped him.

Thomas smiled. "Careful. You'll give yourself a heart attack."

"I swear, if he's hurt her, I will kill everyone down here." Spittle caught in the corners of Roman's mouth.

Thomas's smile widened. "That would be a neat trick."

"Remove these chains. I'll show you a neat trick or two."

"Now where's the fun in that?" Thomas steered Roman around the stalagmite and forced him backwards again.

Roman shuffled along with him and tried to calm down. Tried to gain control. But he wanted to scream. His vision clouded and the image of Eliza's mutilated body took hold of his mind. He needed to know whether the Sheriff had caught her. He clenched his teeth and tried to stem the tremors that dominated his body.

He was awash with memories of the torture chamber. He'd be there soon. Did the Sheriff have something up his sleeve? Would Eliza's strung-up body be there to greet him? Sweat drenched his skin. He tried to turn, suddenly convinced the Sheriff was standing somewhere behind him ready to inflict his torture, but the spike forced him to face forward.

Thomas manoeuvred Roman around another stalagmite and Roman fought to keep his balance. His legs couldn't move the speed he needed them to go and his hands couldn't reach the pole and hold on for stability. Roman was fucked.

Back he went, his fairy steps moving at such speed his heels barely had time to touch the ground. The passageway was an endless parade of identical rocks. Thomas shoved him around further stalagmites and sometimes he forced Roman straight into them.

Finally, the screams came.

Roman's blood went cold. Gurgled cries echoed along the corridor as a whip cracked down upon bare flesh. Roman saw it. Not physically – he hadn't quite reached the torture room yet. But the familiar sound brought with it images from scores of buried memories. He struggled against the jaw clamp. Inside his mouth, his tongue ran across the tip of the spike. He tilted his head but couldn't lift his chin off the pointed spear.

Thomas pulled on the pole and Roman halted. He heard a handle turn and a door creaked open behind him. He was here. His final destination: The dungeon. The prison. Purgatory's hell hole. There were many names this room went by. Roman preferred to call it the torture room, because that was exactly what it was – a room where fucking torture happened.

He readied himself. Even if he did fight for freedom and make it to the waiting room, he had no idea what souls, if any, were due to be returned.

Thomas pushed again on the pole, but Roman dug his heels in. A guard grabbed his shoulder, but Roman struggled and resisted. Slowly, the men pushed him backwards. Roman's feet slid through the dirt. He pulled on his restraints and stretched for the doorframe. His fingertips brushed the aged wood. The spike ripped through his chin and a rush of blood filled his mouth, seeping down his throat and into his lungs. Roman coughed and spluttered, gasping for breath. His fingertips managed to grab the frame. Another guard joined the scuffle and pried Roman's hand from the wood.

Thomas pushed on the pole again, shoving Roman backwards. The guards clamped Roman's upper arms and together they dragged him through the doorway. Roman struggled for air, coughing the blood from his lungs. His fate was inevitable.
He closed his eyes and the Lord's Prayer whispered from his lips.